T0246217

THE WINTER VISITOR

Also by James Henry

THE DI NICK LOWRY THRILLERS

Yellowhammer

Blackwater

Whitethroat

THE DI JACK FROST PREQUELS

Frost at Midnight

Morning Frost

Fatal Frost

First Frost (with Henry Sutton)

THE WINTER VISITOR

James Henry

riverrun

First published in Great Britain in 2024 by

riverrun

an imprint of

Quercus Editions Ltd
Carmelite House
50 Victoria Embankment
London EC4Y 0DZ

An Hachette UK company

Copyright © 2024 James Gurbutt

The moral right of James Gurbutt to be
identified as the author of this work has been
asserted in accordance with the Copyright,
Designs and Patents Act, 1988.

All rights reserved. No part of this publication
may be reproduced or transmitted in any form
or by any means, electronic or mechanical,
including photocopy, recording, or any
information storage and retrieval system,
without permission in writing from the publisher.

A CIP catalogue record for this book is available
from the British Library

HB ISBN 978 1 52943 173 5
EBOOK ISBN 978 1 52943 175 9

This book is a work of fiction. Names, characters,
businesses, organizations, places and events are
either the product of the author's imagination
or used fictitiously. Any resemblance to
actual persons, living or dead, events or
locales is entirely coincidental.

10 9 8 7 6 5 4 3 2

Typeset by CC Book Production
Printed and bound in Great Britain by Clays Ltd, Elcograf S.p.A.

Papers used by Quercus are from well-managed forests and other responsible sources.

For my brother, Matt

'A profound impression was made upon me, I remember, by the roar of the voices in the school-room suddenly becoming hushed as death when Mr. Creakle entered after breakfast, and stood in the doorway looking round upon us like a giant in a story-book surveying his captives.'

CHARLES DICKENS, *David Copperfield*

PROLOGUE

December 1990

Chloe had not been to a Christmas party in ages.

The venue was a hotel in Marks Tey, about five miles west of Colchester. Despite an effort with festive lighting, the hotel bar had the mood of an airport lounge as they all arrived. Women filed through the foyer, boldly coatless, in heels and slinky dresses, lads in pressed Farahs and open-neck shirts flicked snow from bouffant quiffs. Chloe walked along the orange patterned carpet with her boss, still in her work clothes. Alan was wearing the same cheap navy suit he wore every day of the year, come rain or shine.

She liked a drink and a dance, but experience had taught her the workplace was the wrong place for both. In the five years she'd been at CBS she hadn't been to a single party. At her previous job at Whybrows in the centre of town, there'd been some inappropriate behaviour with one of the senior managers during a slow dance and she had never lived it down. Drunkenly enamoured, she had made a play for the man knowing he was married and was thereafter tarred with accusations ranging from being a home-wrecker to attempting to sleep her way up. He hadn't fought her off, though – was more than up for it – but, as is the way, being a man he was deemed blameless. The following year, Chloe moved to a distribution company in the boondocks, vowing to keep herself beyond reproach.

Back then at Whybrows she had still been free and single, several years after her disastrous marriage ended. Now, at CBS, three years going steady with Paul, her new colleagues thought her snooty, aloof – and ambitious. The latter at least was true. And so what if they thought her a frump in a boring dress? That was fine. Apart from that one blip at Whybrows, Chloe had been painstakingly careful to establish a quiet life for herself. Having been noticed by head office, she'd been encouraged to study for a company-sponsored professional qualification. At the age of thirty-two she was a relatively late starter and had crammed intensely, taking exams each June and December, and had passed her finals that summer. Proper study had precluded frivolity, but now she was a qualified accountant there was no reason to duck out of the Christmas bash; quite the contrary. The exam success had boosted her self-worth and moved her to let her hair down, live a little. So here she was.

'What you fancy?' Alan asked.

'Vodka and coke,' she said. Whitney Houston's 'How Will I Know' tempted feet onto the dance floor. Alan, fag in mouth, turned from the bar and handed her the drink. He grimaced at the music. 'I'm too old for this racket,' he said, Superking flipping up and down between his lips as he spoke.

Me too, she thought. The tight circle of twenty-somethings start to bop cautiously under the glitter ball. Chloe's features glazed for a moment sentimentally as refracted light danced around the room. Her memory flitted back to her fourteen-year-old self, having blagged her way into the Colne Lodge with a wrap of speed in her bra. Another twirl of the glitter ball, and she was transported to the first time she met Bruce Hopkins working behind the bar in Valentino's – his eyes in shimmering light.

To wipe the past from her mind, she turned to her boss and said, 'I don't believe you, Al; wait until you're a bit juiced – bet you'll be chucking shapes like the best of them.'

Alan's cragged features remained unchanged; that of a stoic sea captain, watching an approaching storm. Chloe scanned the dark perimeter of the room where the majority of the seventy or so employees still lurked, fuelling up on free booze. There was no one she was comfortable to mix with, let alone dance with. The accounts department was broadly made up of two age groups: either grey-haired senior bookkeepers in their late fifties, who had been with the company for donkey's years and had no truck with Chloe's kind coming in over their heads; or youngsters, the carefree generation currently undulating on the dance floor. Each acknowledged the other, recognising their past or future. Chloe belonged to neither.

Nevertheless, she knew she'd made the right move. Anonymity was what she craved and where better than working as an accountant in a warehouse in rural Essex. By now she was sure no one would really care if the identity of her infamous husband ever came to light: shortly after starting at CBS, the White House Farm murders happened in Tolleshunt D'Arcy, just down the road from Tiptree. It was all anyone would – and still did – talk about. Jeremy Bamber.

By standing next to the boss, Chloe hoped to find an ally, but Alan was more at home with the older ladies in party hats and glittery frocks for whom he qualified as 'a young-ster'. Chloe sensed his discomfort – recently promoted by head office, Chloe had a future, while her immediate line manager, who had never ventured outside Tiptree, sniffed danger. She turned back to the bar, allowing him the chance to engage with somebody else, and ordered another drink. Vodka didn't really taste of anything and nerves had allowed her to drink the first without noticing. The bar, she realised, was populated with unfamiliar faces, some the same age as her. These people stood alone and regarded the room with a mixture of amusement and annoyance. They must be hotel guests. One bloke stood out as good-looking; tall, fair, with a moustache. He was joking with the bar staff. Chloe caught a Manchester accent.

The man had twigged her stare and gave her a playful wink. She looked down at her drink embarrassed, then sideways searching for Alan, but he'd gone. The next thing she knew the man with the moustache had snaked round to her side.

Confused, she made an excuse to go to the loo, promising to be back shortly and asked for another drink – even though she'd barely touched the last. In the ladies she retouched her make-up, something she had not thought to do before leaving the office. When she returned, another younger woman was at her place at the bar. She turned to go, but the man smiled, passed her a fresh vodka, and began to recap the story he was telling.

At some point the other woman melted into the background and Chloe, encouraged, found that she might just have one dance after all.

PART 1

CHAPTER 1

February 1991

'They've gone,' Kenton muttered to himself.

Alone he stood at the water's edge. Mersea Stone, sculpted of crushed shells and sand, gave abruptly into the sea as it washed through a bank of pebbles, leaving them polished in the white spray. The rhythmic rattle of this rinsing was now, by degrees, drowned out by the increasing wind. Kenton looked to the cool grey sky, sensing the change in the weather. Beneath the cloud a bitter north-easterly whisked across the dark river mouth, pushing up white caps colder than ice. He moved up from the shoreline, his boots sinking in the shingle with each step.

It was quite likely that the birds he sought had moved on. He'd been here fifteen minutes or more, and he knew that if they were on the spit, he'd have seen them, scuttling about. Snow buntings could be seen at close quarters, without binoculars. The difficulty was finding them in the first place. With rusty yellow-brown plumage, they blended in perfectly

with the beach surface, camouflaged, invisible in their surroundings, hiding in plain sight. With patience, however, they
would appear, like shingle clusters rising from the beach and
tumbling along the shoreline. And once in vision it was hard
to lose them.

But not today, it seemed, and now the chill air had made
its presence felt to the detective's hands and feet. He stood
motionless on the beach, watching the sea surging up into the
Colne. The wind was against the tide, churning the water; its
resistance flaying aggressively up off the surface, a salty tang
stinging Kenton's chapped lips. The weather was due to turn
nasty in this part of Essex. If he didn't see the birds now, that
was it. These bunting were migratory, here only for the winter,
and their seasonal clock ended early before the bad weather
set in; he'd only ever seen them late November until January.

They'd gone, he knew it.

He turned round and began the slog back inland, seeing the
unmistakable orange red shape of a fox meandering through
the long grasses raked back across the sea wall. Further off,
a cluster of crows threw themselves crazily into the wind,
followed by various waders and waterfowl scattering wildly
in all directions. Kenton raised his binoculars and searched
the sky above the horizon; the fox, being this side of the sea
wall, would not be the source of the disturbance – a raptor
must be overhead. And there it was, high up; the purposeful
thrust of a peregrine. A tingle of excitement shot through
him. It wasn't a wasted day after all. Abruptly it stooped and

he lost it in the melee below. Whether it was successful he did not know. Aimlessly, he panned across the estuary for the falcon – he caught something darting off but the image suddenly began to blur as the quality of the light diminished. 'Snow,' he muttered to himself, bringing the binoculars down to rest on his chest. The falcon had disappeared into the murk, where it was now impossible to separate the sea from the opposing shore. Thick snowfall, tumbling in from the North Sea. He breathed in the cold briny air and shivered. The snow was certain to reach his side of the estuary. The forecast was for several inches across the region.

Kenton reluctantly continued to re-tread his path to the car park. The wind at his back was now carrying large snowflakes and urged him on. The snow would settle quickly, and within a short space of time, the narrow lane leading off the island could be impassable. This was his first time out since . . . he could not, in fact, recall. Still, it was nice to be out in the open air; fresh though it was, birdwatching always gave a sense of purpose to a stroll. Even if he saw nothing, it was a distraction. Emptied the mind, if only for a moment.

As Kenton approached the sea wall, he saw he was not alone. Up on the path, he recognised the nature reserve's warden, Mr Young, and another man, sedge grass whipping around their legs. They had their binoculars directed across the estuary, where minutes earlier his had been focused beyond the point, upriver, towards Brightlingsea. Kenton turned into the weather.

'Nice to see you, Mr Kenton.' Mr Young, ever formal, called above the wind. 'Been a while, eh? Picked a day for it.'

'You know how it is, have to strike when I can.'

Kenton forced a smile and nodded at Young's companion, a die-hard twitcher of advanced years with patchy white stubble. Eyes pursed against the weather, he made no motion of acknowledgement.

'Watching the peregrine?' Kenton shouted across. 'I lost him in the snow.'

'No . . . fire, across the water,' said the old man. 'Brightlingsea.'

Kenton turned around and raised his binoculars. Sure enough, there was a lick of bright orange reaching up through the frozen landscape. 'Must be fierce to withstand a blizzard like this . . . what on earth is there that could possibly catch fire, and tower up like that?'

'Only things over two storeys high that side of the water are churches.'

CHAPTER 2

'Ladies and gentleman, we shall shortly begin our descent into Heathrow. Expect a few bumps as we go through a very wintry weather front moving in from Scandinavia.'

Bruce Hopkins heard the captain's announcement on the fringe of his consciousness and was untroubled by any turbulence; it wasn't until the plane touched down with a proper jolt that he was disturbed from his slumber. Not a fan of flying, he'd dosed up on duty-free gin before take-off, and again soon after. The flight was only two hours, but he'd been zonked out for a good hour and a half, and now on arrival in the UK was decidedly groggy. Through the cabin window was a typical murky English February afternoon, much the same as he'd left behind ten years ago. He chuckled to himself as he reached overhead for the holdall and carrier bag. God, he'd not missed this country one bit.

As he descended the steps onto the tarmac the cold bit in sharply, and his smirk disappeared. This drop in temperature was something he'd overlooked. Dressed in only a linen jacket, he realised he was ill prepared.

Being over six foot, Bruce had passport control in view in spite of the sombrero-headed passengers in front of him in the queue. There were no police lurking that he could see. When his time came to step forward, he slid the black booklet under the glass, and glanced the other way so as not to engage the eye of the border officer. The photo was good. He'd used women's foundation to cover up the deep decade-long tan, to give the appearance of a pasty Brit.

'Retired, sir?' said the man behind the glass.

'Sorry?' Bruce's heart galloped. 'Err, yes, I took early retirement. From BT.' He was forty-eight, but the passport gave fifty-five. Bruce was 'worn in', the forger had said, and with patchy cropped grey hair, he'd easily pull off the extra years – another layer of cover.

'Early to come home, then,' the official continued. 'Don't usually catch a pensioner returning in the middle of winter. Like birds, come back in the spring.'

'Only a short break, I'm afraid. Wish I could stay longer.' Bruce was well-spoken and replied in a clear authoritative voice, which may have led the officer to assume it was not lack of money that curtailed his visit.

'Welcome home, sir.' Passport stamped and returned through the window, with a smile. 'Wrap up warm.'

Bruce nodded and passed on through, shivering with cold. With no luggage in the hold he set off in the direction of the taxi rank. It wasn't until he was safely inside a black cab and had, admittedly, breathed a great sigh of relief, that he reached inside his jacket pocket to retrieve a letter inviting him back into the country, and realised he'd left it on the plane. He could see it now; the pale blue envelope poking out between the sick bag and in-flight magazine. Damn. There's no way he'd get it back now. Would anyone read it? He doubted it, straight in the rubbish bin. And if they did it'd have no significance to whoever it was that cleaned out airplanes.

'Where to, squire?'

'Colchester.'

'What, in Essex? That's going to cost you.'

'I'll see you right, fear not,' he said and proceeded to remove the wedge of banknotes in the seat of his trousers, 'should I not freeze en route, that is. Perhaps you'd be good enough to flick the heater on back here, old chap, thanks awfully.'

CHAPTER 3

Detective Sergeant Daniel Kenton drove the twenty-odd miles to the other side of the estuary within forty minutes. He'd learnt via police radio that Brightlingsea fire department had been called to the neighbouring hamlet of Kempe Marsh, where the church was reported ablaze. The old birder had been right. By the time Kenton reached the main road into Brightlingsea, snow had settled and banked high on the hedgerow. He'd need to be careful or he'd be marooned. Kempe Marsh was out on the crutch of the creek, the road without tarmac.

The snow eddied through the empty streets of Brightlingsea. The old fishing port was deserted. He passed by the town centre and the war memorial, its wreaths gradually disappearing. Beyond the lido and the snow-capped beach huts was the sea. Inland upriver, lay the marshes. On a clear day, Kempe Marsh church tower was evident in the near distance. Today, nothing.

The Vauxhall's tyres crunched slowly over the unmade road. The blizzard, unhindered by man-made structures, blasted across the frozen heath unchecked. The view through the windscreen blurred and so too did Kenton's spatial awareness, leaving him almost queasy behind the wheel.

Abruptly, a huge oak loomed into view, signalling the Jolly Sailor pub and a bend with a slight dip down into the hamlet. Kempe Marsh was little more than a track with a pub at one end and a church at the other. St Nicholas's was soon in view, its stone tower charred black and the roof entirely gone. The fire was out, and smoke fought against the snow tumbling heavily into the building unhindered. Kenton's first impression was that this was a purposeful attack, not just a couple of kids and a box of matches.

He spotted the vicar by his dog collar (and lack of a coat). He was a thirty-something chap, and was in heated discussion with a uniformed policeman under cover of the lychgate. Kenton was late to the scene; the fire brigade were reeling in hoses and newsmen were already disassembling their equipment. A huddle of onlookers remained at a respectful distance this side of the church wall. He drove past the damaged building before stopping beyond two police cars. The churchyard reached the creek, which flooded at high tide, and on the other side of the inlet some distance away were the villages of Alresford and Wivenhoe. The marsh was impassable on foot.

He strode back towards the church through the snow, now several inches thick, and pushed the waist-high wrought-iron gate open. He gazed up at the stained glass windows, seemingly untouched by the flames, overhearing the vicar berate the police officer. The church was Norman, the nave walls of flint rubble also remaining unmarked by the fire. The tower was stained with smoke, bereft of a roof but intact beneath, as if it had been bombed.

'Who are you?' the clergyman demanded, his ears pink with cold, snow catching his eyelashes.

'DS Kenton.' He stepped forward.

The uniformed officer nodded in recognition.

'Forgive me,' the vicar apologised. 'I mistook you for a curious rambler.'

'No problem,' he said. 'Caught sight of the blaze from East Mersea.'

'I'm not surprised,' the vicar's voice misted in the snow, 'it went up like a veritable beacon.'

'Kenton!' A broad Essex accent called to him from the porch entrance into the church. 'Thought you were off today?'

Kenton's heart sank on impulse. Nevertheless, he raised a gloved hand at the stocky figure of DS Brazier under the archway. The two had been assigned to work together at the beginning of the month, but as yet nothing significant had brought them into contact.

Kenton and the vicar made their way over to the porch to meet Brazier.

Snow swirled busily down to greet them through the void where the roof once was.

'I'm not sure I can bear to look,' the vicar said glumly.

'I'm sure the roof has been replaced numerous times over the centuries,' Brazier spoke through a scarf he wore high, covering his chin and ears. Snowflakes rested on his upright spiky hair.

'On the contrary, Detective, that roof was a hammerbeam, one of the finest examples of medieval carpentry in the country. The exterior tile cladding was updated perhaps, over the years, but only with the express purpose of protecting what was beneath. The carved angel bosses depicting the disciples on the braces were unique . . .'

'Oh.'

'Oh, indeed.' The vicar sniffed.

Inside the church, out of the wind, the combined odour of charred wood and wet stonework generated an unpleasant clammy chill. The fire had been out only half an hour and snow was already banked up in the most exposed corner. Elsewhere it settled steadily. Kenton hung back behind a stone octagonal font as the vicar, Brazier and a uniformed officer ventured further into the carcass.

'How the heck did this happen, eh?' Brazier's loud voice carried as he clambered over splintered timbers and broken terracotta roof tiles. His pale green bomber jacker caught a sharp blackened edge of what was part of the once exemplary roof, 'Oops. I mean, how did—'

'Be careful, sir,' the uniform called. 'The remains of the roof isn't safe. I don't think we should proceed any further,' he said, following Brazier even as he warned against doing so. 'More may come down as snow builds up on what's left. The fire brigade warned—'

'Yes, where are they?' Brazier stood in the centre of the nave, under a circle of weak light, blinking up at winter sky. 'I wonder how the flames reached from down here up to the roof. That's a good fifty foot. There's not much in the way of flammable material between the lectern and the roof – eh, vicar? Apart from the hymn board. And look at the walls – no scorch marks.'

Plaques honouring past nobility and war heroes were clean of fire damage.

'Petrol,' the vicar replied, as he too stepped forward into the nave and looked up into gaping absence above. 'The fire brigade say petrol. How do you propose to catch these vandals?' he said. 'The fire raged untroubled for a good hour because of the weather, and because the fire engine at Brightlingsea failed to start – that's what they told me anyway. A flat battery if you can believe it.' He backed away from the nave towards Kenton. 'What are you going to do?'

'Nothing,' Kenton said, calmly. 'In here at least. Until the snow abates there's nothing we can do.'

'What do you mean, nothing?'

'We don't want to mess up what might be underneath,' Brazier said.

'Wait for the snow to thaw?' The vicar was aghast.

'Don't blame us, Reverend. The weather is God's work, eh?'

The Lord's servant ignored this remark.

'In the meantime, we'll look into the surrounding area,' Kenton said. 'Anything out of the ordinary happen in the run-up to the fire?'

'Nothing, nothing whatsoever. There was a funeral, and that's nothing special given the age of the population here. What with the weather, I made swift work of it; most of the mourners were of a similar age to the deceased. It was imperative to get them back into the warm soonest, if you follow me.'

'Understood. Name?' Brazier pulled out his pocketbook and a stubby pencil. He wore navy woollen Steptoe gloves.

The vicar's features relaxed at the sign of note-taking. 'War veteran, Colonel Bulmer-Jones. Lived in the fisherman's cottage on Foundry Lane. Ninety-three. We were done and in the Jolly Sailor for the wake shortly after midday, myself included.'

'And that was when the fire started?'

'So your colleagues believe, while the whole village was in the pub.'

'If it was an outsider, and let's say for argument's sake it was,' Kenton said, 'he or she would have come through Brightlingsea? There's only one way in and out.'

'Yes. The marsh would be sheer madness . . . or there's the possibility of a boat?' the vicar added doubtfully.

'A boat?'

'There's a jetty attached to the old rectory.'

'Old rectory . . .?'

'Yes, as opposed to the vicarage, where I live. The original rectory was deemed no longer safe. Are you familiar with coastal erosion?'

CHAPTER 4

As the taxi emerged from the Dartford Tunnel into Essex it started to snow. Steadily, thick and fast without warning, and the traffic slowed accordingly. The driver changed his tune, a jolly chirpy banter was abruptly replaced with sombre mutterings about road closures and problems getting himself and his black cab back to the East End. Bruce made the appropriate noises of concern, then sidetracked him, 'Good lord, will you take a look at that!' he exclaimed, turning round. He'd missed it on entry in the murk; huge pillars of concrete, and cranes disappearing up into the grey. He rubbed at the window to get a better look. Men in hard hats and high-vis, tiny by contrast, moved about a construction site so vast, that even in this poor light, it was plain that something of epic proportions was under way.

'Bridge, ain't it? Cable one. Reckon the towers near five hundred feet high.' A bridge over the Thames, this far out. Impressive. When Bruce skedaddled, they'd just opened the second tunnel. As they exited the M25 – itself far from complete in 1981 – onto the A12 heading east he had steered the driver off the problematic aspects of the weather, back onto altogether safer ground of the traffic levels in general.

In all this time Bruce had been back only the once, in 1984, and then his feet had barely touched dry land. Gazing out the window, he wondered if much had changed. Thatcher had gone – just – but the Tories ran the country still. At first, he'd kept abreast of what was going on – Charles and Di, the Falklands – but he soon ceased to care. The papers often lay unread for weeks unless something major occurred that the holidaymakers obsessed with, then he'd make the effort for conversational purposes. The Poll Tax. As if he gave a fig about that. He yawned elaborately and dozed, waking only as the taxi slowed in Colchester High Street. Bruce revived immediately and asked to be dropped just ahead of the hotel, outside Williams & Griffin, the upmarket department store. Delighted to see Willie G's still as he'd remembered it, Bruce made a beeline for men's clothing to see what they had in the way of overcoats. And hats. A necessity, given the weather and the imperative to make him less conspicuous in the brief time he was here.

He pulled out his spectacles in order to read the sizes on the hangers. There was no denying he'd put on weight, but from a 44 chest to a 50. Jesus. And not from pumping iron – more poking patatas bravas in his mouth. 'Bit stiff after the flight,' he stood erect and pulled in his stomach, 'not enough leg room for a chap like me, plenty for a dainty thing like you,' he joked with the sales assistant, who tittered. They bantered as he worked his way through to the most expensive coats in the shop. He might be past his prime, but Bruce could still charm the birds from the trees, even ones half his age, with his polite well-educated voice. From dustman to duke, he could flit across the social scale with ease. Choosing a Crombie with a velvet collar, he elected to keep it on, and grabbed a black woolly hat at the check-out. On exiting the store, he ambled along the High Street in a jolly mood. Though some of the shop frontages had changed, the centre of town was much as he remembered it, a timeline of buildings throughout the centuries, from the timber-framed coaching house of the Red Lion to the elegant Edwardian Baroque of the town hall. At the George Hotel, he checked into a first-floor suite that overlooked the High Street. He had the room for the week; whether he stayed that long remained to be seen. There was no warrant out for Bruce, but if the police got wind he was in town they would have plenty of reasons to detain him. He didn't think this likely – for one, it was Chelmsford police who had busted the Crouch haul and he doubted anyone round here would remember him. The super from those days had since retired. And it wasn't like Bruce was at Brink's-Mat level.

He threw the holdall onto the bed and pulled a bottle of duty free out of the carrier. He had three hours to kill before the appointed time. Too long to do nothing and too short to do anything useful, like get over to Fambridge. Too risky to call on old acquaintances for the same reason. Standing in front of the mirror, he splashed his face to freshen up. It suddenly occurred to him there was one person he could visit without straying too far. One who he could trust not to blow the whistle: Chloe's mother, Margaret. According to Chloe's letter, it was at Margaret's insistence that she was writing to tell him to come now before it was too late. Little Margaret rattling around in that big old house. Yes, he was quite fond of the old duck, terrible snob though she was, and she wasn't far from here.

He set off towards Lexden, down Head Street towards Crouch Street. The landscape had changed; new shops he'd never heard of; pubs with different names or gone altogether. Finding it to be slow going underfoot, his hand-sewn leather-soled loafers coping poorly on the fresh snow, he craved a steadying drink. Curious, he paused at the allure of a new 'wine bar' but found the noise inside deafening with chatter and left without ordering. Instead, he'd try find a chemist, as his mouth ulcer had started to give him gyp in the cold weather, and he'd left his painkillers in Spain.

CHAPTER 5

'This is your case,' Kenton said as they finished making their way around the church perimeter and arrived back at the lychgate entrance, having found nothing but animal tracks of some kind. This was to make it official; Brazier had already handed over his card with the CID telephone number as the pair parted company with the vicar, Father Symonds.

'We'll handle it together, surely,' Brazier said as they stepped out of from under the gate, pulling his scarf up over his nose. They passed under the yew trees that lined the already cleared pathway, between snow-capped headstones. Brazier pushed open the rusty iron gate through which they had all entered. Outside in the lane, he leant back and looked up into gloom. The cloud seemed lower than it was twenty minutes ago, as the night seeped down upon them, obscuring the tower and coating the high flint rubble walls with wispy mist. There was not a sound to be heard, the churchyard was cold and silent. The rafters having caved inwards, the perimeter was clear of debris. The south side of the church gave way to the creek and somewhere beyond, under an icy fog, lay open water and the North Sea. In between was salt marsh. With the snow covering everything as far as the eye could see, which wasn't far, it would be madness to try and cross on foot.

Leaving the church grounds, they trudged up the lane past Kenton's car to the old rectory, an Edwardian villa in a state of dereliction, to check out the jetty. They paused. The snow was coming down thick again and it would soon be very dark. There was no way they would find the jetty in this.

'Sod this for a game of soldiers,' Brazier said. 'Terrible, this fire, but nobody has been hurt. We go down there in this, we may never come back.'

Dramatic though this sounded, Kenton was inclined to agree. 'I'll put a press statement together for Watt tomorrow morning if you like?'

'Be my guest. Let's check the boozer, then we won't need to come back.'

The Jolly Sailor did not live up to its name. The place had a stale, smoky interior, and Kenton doubted any of the punters would know their way around a laser dinghy. There was one customer at the bar reading a paperback, with a dog at his feet, and two playing dominos in an alcove. The walls were of thick, alabaster-coloured stone, and glistened with moisture, as though in a cold sweat despite the open-hearth fire.

Nobody stirred as the police entered.

'Evening, all,' Brazier said, cheerfully. 'Two pints of Guinness, please,' he said to the woman behind the bar.

'I'll have coffee, if you don't mind . . . if that's possible?' Kenton said.

The woman went about pouring a pint without a word. At the end of the bar the old chap put down his book and began to knock a pipe noisily on the bar.

'Any good?' Brazier glanced at the paperback: *The Kingdom by the Sea.*

'Grand,' the man said, placing his pipe between his teeth. 'We ain't in it.'

'Prefer to remain a secret, eh? Don't like strangers.'

'Who does?' He puffed on the empty pipe.

Kenton was bemused by Brazier's approach. If not trying to rile the locals, exactly, he was at least messing with them, trying to bait them. He himself preferred the direct approach; everyone knew where they were.

'Small enough here that a stranger would stand out, I guess.'

'If you're of a mind to look out for them, yes.'

'I reckon a fella like you would spot one from here,' Brazier said.

The man shrugged, he wasn't taking the bait.

'The vicar said the whole village attended a wake in this pub earlier today?' Kenton said.

'That's right,' said the woman behind the bar, 'in the room out back.'

'Just villagers? Visitors come in from outside for that?'

'No cars. Two old soldiers come in from town on the bus. Went back on it too. Turns round at the war memorial.'

'The fire was started while you lot were in here.' Brazier had Guinness cream on his top lip. 'So we are looking to talk to people, villagers, strangers – anybody who was in the vicinity but not part of the wake.'

'I saw two people hurry along the seafront when I went to fetch some more bread for sandwiches,' the woman said. 'Didn't get a good look at them – it was coming down in torrents. Kept me head down, as did they.'

'In the middle of the storm?' Kenton asked. The snow had come across the estuary, reaching Kempe Marsh before striking him on East Mersea. 'Towards Brightlingsea – away from the church?'

She nodded.

'Any description? Coat colour? Hats?' Brazier said.

'Sorry. The snow was so thick I could barely see my own hands.'

Two individuals abroad, but no description.

'Thank you,' Kenton said, readying to go and not fancying the instant coffee before him. 'You've been most helpful. Anything else, before we leave?'

'The vicar's ordered some heaters in,' said the old man.

'You what?' Brazier said.

'To melt the snow, inside 'is church.' He removed his pipe, and smiled. 'So he can look for clues who done the fire, he says.'

CHAPTER 6

Roland Beech was paid to drive cars, and was proud of it. First as a Formula 3 racer, until a crash took him out, then as a getaway man and car thief. In his day there was no one in Essex as nimble as he, even with a gammy leg. To be offered this job after five years in the nick was a testament to his reputation, beyond the screw-up with the immobiliser alarm that did for him in eighty-five. Roland parked his own battered Capri down a residential street in Marks Tey village and hurried along the main road towards the hotel. He pulled his jeep cap down to reach his ears; it was bitterly cold. Snow was banked up everywhere, but the roads had been gritted and were reassuringly black, not white.

The Copford Hotel was further away than he thought, out on a limb it was practically on the roundabout for the A12. The effort it took to be quick on his feet because of his knee made him sweaty beneath his black leather biker jacket despite the temperature, as he hugged the shadows cast by the conifers that screened the hotel. Beyond the trees and car park, a soft pool of light illuminated the hotel forecourt – although to call the flat-roofed three-storey building a hotel was pushing it. More of a motel to his mind, stuck out here near the motorway. The trees shielding the Copford from a noisy road also cut out the glare of the street lamps, leaving the car park in darkness. The forecourt lights were weak and did not reach beyond the entrance. He'd bear that in mind for the future. Good odds on stealing a car.

The wind had died. Sound travelled easily through the still evening air, between the breaks in the early evening traffic, which was slowly but steadily increasing. Slipping inside the main entrance he kept close to the evergreens, the foliage tickling his back. Once certain he was concealed in the dark, he paused, his breathing laboured, lungs bursting, scratched with the cold air. His glasses had steamed up too. Jesus, he was unfit. All that time inside. The moonlit frosted windscreens glittered. The car was easy to find. He'd memorised the reg number: blue Sierra, G plate. Why this car he didn't know. It wasn't even locked. The less he knew the better. His chin resting on the steering wheel, he slipped in the skeleton ignition key. It started fine, despite the cold. As he edged the motor forward, however, he realised he couldn't see. Shit. Ice on the windscreen. He should have realised. He stopped, rooted around for a scraper, found one in the side pocket. He jumped out and thrashed it across the glass, the sharp rasp reverberating across the car park. Jesus. Jesus.

Another engine started. He paused as a car exited ahead of him. Back in the car, he turned the heater on full whack and tried demisting the inside of the car with the sleeve of his jacket. Stay calm, he told himself. If they've not come by now, they're not coming – the time was safe, he was assured of that. He had been given a specific time slot in which to act – whoever owned this Sierra used it during the day and was presumably now in the bar. He sat back and let the engine idle for a few moments, the heater getting some warmth, and took stock of the interior. The car was new or newish, still had the faintly polished smell to it. The instrument panels were the same as ever. Hold on. He leant forward and tapped the facia with his knuckle. The petrol gauge hadn't moved. It sat at the bottom of the red. Bloody hell.

Friday Woods, his drop-off point, was a good five miles away. There was a garage off the slip road on the A12, or another twenty-four-hour place on the main road into town. Although the former was closer, it was in the wrong direction and he'd have to continue south up the carriageway until the next junction. The less time on the road the better.

He slipped seamlessly into rush hour. The Elf garage was less than a mile away, and he made it easily. In fact, it was on the corner of the road where he'd parked his Capri. The petrol station was busy; good – he'd blend in. He took the car in at a crawl and stopped, taking a moment to wrap his scarf high around his neck; but not too high – he didn't want to look like he was going to rob the place. Right. He scanned the pumps before getting out. Hello, what was this? Instead of the usual four- and two-star petrol, there was another option. Unleaded. *Unleaded?* What the bloody hell was that? Did this motor run on that – did it make a difference if he got it wrong?

CHAPTER 7

Kenton drove cautiously in the dark. The snow was beginning to freeze, he could feel the tyres slide on the bends. Who would set fire to a church? The vicar was rightly upset. And impatient. (Wasn't patience a virtue?) Then there was Brazier, there on the scene before him. Fair enough; he was on duty. They'd yet to work a case and Kenton was determined to be positive. Seemed all right, but didn't hang around for a chat. Sped off in a Citroën, wheels shooting slush as he went. Weird how forthright he was in the pub with the locals, and then disappeared like that. Maybe Brazier had taken a dislike to him? What could he have done wrong so early on in their relationship? Kenton's mind meandered here and there along with the country lane. When he reached the main road it was empty, and snow had settled across the dual carriageway. Alone with his thoughts he motored home, blissfully unaware of the lateness of the hour.

He was greeted with, 'Where on earth have you been?!'

Lindsay's outburst broke the silence like a thunderbolt. He closed the door behind him as his elder daughter scampered up the stairs for cover. Their one-year-old stared at him in awe from her high chair, then released her spoon, which clattered to the floor. Kenton stood watching as Lindsay scrabbled to pick it up before the child began to scream. Lindsay rose, her broad mouth, capable of the warmest of smiles, was down-turned and miserable. Like a fish caught on a hook.

'I . . .' There wasn't anything to say. It was nearly seven. He hadn't thought to call. It was dark by four, the latest he could conceivably have been home from East Mersea was five, and that was on a clear day with decent visibility. Not an almighty dumping such as they'd had today.

'Come here,' Lindsay commanded. He edged forward and she made as though to kiss him but instead took a sniff of his breath. 'Makes a change.'

'Hey, it was my day off, so what if—'

'You had gone in the pub and not told anyone? Even though it's the worst weather we've had all winter? Give me strength.'

But he hadn't been drinking.

'I saw this fire across the water.' He moved sheepishly off.

Lindsay Kenton watched her husband's broad back fill the narrow galley kitchen and heard the tap fill the kettle as he told a story about whizzing off to Brightlingsea. Did he not see that her worry had percolated into anger as the hours had drawn on? She'd had no idea where he was.

He finished dunking a tea bag and then blew his nose on a piece of kitchen towel with such ferocity that the baby gave a start and almost lost her spoon a second time.

'Oh well, you're back now,' she said. 'Did you see what you wanted on the beach? Snow goose or something?'

'Bunting. No,' he said sadly, 'they'd buggered off.'

CHAPTER 8

Margaret was aghast as she opened the front door – a small, prim lady of sixty, she was unaccustomed to surprises at her time in life.

Under the porch light loomed a large snow-dappled figure; though it had been many years, it was unmistakably that of her son-in-law.

'Aha, hello darling, been a while,' he said breezily.

'What in God's name are you doing here?' she said, nervously touching her short stylish terracotta hair, as if the intruder's first move would be to muss it up.

'That's not the sort of reception I was expecting. May I come in?' He barged past her and stooped in the marble hallway. 'The old place is unchanged, I see.'

Unlike you, she thought, as he pulled off a woolly hat to reveal that the thick charcoal hair that once swept across his brow had gone, leaving a sparsely covered dome with fine cropped grey stubble. 'What do you want?' she said sharply.

'Chloe wrote and asked to meet. I'm surprised she hadn't mentioned it.'

'No, she's not said a word . . . Why would she want to see you? She has a wonderful life now.' Margaret halted herself. She was not going to impart details of her daughter's life to this man.

'She wants to make her peace with me. She's dying, no?' He said this as though she were popping to the shops. 'To be precise, she said *you* told her to pass the olive branch.'

Margaret made a noise, part choking and half-stifled laughter. 'She's not in the slightest bit ill. Show me this letter.'

'Can't. Left it on the plane. I swear she said she's terminally ill.' He flopped the hat about in his big hands, loosening snow onto the floor. 'Well, if she's not, she's not – jolly good. Aren't you going to offer me a drink, raise a glass to good health, one and all?'

'Preposterous. Get out. Get out now! You are filth, a thieving villain. I don't believe a word you say.' She pointed to the door, causing an impressive sapphire ring to wink in the light at him teasingly.

'That's all water under the bridge now; my crimes are long ago. Chloe's forgiven me.'

'I rue the day you walked into our life, a con artist. For all your la-de-da, you were then as you are now, nothing but a common thief – only a common thief doesn't have the advantages you have had and squandered.' She could feel her colour rise with anger. 'The shame you brought on this family. Of all the rotten luck, that Chloe had to meet you of all people in the world.'

'Luck? Well, you'd know – Chloe had had a big dose of bad luck before I rolled up,' Bruce ruminated. 'But it was more planned than that. Don't pull that face – of course there was a motive. I did love her in the end though; even I didn't expect that. Remember, Margaret dear, you told me how pleased you were that she happened across me. How did you frame it, now?' he consulted the chandelier on the ceiling above. 'Ahh, yes: "Chloe hasn't had the best start in life, got herself in a bit of a bother, it's so fortunate that she met you." Or words to that effect. And let's not pretend I don't know exactly what that *bit of bother* was. Oh yes, I know, so don't you talk to me about shame.'

'What do you mean?'

'It was quite by chance. There was someone special in my life before Chloe, believe it or not, who led me here.'

'I don't understand . . .'

'Your little secret,' he smiled unpleasantly, 'became the source of much joy to me.'

'I am calling the police, this instant.'

'Okay.' He held up both hands. 'But darling, I think you really ought to hear me out before you do. Just five minutes – and then I'm gone.'

She nodded dumbly, still in shock.

'Good girl. Now that drink – and pour yourself one too. You might need it.'

In a little under five minutes, Bruce Hopkins had turned the tables on Margaret. What he'd just told her was so appalling, she couldn't believe it to be true. And yet, what he said did explain things that at the time didn't quite make sense. Now, as she stood glued to the spot, watching him in the doorway, about to leave, she saw with a terrifying clarity just what Bruce Hopkins was.

Calmly, she said, 'Aren't you worried the police will find out you're back in the country?'

'I won't tell if you won't – and I know you won't.'

'When are you meeting Chloe?' she asked.

'Later, somewhere neutral, out of the way . . .' he paused. 'Now, if Chloe hasn't spoken to you, I think it best for all that you don't speak to her. Got that?'

'The police will have you,' she said, as he turned and left.

He didn't respond, and she remained unable to move long after he shut the door.

At eight thirty, a taxi collected Bruce from the front of the George Hotel.

He was preoccupied with the reception he had received from his mother-in-law. Little Margaret. Still dressing like a starlet from the Swinging Sixties. Margaret was, to put it mildly, horrified to see him back in the country. It was only when Bruce declared knowledge of the skeleton in the Moran closet that she had payed him due attention. Even so, there were elements that didn't make sense. 'Not ill in the slightest,' he muttered to himself. Maybe the illness was a ruse just to get him here? Come to think of it, if she were that ill, would she have picked such an out-of-the-way pub to meet? There was surely neutral ground closer to home . . .

'Want picking up, mate? Better to book now with this weather. Word on the radio is not to travel unless necessary.'

The snow had abated for now, but he had a point. 'Yes, well, perhaps.'

The pub, one he was unfamiliar with, was surprisingly busy for midweek. He ordered a Guinness, and plonked himself on a free bar stool. There was a TV strapped to the wall, flickering away soundlessly. Vanity had prevented him bringing his specs – he couldn't rock up to meet the ex wearing bifocals.

'Excuse me, are you Bruce?'

A pale woman in her twenties with pink lipstick and streaked frizzy hair tapped him on the shoulder.

He was momentarily stunned, weak eyes darted nervously around the bar. Regaining his composure, he said sweetly, 'Who wants to know?'

'I'm a friend of Chloe's. She asked me to come and find you. Unfortunately, she's too sick to come out.'

'Yes, I understand . . . oh, I'm sorry.'

'Yes, she says you're welcome to come round.'

'To her home?' he said, amazed.

'Yes.'

'Absolutely!' He slipped off the bar stool.

'Mine's a rum and coke,' she said playfully.

'Why, yes, of course, how rude of me.'

He ordered her a drink, and another pint for himself. As he held out a fiver she placed a hand lightly on his arm and moved closer to allow another punter room at the bar. Her kind were not to his taste; he was more interested in seeing Chloe herself than drinking with her young friend.

'How do you know Chloe?'

'Pals at work.' She glanced away.

'Oh yes? Doing what?'

'We don't want to talk shop, I'm more interested in you. Bit of a mystery, aren't you?'

'I haven't the faintest idea what you're on about.' The corner of his mouth ticked involuntarily.

'Don't worry, I'm not going to say anything in here,' she said, then in a lower voice, 'Good on you, I say.'

Nice as it was to hear, Bruce grew aware of his vulnerability. As though reading his mind, the girl said, 'Come on, knock that back and we'll scoot.'

The air was taut with cold. Wisps of snow caught under the outside lights before flicking off into the dark. They made their way to the rear car park. Bruce couldn't tell the colour of the woman's car, let alone the make. He slipped into the front seat, which happened to be quite low, suggesting something sporty. Feeling warm and comfortable, he was pleased to be seeing Chloe after so many years. He was relaxed. Very relaxed. In fact, the journey and the drinks had caught up with him, and he felt tired and heavy.

He woke abruptly when the car had stopped, with a dry

throat and unnatural wooziness. As a man whose business experience included drugs in all their many guises, Bruce knew in a flash that he'd been spiked. Soporific, he could barely raise his eyelids. The experience would, under ordinary terms, be pleasant.

'What have you given me?' he mumbled.

The answer surprised and scared him.

'Ahh . . . that's medical. Why?' At that moment he felt a cord round his neck.

'*Kill the beast, slit its throat.*'

These words, hissed in his ear, he knew them, buried deep in another lifetime. Not the voice, but that line was enough. He'd been tricked.

Movement behind as his attacker shifted position. 'Not literally, that would be too messy. But you get the picture.'

'Where have you been . . .?' Bruce rasped weakly.

'You know. You put me there.'

And although Bruce did know where this man had been, he never suspected for one minute that he was responsible. 'But I tried to help you.'

The cord only tightened in reply.

He fumbled uselessly at his neck to try and free himself. It was futile. 'Let me speak,' he gasped. 'Just for a minute, then do . . . as you wish.'

His assailant relinquished his grip. Bruce gulped for air. 'It's not my fault, you see . . .'

'Out of the car you come. Tell me as you take off your clothes.'

Powerless, Bruce did as he was instructed and stepped feebly out into the freezing night air.

CHAPTER 9

At nine fifteen, Chloe saw the estate agent out with a false smile. Last week, the sale of her two-bedroom Lexden flat had collapsed. Nine months of messing around and now this young lad had rolled up for a revaluation; only to then politely inform her that her home of the last ten years was worth five grand less than when it was placed on the market a year ago.

She looked forlornly at the boxes piled in the living room, where she had started to pack. Damn. *Damn*. More time wasted. A new house was a milestone – whether the builders at Friday Wood Green would hold the new house while she tried to sell again was the question. At the reduced price, the flat would go quickly, wouldn't it? She had hung on to this place for too long; it was the last thing still stained by his memory, she had fought so hard to cleanse her life of him in every other way. Chloe felt as if she had always been trying to erase sections of her thirty-five years. Too many. And yet while trying to escape the past she had always remained rooted to the spot. Now, more than anything else, she wanted – as promised on New Year – to start a family with Paul. Paul. She would have to tell him the news about the flat. Bless him. She'd always been straight with Paul, apart from that one time at the Christmas party.

Someone had called while she was buttering up the estate agent and she could see the red flash of the answerphone. She pressed play. '*Sweetie, we need to talk. Are you okay?*' Her mother. Strange time for her to call? No matter, it would have to wait, whatever it was.

Having arrived at work mid-morning because of the estate agent, Chloe spent the rest of the day catching up and returned to the flat late that evening. Too late to cook anything from scratch. She had picked up a takeaway for the second time that week. As she eased the door open, the murmur of the TV greeted her, causing her a small start, forgetting she had given Paul a key. She was glad he was there; it allayed her worries that he might be despondent over the flat falling through. What better reassurance than this. Happily, there he was among the boxes, watching something or other. He called out to her: 'Phone your mother. 'She'll call back otherwise.'

As if on cue the phone rang. She put her dinner plate on top of a box and weaved among them and Paul's long legs to the telephone. 'Sorry, Mum, I've just got in from the office.' It's year-end and we're trying to finalise—'

'Hush your excuse, girl.' Not her mum. It was Sandra. 'You'll never guess what. Are you sitting down?'

Sandra was her best pal and she loved a gossip. They had

grown up together. Tearaways as kids, both had suffered from mistakes made in their teens and a sharp correction in behaviour after trailing around with rock bands and sleeping in VW vans when they should have been at school. Now, both women were the prim side of respectable, albeit in very different ways. Sandra was a parish councillor in Wormingford and unable to leave the house with a hair out of place. Married to a banker, her immaculately kept house was a source of much discussion at the school gate, so Chloe heard; writing on the V&A kitchen calendar, for instance, was forbidden, as any practical use would render the month untidy. Tittle-tattle and the misfortunes of others were her mainstay for entertainment; vicarious pleasure, wilful ignorance of the consequences.

Despite their paths having diverged so dramatically from their rebel teen days, it was the will to reinvent and survive that bound them both together. They were inseparable, and prided themselves on the fact that nothing could shake them. Chloe could do with a laugh, and nudged Paul on the shoulder to budge up.

'Go on then, I'm ready.'

'It's Bruce. Your ex – he's in Colchester.'

Chloe froze. Why would Sandra be so callous? This flat had originally been Chloe's ex-husband's; the joke was in poor taste given her sale had collapsed. Why would she say that anyway? Sandra knew well enough mere mention of his name triggered anxiety. Chloe composed herself.

'Ha ha. My sale fell through, by the way,' she replied sourly.

'No kidding. Serious. Someone spotted him in town.'

'Fuck off.'

Paul flinched.

'Who?'

'One of the make-up girls in Willie G's, strolling through, bold as you like.'

Chloe took a deep inhale. Vinegar from the remains of their fish and chips cloyed at her nostrils. What had been an enjoyable meal now sat like a solid lump on her stomach. The room was too warm and she began to feel vaguely sick.

'Chloe, you still there? Chlo?'

'He is a wanted man, Sandra. If the police got wind of this . . .'

'No joke, hon.' A wail erupted in the background. 'I gotta go. Kids eating each other.'

Chloe sat there staring at the figures on the TV as the events of over ten years ago came flooding back. Why? Why would he risk coming back? Perhaps there's something left of his aunt's jewellery, squirreled away for safe keeping in town. On reflex, Chloe looked to the door.

'Who's a wanted man?'

She'd completely forgotten Paul was sitting next to her.

CHAPTER 10

It was 7.45 a.m. and the central heating had yet to be felt by Superintendent Watt, chief of Colchester's police force, who sat in his pristine, empty second-floor office on Southway, awaiting the arrival of his men. At this time in the morning, he had only the radio for company, but he regarded keeping abreast of the news as part of the job. The IRA threat was very real here. He had already planned to open his morning brief with a few words on the subject. The recession was deepening, with two million expected to be out of work by the end of the year. The financial services and car industries were widely reported to be making redundancies; both were big employers in the area. On top of that, the health service was undergoing a shake-up, which meant that the closure of Severalls – the huge psychiatric hospital – was full steam ahead.

He switched the radio off, having had enough doom and gloom for one morning. Its silence allowed his new desktop computer to become audible, whirring away contentedly on its own portable desk in the corner. The station was a new purpose-built structure with an exit onto the Southway roundabout. Modern in the extreme, it boasted split-level rear access; a ramp up to the senior ranks' car park and a lower drop-off point for squad cars to bring in suspects. This latter entrance was equipped with a motorised turntable to rotate vehicles after depositing their cargo. An inspired idea, keeping the main entrance free of dramas and more hospitable to the general public. There was also an inbuilt gymnasium and badminton court two storeys high, which had proved popular with young members of the force.

In short, the new station was a far cry from their old quarters in the centre of town, where most of the senior officers had served. Watt himself, the most senior, was not one of them. At thirty-six, he had been in the position only a year and was by far the most enthusiastic about the building, although even he privately wished for real walls; the corner panoptic view swung both ways and on balance he'd rather not sit in a goldfish bowl. Aesthetically it was inoffensive, and nowhere near as brutal to the eye as the new one he'd worked in at Chelmsford.

Brazier and Kenton marched in at eight on the dot and sat down. The three men exchanged cursory greetings. Brazier gave the commentary and read through the press statement calling for witnesses. Watt was curious to hear of Kenton's surprise appearance.

'Very good of you to visit the scene, Sergeant,' Watt lifted his gaze from the typed sheet of paper, 'on your day off.'

'I saw the blaze through a blizzard across the water and was curious to know what could possibly go up in such a location. My interest was piqued,' Kenton said evenly. He sat with arms crossed, defensive.

Brazier eyed the frosty exchange. Maybe Kenton fancied he could do a better job running the place, hence the attitude. Maybe he could – Brazier suspected there was no real intelligence behind Watt's shiny face.

Watt sat hunched forward across the bare white desk, fingers laced. His training decreed he present a posture of authority, enthusiasm and energy.

The men opposite saw a nervous penitent seeking absolution.

'What do we think? Arson?'

'No doubt.'

'Any clues? Satanists, kids, Welshmen?'

'Nothing, yet. Two figures were seen on the waterfront in the blizzard, but it's not conclusive. Only they happened to be out at the time and not at a wake with the rest of the village. Whoever did this knew what they were doing – the roof is a good ninety feet up. Not even a military flame thrower would reach it.'

'Yes, the roof,' Watt said. 'Its unique design was mentioned on the news last night. Hammered wood, or some such from the Dark Ages.'

'Hammerbeam,' Brazier corrected.

'Thank you, Sergeant,' Watt couldn't quite make eye contact with Brazier. 'Questioned the locals, these chaps at the wake?'

'Brightlingsea local plod are on it.'

'Hmm. Let it thaw, as you rightly say – we don't wish to disturb what lay underneath, but let's be frank,' Watt said, 'if we've not nabbed anyone within the first twenty-four hours it's bloody unlikely, especially with this weather mucking everything up, we ever will.'

Nobody argued otherwise. One thing Watt did know, and that was statistics – snow or not, if they hadn't a lead by the end of the day, chances are whoever did it would remain a mystery.

CHAPTER 11

Watt delivered his weekly catch-up from his podium platform as per usual, at 9 a.m. sharp. The briefing room on the first floor was the largest space in the building excluding the gym – at thirty feet deep it could easily accommodate two shifts between changeover. Before him now were the majority of C and D shift, around forty-five heads in total. The super was not a tall man, and neither was he conscious of being short, but he did believe the extra six inches afforded by the podium allowed his voice to project better. Once he was up on what was essentially a plastic step, they knew he was about to speak. The assembly as usual was seated and divided, plain clothes to his left and uniform to his right.

He opened with a plea for vigilance in the town.

'As you are all aware, there was an IRA mortar attack on Downing Street last week, and we, being a military town, are mindful that the garrison will remain in a state of high alert. The army depend on our support at times like this, when the mainland is, once again, under siege.'

There was little acknowledgement from his audience. They

knew the score and rubbed shoulders with Military Police practically on a daily basis. He didn't dwell on this and moved swiftly on to good news stories, of which there were precious few. Here, the weather came to the rescue.

'Well done those officers out in the community during the inclement weather. Power cuts have been widespread across the northern rural parts of the county. Grandmothers have been dug out of cottages in Coggeshall and Feering. Roads re-opened with officers assisting the fire service.' Watt then held up the local paper, featuring a constable with shovel outside a retirement home in West Mersea. A cheer went up for the officer involved.

CID sat morosely quiet. The cold snap had deterred would-be criminals, but as a footnote Watt said not to be complacent.

The super followed the same formula every week: top and tail with serious business, a bit of banter in the middle. He patted himself on the back for taking the editor of the *Evening News* out for lunch – the courtesy had been repaid with news of the church fire being kept away from the front page in favour of a story on a local care home.

'Brazier! Kenton!' he called out as the room emptied.

Kenton cringed and halted at the super's call behind him, like that of public-school prefect. Brazier, still seated, continued chatting to uniformed sergeant Wilde, a recently promoted woman with a dark bob like pop singer Betty Boo. At the sound of Watt's voice, she upped and left.

'Senior clergy have been bending the ACC's shell-like, complaining our investigation is lacklustre.'

'Eh?' Brazier grunted.

'That was the word.' Watt rocked on his heels. 'The Reverend is getting antsy.'

'He was getting heaters in,' Kenton said, 'to speed up the thaw.'

They had omitted this tiny detail from their report earlier that morning.

'What the hell? He can't be doing that. Get down there with a panda car and a couple of shovels and clear it.'

'What about disturbing the—' Kenton began, but Watt cut him off.

'We all know in all probability there's bugger all to find. Get back down there, Kenton. I'll give them "lacklustre".'

Wilde made her way to her locker to get her Gold Blend before heading to the kitchen. She needed a proper coffee before engaging with anyone, none of that hamster grit they served up. Brazier's nattering had brought her headache into sharp relief – she couldn't make up her mind about him. Out last night, she'd barely made it in for the briefing. After caffeine, she'd go downstairs, check the cells. Nine of them, only three currently occupied.

'Constable, a member of the public has reported seeing a vehicle being pushed into Abberton Reservoir.'

Sergeant Philips' nasal voice boomed behind her. Ugh. The

last person she needed. She tipped her head back with a sigh then spun round. 'Philips, see these stripes on my arm, they're the same as yours, right?'

'Please don't take offence, *Sergeant* Wilde,' he said sweetly. 'I have trouble seeing you as a sergeant; your youth . . .'

Philips, bum-licker supreme, ran the Control Room and was Watt's right-hand man. A nasty combo.

'I'm twenty-five,' she said, sizing him up. 'Or does everyone look the same to blokes your age? What are you, forty-five? Fifty? It's so hard to tell. Call me Wilde, that's my name.' She had made the mistake of going to the pub after badminton last night and now Christie had called in sick, leaving her a man down. She didn't have time for any nonsense.

He nodded. 'Of course.'

'So, where on the reservoir are we talking exactly? It's a massive body of water.'

'Gent who saw it was on the causeway and saw it through a telescope this evening.'

'Christsake. What was he doing out there in this weather?'

'Watching for birds.'

'Lunatic.'

'Sergeant Kenton saw Kempe Marsh ablaze while pursuing the very same activity only yesterday.'

She had no comment to make on that, and said simply, 'Insurance job?'

Either that or it was stolen; joy riders got tired and ditched it.

Philips shrugged.

'Not my place to say.'

'Hmm, well it can bloody wait until the weather improves.'

'Not wishing to influence you, Sergeant Wilde, but the man did say he'd reported it to the water board too, for fear of contamination.'

'Jesus.' Wilde cursed as her badminton racket clattered onto the floor as she opened her locker. She banged her head on the locker door and mentally repeated her encounter with Philips, with added expletives.

'Temper,' a WPC called over, pulling on her overcoat, about to go into town.

Head resting on the locker, Wilde grunted underneath her thick black hair.

'I sometimes wish he'd never promoted me. I'm a token, and he's just ticking boxes.'

'Philips wouldn't have nailed ravers partying in farm out-buildings at dawn, like you. You know you deserve it. Watt knows you deserve it. At least they're the right boxes. You're hungover, and maybe a bit paranoid, that's all,' the WPC, Keeley Corbett, said. Married young, to a doctor, Keeley was rumoured to be gay, and the marriage was considered to be in some way practical or strategic; stopped blokes pestering her for a while. Wilde herself, though certainly thought of as a looker, was not troubled by the lads. Her black belt in Judo helped.

'He's never spoken to me, Kee,' she replied, shoving the locker shut.

57

'Has he squeezed your arse?'

'Watt? No, he bloody well hasn't.' Watt was many things, but not a groper.

'Well then. Don't look a gift horse in the gob and ignore Philips. He's jealous. No, not jealous – threatened. Watt is his baby and he's just worried you might be after stroking the chief's balls, and that's his job. Assemble your team, recovery vehicle, put the call in now for frogmen. Contamination? Hell, too late in the day to be worrying about that – God only knows what's been dumped in there over the years – it'll take more than some crappy old motor to poison us. He's a pen-pusher, that one, no idea what's involved, trying to unsettle you.' Corbett stepped up to her, doing her top coat button up. 'Beats chasing drunks out of Debenhams, eh?'

'You're right.' Wilde took a breath. 'Sorry. There aren't enough of us, women, in this game.' Grabbing her own coat, she followed Corbett out.

CHAPTER 12

Mrs Margaret Moran lived in one of the grandest houses in Lexden. The family had moved into the nine-bedroom Edwardian mansion when Chloe was five. It boasted three cellars and a turret, and had made Margaret feel terribly lonely since her husband had passed away. She'd surrounded herself with ladies in similar circumstances in the hope of staving off the gloom.

As such, when Chloe approached the house a group of women in brightly coloured clothing were just leaving, gingerly crossing the snow towards their various Mercedes and BMWs. It would take more than an Arctic blast to curtail the bridge mornings that were etched in her mother's weekly routine as surely as the sun would rise each day. The inconvenience of her army major father's death was the only thing she could ever recall having caused proceedings to be cancelled, and then only for a week.

Wilson, her mother's odd job man, answered the door and ushered her through the main reception to the rear drawing room before going to fetch Mrs Moran. That Wilson was still here, Chloe took as a good sign. Margaret had not driven him away. Chloe moved to the window and stared out across the unbroken snow at the naked birch trees, their usually crisp white trunks now looking dirty by comparison.

'Ah, Chloe, what a nice surprise.' Margaret Moran not being one for slippers, her daughter had heard her firm step across the marble hall before she had to face her. She turned slowly. Petite, Margaret always made sure she was noticed – even now, at sixty, her neat burnt-orange hair tastefully matched with a green one-piece. Chloe was the opposite, much to her mother's chagrin – still shirking attention and with no real interest in fashion or clothes.

'Morning, Mum, put the kettle on, eh?' Chloe moved away from the window and sank into her mother's recliner. 'Sorry I've not called – busy time of year for us bean counters.'

Margaret, who had remained standing, wore a quizzical expression that Chloe couldn't read.

'What's up?'

'You look well,' her mother said in response. 'You're not ill?'

'No. Of course I'm well. You sound . . . disappointed? Are *you* okay? You look, well, a bit funny.'

Margaret tutted. 'I thought you might have mentioned Bruce was back and you two planned a clandestine meeting.'

Chloe's mouth opened but no words came, and for an instant she remained slack-jawed.

'I mean, after all that business, the stealing and so on, you know how me and your father felt . . . perhaps that's why?'

Margaret's pencilled eyebrows moved tentatively upwards. 'Regardless, I thought you might be at least curious to hear our side—'

'Mum, what on earth are you talking about? No, I am not meeting with Bruce, for heaven's sake!'

'He said you'd written, asking—'

'Written!' Chloe jumped up from the chair. 'I have never so much as written Bruce a Christmas card in ten years. Jesus . . . Mum?' She slipped from indignation to a plea in a breath. 'Mum . . . have *you* seen him?'

Margaret tilted her head in shame, or embarrassment.

'Have you?' she demanded.

'He came here yesterday.' Theatrically, Margaret reached for the mantelpiece to steady herself, then changed her mind, and turned to her daughter. 'I telephoned you immediately, Chloe . . . I wanted to speak to you, before you met. But then when I called a second time and you did not respond, I thought, she doesn't want to . . .'

Chloe took a deep breath. 'Mother, I have not seen Bruce in over ten years. Sandra only just told me he'd been seen in town. Why he's here, I have no idea – whatever it is, it has nothing to do with me. Is that clear?'

'Yes, dear, I'm sorry.'

'Why did he come here? What did he say to you?'

'Well, that's just it, he said he was meeting you somewhere, I can't recall where, and not to come to the flat . . . that was it.'

'When?'

'Yesterday.'

The word hung there, between them. He had been here, perhaps in this room.

'Presumably he wanted something?' Chloe said eventually.

'All he said was she's forgiven me. For everything.'

'What?'

'He looked absolutely dreadful. Come, let's get the kettle on. When's this beastly weather going to end? The girls had a devil of a job getting here. Madge's chauffeur slipped in the snow and dislocated his hip.'

Chloe, in disbelief, watched her mother leave the room.

'Mother!' she called. 'You should have called the police!'

'The past is the past, darling,' she heard echo in the hall.

CHAPTER 13

Kenton was despondent at returning to Kempe Marsh. He felt Watt was punishing him for answering back – the super knew it to be a waste of time – and Kenton wasn't even meant to be there in the first place. Brazier took the call. Watt had not mentioned him. In fact, Kenton wondered if Watt was wary of Brazier. He was unusual.

Kenton climbed into his car, which responded with an equal lack of enthusiasm. The Vauxhall's battery couldn't take much more pounding on the electrics; lights, heater and wiper. It took several turns of the ignition before the vehicle reluctantly whirred into life, allowing him to cautiously exit the station down the ramp. Most of the snow had been cleared in the town centre by the movement of traffic and people, but the sky was ominous and heavy with more. There was not much evidence of a thaw in the countryside; the occasional dark muddy smudges on the landscape. The wind had got up and whisked the skin up off the snow, producing a veil-like effect across the fields.

The church interior, on the contrary, was warm and damp

when he arrived. Much of the roof debris had been cleared and lay piled up outside, leaving pools of melted snow across the flagstone floor. The vicar's electric heaters had been effective, apart from unleashing a wholly unpleasant smell. An inch-by-inch search of the wreck of St Nicholas-on-the-Marsh was in progress. Floor brasses cut into the flags shimmered dully underfoot as Kenton splashed across their surface towards the huddle of uniformed men on the chancel step.

'Could be sprayed up the walls. Petrol, through a hand pump of some sort,' a red-nosed fire officer said, watching one of his men climb a ladder up the nave wall, 'to get the roof to catch.'

Weak sunlight slipping through the gaping roof cast a long slim shadow of the ascending man, as he continued examining the burnished-barley plaster of the pillars behind the pulpit.

Kenton nodded. It seemed feasible.

'How's it going?' he asked the uniform sergeant.

'It was a helluva of mess, but underneath all this roof debris, the vicar's pews appear to be intact, so that's something.'

'Anything out of the ordinary?'

'One tiny thing.' He beckoned over a young PC, who'd been resting on a shovel while in conversation with another fire officer. Both came over. They had found what was believed to be a feather fragment lying on the surface of the water in the nave.

'Were there pigeons in the roof?' the uniform sergeant asked.

Kenton stood next to the fire officer, considering the charred remain lying on the PC's gloved palm. Blackened and seriously damaged, there was not much to go on. A tiny segment of a feather's vein, none of the rachis or stem was present.

'The vicar's the fellow to answer that,' the fire officer said.

'And that's it? All you've found in four hours?' Kenton asked.

'Combed the entire floor space, sir,' the officer said defensively in a broad North Essex accent; more East Anglian than townie Essex. 'Not so much as a Swan Vesta.'

'Of course – bloody good work to find this. I just meant – where's the rest of the bird?' Kenton frowned and raised the constable's hand into the light. 'This doesn't look like a pigeon feather to me . . . there's shades of brown in there. Barred . . .'

The PC moved closer, until their heads almost touched. 'You're into birds, aren't yer, guv? What d'you reckon it is then?'

The light now blocked by the policeman's helmet, Kenton stepped away and scanned the unblemished walls, lined with memorials of patrons through the centuries, and alcoves with sombre alabaster figures. 'I don't know, I'm not an expert. It might be the remains of a seasonal display . . .'

'All by itself?' the constable said, echoing his own observation.

'So it seems,' Kenton said, attaching little interest to it, and wanting to get back to Colchester before the lanes turned to ice. 'Bag it.'

CHAPTER 14

The small party of police and reservoir men stood at an open section of the water's edge, half a mile from the causeway. It was here, at this small break in the reedbeds, guided by the birdwatcher's approximation, that they'd found direct access into the water was possible, and conducted their search. It had taken frogmen fifteen minutes to locate the vehicle. Realising the situation was more serious than someone dumping an unwanted motor, Wilde had called in CID. This wasn't an insurance job; it was a burial. As the car was winched out of the reservoir in a blizzard, the boot had popped up and, to the surprise of all, revealed a huge dead man, naked apart from his underpants.

'Are you sure it's him?' Wilde asked again.

'Reckon so.' The wind raged between them. Brazier's baggy trousers flapping widely as they watched three young officers negotiate the body out of the car. 'Put on a few pounds since. But yep, it's Bruce Hopkins, all right.'

The Water Board's engineer finished circling the vehicle and made his way over to her.

'What you thinking?' Wilde asked.

'You need a four-wheel drive the majority of the year to get across this terrain,' the engineer said. 'A regular vehicle like this wouldn't cut it.'

'But if the ground were frozen?' She inclined to catch the man's words as snow blustered around the synthetic fur hood of his snorkel jacket. 'Would an ordinary car manage it?'

'Yes, it's possible – evidently.' The engineer raised his mittened hands demonstratively. 'But you'd need to know the way. Be very familiar with the landscape.' Beyond the icy rim of the reservoir, flurries of snow like confetti tumbled across its tight corduroy-grey surface, over which brent geese flew low and stoically into the weather. She could hear the occasional soft squabbling of waterfowl, hunkering down, hidden within the snow-laden reeds yards away from where they stood. They may only be a few miles from the outskirts of Colchester but the weather had transformed the area, giving it the semblance of a Siberian lake: the snow had drifted, and the landscape was a white smear for miles around. Wilde pulled out pocket binoculars and saw nothing to distract the eye other than the blue of the Ford Sierra before them, which appeared as out of place here as it would on the moon. Brazier moved over to examine the body, now on a stretcher.

'Hopkins was one of the River Crouch cannabis gang, responsible for one of the biggest drug hauls ever, found in a yacht moored outside North Fambridge,' he said loudly over the weather.

'Wasn't he meant to be in Spain?'

The body had discernible tan lines at the elbows and knees, but the bloated face was a bleached puce, with a network of burst blood vessels like a road atlas. Beneath a bulbous chin there was an unmistakable mark of where a cord or rope had been used around his neck. Sutton, the SoCo doctor, could be seen making his way towards them.

'Yup, that was what we all thought,' Brazier said. 'Who'd want to come back for this?'

Wilde wasn't sure whether he meant the snow or the fate that awaited him.

Roland was dismayed; worse, he was in shock. He'd popped over to the Gladiator for a pint with a few mates after picking up the envelope on the doormat with his wedge as promised, only to hear the worst news imaginable. The Sierra in the reservoir had already been retrieved, within twenty-four hours of him shoving it in. The pub was a-titter with it as he'd arrived.

'You all right, pal? You look a bit pale.' Fat Roger, a car mechanic friend, said, placing a big palm on his shoulder.

'I'm sound, Rog. Parky out, that's all.'

'Another pint for me mate here, love, when you're free,' Roger called across the bar.

'Probably an insurance job, eh? Wouldn't be the first,' Roland said.

Roger shook his head and his jowls followed. 'Nah,

mate – something fishy in there, an' not the resident pike – there was an ambulance. Scouse saw it when he was on his mountain bike.'

'Ambulance?' Roland said, barely audible. What on earth was cause for an ambulance?

'Can mean only one thing,' said the barmaid, wearing her customary hooped earrings, large enough to contain a perching budgie; she was the disseminator of all gossip on the Monkwick Estate. 'Gotta be a body in there. Mark my words.'

Roland hid his surprise in his pint glass. Making quick work of the second pint, he made his excuses and hurried home.

The rule when nicking motors to order was never to ask questions. So Roland hadn't. The less you know, the better. It might have been insurance, it might not, but when the bloke said the Sierra was now no good – 'What we want the vehicle for may draw attention to it – and heat on you' – Roland assumed it had been intended for a job. He thought that would be the end of it, left for somebody to find in Friday Woods, where he'd been told to abandon it. But no: fella had said that if he made it disappear proper, he'd be paid half the final wedge again as a bonus. This change in plan by his employer had come after Roland's confession on the phone that he'd had to stop to stick a few quid's worth of juice in the motor.

Fair enough, he'd thought then, the reservoir was just down the road from the woods. But now he smelled a giant rat . . . he'd been done up. Ask no questions was one thing, but leaving him exposed like this? If the job was to dump a body, they should have been upfront. Then again, he'd have said no way . . .

Roland, dazed, stumbled into the house, passing his sister glued to the TV in the front room.

'You'll never guess what,' Mandy called out.

He wasn't in the mood for surprises. Ignoring her, he made straight for the kitchen, and the top shelf.

'I said, Rollie, you'll never guess what,' Mandy said again, louder this time.

He poured cheap vodka into his Spurs mug with a shaking hand, filling it about halfway, took a gulp, then another, breathed out. He waited for the warmth to flow and steady him, before strolling with a determined confidence back into the front room.

'The IRA have bazooka'd John Major?' he said.

'No, bigger than that – the Old Bill have pulled Nicetoseeyou out of Abberton Reservoir.'

CHAPTER 15

'Bruce bloody Hopkins!' Watt guffawed, as if the name brought to mind a mischievous long-lost friend. In truth, the super knew nothing about the case; it was way before his time. He scratched the back of his head thoughtfully. 'When was that now?'

'Eighty-four,' Kenton said, knowing the boss's ignorance.

Brazier, Kenton and Wilde stood before Watt in his office. He pushed his chair back and frowned out of the huge window as darkness descended on the town.

'What is there here to lure anyone over from the continent in February, I wonder?'

'Another job, sir?' Wilde suggested. 'Smuggling, like before.'

'Unlikely,' Brazier said. 'They blew it that time and lost his boat with the cargo.'

'Essex in February,' Watt said. 'It's not a destination hotspot for the winter, is it?'

'Unless you're a goose, sir,' Kenton said.

'Yes,' Wilde said, 'plenty of them on the reservoir.'

Watt smiled. Training told him that officers working murder

71

often had a twisted sense of humour. He wished the three of them would sit down – he found it vaguely threatening, them standing there like that. But there were only two chairs. He played along. 'They'll feel right at home – like the Siberian tundra out there right now. Twitching is all the rage.' He was not immune to society; one of The Goodies had been on the local news, banging on about it, the little bearded one. 'Anyway, back to Hopkins. Why leave Spain now?' On his desk lay the scene-of-crime photos. 'Not with any intention of ending up garrotted in the boot of a Sierra, I imagine. Anything on that?'

'Manchester plates. And Didsbury tax disc, valid. Can just make it out,' Brazier said.

'Stolen, probably,' Wilde added.

Stolen cars travelled the country easily, usually to order. And Sierras were the most nickable there were. Watt's phone flashed from its position on the right-hand side of the desk. He eyed it uncertainly, hesitating whether to answer. He took the call: indecision was a weakness.

'We've located Hopkins' next of kin, sir,' the familiar voice of Philips informed him. 'An ex-wife. Chloe Moran. Lives in Lexden. Uniform have gone to collect her.'

'Very good,' he said and hung up. He considered the three officers. 'This is the first major outing for you two,' he began, wagging his finger between Kenton and Brazier. 'I want to see teamwork here. You're equal rank, but Kenton, I expect you at the fore, knowing the town. How was Kempe Marsh?'

'We found a feather.'

'A feather?'

'Sir, the remains of one. I have sent it to the lab.'

'A phoenix, perhaps?' Watt suggested. 'Very well, we can do only so much. Onwards with Hopkins. Any questions?' He waited for a reaction. Kenton was educated, like himself. Brazier had no qualifications to speak of, but at twenty-seven came with an impeccable record. He was regarded as a bit eccentric, and according to his old Clacton gaffer, exhibited signs of 'attention deficit disorder' – 'but don't let that put you off'. With spiky hair and scarf still wrapped high, Brazier was gazing absently out the window.

'Very well, off you all go. Accompany DS Kenton to the morgue to assist and deal with the ex-Mrs Hopkins. You too, Wilde – be on hand once she officially identifies the body.' Good to keep her involved – Watt had been tasked with having two women in CID by the end of the year. 'Philips will notify the press. Expect a fanfare.'

Kenton exited, followed by Wilde. Brazier eventually roused himself, stared at Watt keenly, then left without a word.

The Clacton gaffer had not mentioned the funny eye.

CHAPTER 16

Chloe's mind was at sixes and sevens as she rounded the corner of her street. She was so distracted that she didn't notice the police car outside her block of flats. As soon as she did register it, she immediately assumed it was connected to Bruce. It was. In minutes, she was conveyed the short distance to the County Hospital on the Lexden Road and escorted wordlessly down the gleaming silent corridors to the morgue.

That he was dead seemed obvious, though she couldn't recall anyone actually saying the words.

She paid little attention to the four people in the chamber – for it was more of a chamber than a room; stark and clinical, with a faint smell of detergent. Two women – a policewoman and a woman in a lab coat – and two men, presumably detectives. The men stepped aside and only then could she see the sheeted mound on the trolley. The lady in the lab coat, who had red hair in a neat bun, stood poised.

One of the men started talking but she didn't take in his words. As the doctor made to remove the sheet, Chloe's eyes were drawn to the nape of the woman's neck and the fine hairs that escaped the bun, before she took in the ghastly sight of her dead husband.

She had to look twice to be sure. His face was so big . . . and unpleasant. And the hair, always so perfect – practically non-existent.

'Yes, it's him. Jesus, he looks rough.' She turned to meet the gaze of a man in his mid-thirties wearing glasses, shirt and tie. 'Life on the Costa Brava is obviously very punishing.'

The moment of respectful stillness now over, the people in the room got to work around her, with the exception of the doctor, who replaced the sheet and disappeared. The shorter male, who was wearing enough product to hold his dark brown hair bolt upright, handed her a card with a CID phone number on it. The woman, a sergeant from her stripes, with a bob not dissimilar to her own, asked if she was okay and if she needed accompanying home. Chloe didn't need anyone right now, but acquiesced anyway, imagining it the expected behaviour, and followed the policewoman out.

In reality, Chloe Moran felt nothing but immense irritation at this unwanted intrusion into her life. Of course her ex-husband remained a burden; even in death she could not seem to rid herself of him. And at the back of her mind she was still annoyed at her mother too; something about Margaret's behaviour niggled her and she didn't know why. She resented her mother and Bruce in equal measure, and cursed them both for imposing this situation on her.

*

Kenton cleared his throat to remind the pathologist, whose back was towards him as she returned to examining the large, marbled body, that they were still present. The lab was marginally warmer than it was outside; a whisker above freezing point – he wondered if she wore thermals underneath her lab coat.

'Strangled,' Dr Nelmes announced without lifting her head. 'On the face of it, that is.'

'What does that mean? On the face of it?'

Kenton heard Brazier sniff unpleasantly behind him.

Nelmes turned her pale face towards him. 'Dry skin around the neck, and . . . swelling. Though not as much as one would expect.' She stepped aside to show the hand. 'And . . .'

'And what?' Brazier asked.

'There's no sign of a struggle. Clawing at the garrotte or cord, you know, telltale signs the victim put up a fight. It was minus five degrees the night before he went into the reservoir – perilous to be out in just your underwear for any period of time.' She let the hand drop indelicately with a thud. 'He's not been dead long. Two days, three at most. The water makes it difficult to pinpoint,' Nelmes continued. 'Am I right to think there's not much in the way of vegetation on the banks of Abberton Reservoir?'

Brazier cast his mind back. All he could see was snow. 'Reedbeds,' he said eventually.

'Anyway, this man may have passed through the great out-doors before being placed inside the car.' She moved around the gurney to a tray and picked up something with tweezers. 'This was found in the car boot.'

She held it in the air.

'A leaf?' Kenton said.

'Yes. Oak, by the look of it.'

Kenton moved in to have a closer look at the corpse. The body was a dirty greenish-white.

'Don't get too close,' Nelmes said, her Scottish accent only coming to the fore when her voice was raised. Nelmes had been with them only three months, replacing the ancient former local coroner, Robinson. Kenton moved back in deference to her authority as she continued to move around the body. 'My guess is that he'd not have been long for this world anyway.'

'What, do you think he had some kind of a condition?'

'Come on, you don't need me to tell you; just look at the physical state of him. A coronary waiting to happen.' She made to open the victim's mouth. 'And here, look at this.' She moved the tongue to one side. Kenton winced. It was inflamed deep red with white sores.

'Nasty,' he said, repressing the urge to recoil in front of the doctor.

'Cancer.' She replied, holding up one of the yellow-fingered hands. 'Quite far gone; he'd lose his tongue in a matter of months. Anyhow, I want to run some blood tests, he may have been on medication or may even have been drugged.'

The doctor released the hand and moved towards the head, now down to a bulbous nose.

'Hello, what's this?' She picked up a pair of tweezers from the utensils tray.

'What's what?' Brazier said.

'Appears to be something lodged up here.' Nelmes proceeded to extract a tightly rolled paper tube. Holding it out, she held it out to Brazier.

'What on earth . . .?' Brazier hurriedly pulled on surgical gloves and took the object, 'A note from his murderer?'

Kenton took it. 'Spot on – a Spanish one to be exact, to the tune of a thousand pesetas.'

'What's that? A fiver? Enough for a couple of pints at least. Bureau de change then pub?' Brazier said, his face alive. 'Situation demands it.'

Kenton was taken aback by the suggestion – the pub was the last place they should be right now, but instead said: 'Sure, let's go over the road to the Tap. And don't worry, I've got sterling.'

CHAPTER 17

The Tap and Spile public house was opposite the hospital, where Southway became Lexden Road, and was a popular haunt for medical staff and police alike. And at times of intrigue, the press could be found here too. Kenton knew it well, but to his mind it was hardly the appropriate time, and he was short on cash, but he wanted to get off on the right foot and hear what Brazier had to say.

'Wait.' Brazier halted, recognising a hack entering the pub ahead of them, and thinking better of the Tap, changed course for the Sun, out of the way on the far end of the Lexden Road.

'Before we get into thick of it, can I just check you're okay with me taking the lead on this?' Kenton said.

'Totally, mate, it's your manor. I'm the new kid on the block. We don't want to stop every five minutes for me to dig out a street map.'

'That's very good of you to be so dismissive about it – but you don't need to be an expert on this town to run the case. Besides, I'm sure you know your way around Colchester as well as I do.'

Brazier marched on ahead, disinterested in discussing matters of command any further.

'Well, I look forward to working with you, Brazier,' Kenton said. 'At first I wondered why Watt put us together . . .' He stopped himself, wishing to phrase it correctly.

'Because we're so different? The old nice and nasty routine? Rough with the smooth?'

'No, no, I'd not dream of saying that. I wouldn't begin to speculate.'

Kenton was a middle-class university graduate from Surrey with a wife and two kids. A known quantity, in the force and the town. Everyone including Brazier knew that.

'I mean, different, yes – complementary – elements to a team.' And teams were the future; Watt pronounced this on a seemingly weekly basis. The powers that be decreed new initiatives for teamwork, over and over. The aim was to overcome the rigidity and draconian hierarchy of the old days. Now it was common practise for officers of the same rank to share cases, just as Watt had arranged here. No matter that the idea was flawed – decision-making grew slower not quicker, as 'teamwork' left the divide between authority and responsibility unclear; and it didn't go unnoticed that the 'management team' that was often referred to had a membership of . . . one. Watt had no qualms about speaking of himself as plural.

'Mate, don't fret. I'm sure we'll be dandy, eh? I'm just a south Essex boy. Scraped into the rozzers with four CSEs.

One of us will have to write the reports up and it ain't going to be me.'

'Oh, absolutely,' Kenton said. 'Here, let me, my shout.'

Brazier pulled up a stool, ordered a cider, and planted a paper bag of boiled sweets down on the beer mat, noticing a tarantula in a small aquarium beneath the optics on the other side of the bar. There was no reason he and Kenton couldn't rub along just as well. They were both open-minded in their way, Brazier more so, being the younger. 'Trying to quit the fags, aren't I?' he said, noticing Kenton frowning at the sweets. 'Right, to business,' he added as the pints were placed in front of them. 'A Spanish banknote wedged up a dead Englishman's hooter. Will attract a lot of interest. Watt's right.'

'Scotland Yard for a start.'

'The Yard, Interpol, absolutely – this has to be a message from the killer? Who else? Hopkins must have been caught skimming in Spain, and so some pissed-off Spanish guy come over here to do him.'

'Perhaps,' Kenton shrugged. 'But why travel here to do it, why not in Spain?'

'Send a warning to other Brits – the Spanish want it all, as the papers here say.'

'Good point.'

Kenton looked Brazier square in the face as he spoke and noticed for the first time that his left pupil was badly disfigured. 'Something bad happened in Spain, he had to scarper back to Blighty. Who knows? If that's right, then it's very good reason not to let this get in the papers – and you can bet we'd lose control of the case before we've even started if there's a Spanish connection. Why now though, after ten years? Must have known he'd been rumbled.'

'The Crouch case was huge, right? Hopkins was one of them that got away, but the skunk was left on the boat, remember, so they left empty-handed – maybe he fell on hard times, had to resort to dealing and got careless. Anyway, will anyone care? The doc said he'd got cancer and didn't have long.'

'Murder's murder. No one was harmed in that haul. Those guys were not seen as villains; more lauded for the size of their balls.'

'A bunch of hoorays, weren't they?' Brazier sucked on his sweet. Then removed it from his mouth and stuck it in the ashtray. 'I don't know much more than that – before my time. Wasn't your old gaffer involved?'

'Sparks.' Kenton smiled as he said the name. 'Yes, he was, in a manner – saved his bacon. And yes, there was a public-school connection of some description.'

'Be interested to see what Hopkins' ex-missus has to say about it all. Pretty stony-faced, wasn't she? Don't imagine they had much of a marriage.'

Kenton gave an involuntarily shrug. 'We will need to rule her out.'

'Without ruffling her pretty feathers will be the trick.'

Kenton turned with a trace of disproval. 'Talking of feathers, the fragment we found in the church was a pheasant I think, probably from a leftover decoration or seasonal display.' He was picturing such displays in the church where he took the kids, in Kelvedon.

'On the coast?'

'You what?' Kenton said, sharply.

'Pheasants are a hedgerow bird,' said Brazier. 'Not coastal – or bog, whatever you want to call it . . . Sorry, this might be splitting hairs . . .' He paused to gulp his pint. 'Another thing – and stop me if I remember wrong – most of the walls were intact, right, the damage was only the roof? Displays are usually tucked away in the alcoves on plinths, right?'

Kenton was dismayed. The man was right – pheasants were not a marshland bird. Jesus, why hadn't that struck him sooner? And he *had* seen the alcoves and the walls for that matter, but not arrived at that conclusion.

'You're right,' Kenton said finally. 'Anyway, I've sent the fragment to the lab, see what they say.'

Their pint glasses sat empty on the bar. Kenton was keen to move; get on with the job.

'What's the plan, then?' The ice broken, Brazier too sensed it was time to go. 'Let Watt know about the banknote, or store that particular detail for now, and go find Hopkins' ex, Chloe Moran, see what she has to say?'

Kenton did not want to see the super until absolutely necessary. 'Watt will have his hands full with the press. Let's try and see Ms Moran before they do.' He rose. 'Do we have her address?'

'Wilde slipped me it – she's just round the corner, Oxford Road.' Brazier smiled. 'Cheers for the pint, good to catch up.'

CHAPTER 18

Having yanked off her boots, Chloe had collapsed on the sofa and not moved in over an hour. A sob was always just beneath the surface. Bollocks – that was not going to happen! Cry over that fat pig, as if . . . How had he got so fat? He was enormous. Bruce was never even close to that size when they met. No way. Tall, yes, slim and vaguely handsome back then. She pinched her nose and felt the tears slide down her fingers, all the same. Tears of self-pity. She propelled herself up and screamed at the empty room.

Chloe spotted the police from the window. The shortish one wearing a woollen peaked hat and a bomber jacket, the other in a duffle coat, like some spod from a university campus. They'd not wasted much time . . . unsurprisingly, she hadn't much time to project the grieving wife vibe.

She had to think carefully what to say. Taking a deep breath, and checking herself in the mirror, she made for the door. Standing there expectantly, she realised her whole body had been tight, rigid with . . . what? Fear? That he'd get off the slab and come at her? He never came after her when he was alive. No, it was the pressure of the way he'd returned to her life, why he had come back, what he might have wanted . . .

Brazier and Kenton re-introduced themselves. They were polite if nothing else. On the front step, Chloe stood several inches above Brazier, proprietorially, arms across her chest, leaning on the doorframe, in command.

'I know he's dead, I identified the body. Remember?'

'Yes, we do . . . understand that,' Brazier said. 'We are now investigating the circumstances of his death, and as his next of kin, we'd like to ask you some questions, if that's all right with you?'

'Hey, that's an unwanted association.' She flicked her hair back and shot daggers at Kenton, who visibly recoiled. 'Let's get that straight.' She moved forward and uncrossed her arms, breathing out, expanding her chest, which he could not fail to notice, being at eye level.

'I'm sorry. You don't use his name anymore, correct?'

'Correct. I go by my maiden name, Moran, but I'm still at the same address, which is why you found me. Everybody knew *his* address, right? And presumably I'm the only kin, there's no one else. Miserable existence he led.' She paused. 'Anyone might have killed him.'

'Maybe we can speak inside?'

Chloe considered letting them in. Brazier glanced back over the forecourt of the block. Thick snow lay on the car windscreens.

'You're letting the heat out,' he said as a neighbour ushered them to leave the building.

Grudgingly, she stepped aside. 'First floor, on the right.' Scrutinising them as they passed through, she added, 'You're a bit short for a copper.' Brazier rounded the stairs without comment. 'And wipe your feet on the way in.'

The flat contained worn eighties furniture at odds with the large sash window overlooking the forecourt. There were half-packed or unpacked boxes everywhere. On the mantelpiece remained a single photograph of her with a man that was not Bruce.

'On the move?' Brazier asked.

'I wish. Been here for eleven years – and he's not lived here for ten of them. And before you ask, I have no idea where he went. I kicked him out before he skipped out of the country.'

'When was the last time you saw him?'

'Not since the day he left. Had to look twice to be sure it was him there on the slab. Barely a year, that's all I spent with him. He spent longer wooing me than our sham of a marriage lasted.'

They remained standing awkwardly in the small front room.

'When did he leave?'

She shrugged. 'October 1980. We'd been married five months. The next time I saw him was in the newspapers along with the rest of the country, the summer of 1984 after the River Crouch drugs raid. When, as it happens, I went through all this same old crap with you lot.'

'Okay, any idea who might have wanted him dead?' Kenton asked.

'Anyone, as I said. He'd been ripping people off for years and years.' Chloe held his gaze, daring him to challenge her. 'He had the gift of the gab, but when you get down to it he was a snake, a cowardly man, targeting the weak and defenceless.'

CHAPTER 19

Brazier saw no trace of a weak and defenceless individual before him now. She'd earnt her confidence and pride the hard way, perhaps.

'Bruce used his own boat for the smuggling jobs, right? Bought from an inheritance? Do you know who left him the dosh?'

'Depending who you believe: a relative, who I never met, or drugs money. He never talked about his family, all I know is he was brought up by a rich aunt who left him a packet shortly after we were married and that's when he did a bunk. You should be in touch with his pals, he spent more time with them than me.'

Kenton raised an eyebrow.

'I'm not jealous,' she said. 'I got this flat out of it.'

'How much money was there?'

'Near a million.' The flat, though in a posh part of town, was pokey and probably worth fifty to sixty grand tops now. Back then, it'd barely scratched the surface of a million quid. She'd not got much. Bruce's schooner would be worth double at least.

'Did he blow the lot?'

'I haven't the faintest. Try his pals, as I said.'

They waited for more.

'The ringleader was Peter, Peter Hart; it was always Pete this, Pete that. Check the papers; they shared the front page together, that photo of them on the boat in Malaga harbour. He's probably abroad.'

Kenton made a note.

'Spain?'

'*Spain,*' she intoned. 'Yes, Spain. That's where they all are, isn't it? Cons that made it.'

'You strike me as bitter, Ms Moran, if you don't mind me saying so,' Kenton said.

'And if I am?' she sighed. 'Look, we weren't that close. He just wasn't that interested.'

'Interested in what?'

'*Me.* What did you think I meant?' Chloe said. 'Everything was fine to start with, but then . . . I don't know. He was quite a bit older than me – but still boyishly charming with a cute babyface on top of slender tall body, he had the gift of the gab, what you'd call a gentleman. Clever, knew stuff, interesting things that the dimwits round here wouldn't have a clue about . . . but the sparkle vanished, went like that, like he couldn't be bothered once we were married.'

'It happens,' Kenton said.

'At the start, people, my mother included, used to think him a loveable rogue – he'd turn the charm on when we were short of cash, all right. We'd been going out together for a couple of months or so before I realised he had no intention of getting a regular job. He claimed he tried various things – bit of journalism, publishing, teaching, drifting from one to the other – but had yet find his "niche", as he put it. He'd get up and disappear mid-morning, and when I asked where and what for, he'd just say, "ducking and diving" in jokey way, like some dolt off the telly.'

'And still you married him?'

'Yes, something of a whirlwind romance, after only six months. I was under his spell, and we weren't at that time short of money. Or so I thought.' She stared out of the window. 'There wasn't a single member of his family at the wedding. I should've realised before then, though. My poor mother found it very odd, but he charmed her all the same.'

It was difficult to imagine the man in the morgue as having once been the man she described.

'What went wrong, then? Apart from the sparkle . . .'

'Things didn't really start going wrong until after we were married . . . Except there was this one instance before. When my mother lost her eternity ring. By Easter 1980, we were busy planning the wedding, and Bruce had practically moved into my mother's house with me. After Sunday lunch, that holiday, he was helping her with the washing up, larking around, making her laugh. She had removed her ring to put on rubber gloves and placed it on the windowsill. Everyone had had a bit to drink, and it wasn't until the next day she realised it was missing. We searched everywhere for it, upturned the bin, you name it. Bruce too, but in a way that I just knew he had it.'

'Did you challenge him?'

'Yes, we had a massive row and he buggered off. Disappeared for days, I had no idea where he went. I was beside myself. What an idiot, I should have got out then . . . but, no. I was too far down the road. My pride was wounded – I couldn't face the prospect of being jilted. Young and stupid – I even told myself if he did it, it was because he loved me. Boy, was I relieved when he returned home!' She held up her hands in cynical amazement. 'The ring never did turn up, and though I never had proof, I reckon he pawned it, to help with the wedding cost.'

'Maybe he did love you?'

'Hah! No. The reality was, my mum had enlisted her nosey old friends in the wedding arrangements, and Bruce was frightened one of them would twig him for a sponger – so he made sure everyone saw an ostentatious gesture of cash.'

'Do you work yourself?'

'Yes, I'm an accountant. Surprised? Bit different from back then, I'll grant you, when I was juggling working in a club by night, a filing clerk by day and trying to re-sit my O-levels in between – having realised that idle bastard was not going to bring home the bacon with any regularity. Then, suddenly, just before we married, the old aunt died, and we offered on this flat – but that held his interest for a millisecond. Having his own money meant he soon forgot about me, my mother's money and, fortunately, this flat. Then his mates resurfaced, attracted to the smell of cash, and – *whoosh* – he was gone . . . Anyway, water under the bridge. I've moved on.'

Although she hadn't; she was still in the same flat, and spoke as if it were just yesterday that he'd pawned her mother's ring.

'What would tempt Bruce back from Spain?' Kenton echoed Watt's words.

'No idea. There's nothing or no one here for him that I know of.'

After forty-five minutes, they left her in peace. Chloe was drained. She had omitted to tell them about Bruce visiting her mother, or about the letter he'd claimed to have received from her. She knew it ought to have been the first thing she said, but caught up in the moment, it somehow hadn't come up. As she watched them talking across the car roof below, she knew two things for sure: one, finding out that Bruce had contacted her mother had given her the jitters, and two, if the police found out that she knew about it – which, if they were worth their salt, they soon would – the implications for her were serious. Meanwhile, the green flash of the answerphone was there to remind her that her mother had seen the news. The news. Press. She'd have to tell Paul.

CHAPTER 20

Brazier and Kenton had left Chloe Moran without a lead; only the impression of a failed relationship, and not an unusual tale at that. Kenton read scarcely concealed anger in her voice, anger at having to unearth all this again; she would have tried much harder to hide her resentment had she murdered him. 'She didn't hold back. I say we leave her for now.'

Brazier agreed.

The death was public by the time they returned, and Hopkins was on the lunchtime news. Events weren't going as planned. Watt was gesticulating wildly at Philips in his office. 'Give him a wide berth,' Wilde's WPC pal, Corbett, advised, pointing to Post-its on Kenton's phone. 'Two leads, boys, to occupy you and keep you on the street and out of here. A publican at the Hare in Layer claiming Hopkins had been in two nights before and a bloke in Marks Tey claiming he owns the Sierra.'

'Marks Tey? You sure? The car has Manchester plates.'

'Yeah, spot on, bloke sounded like Bez from the Mondays. Manc sales rep staying at the Copford Hotel, out near the motorway.'

'I'll flip you for it,' Brazier said.

'All right.'

Brazier spun a ten pence in the air. Kenton won. 'You choose.' The Hare was the exciting lead, who gave a monkeys about the car? But Brazier said, 'I'll take Bez.'

'Sure?'

He nodded and said loudly in the direction of Watts' office: *'Call the cops!'*

Kenton ignored him, and instead picked up the Post-it with the number for the pub.

The Hare was on a rural crossroads south-west of Colchester. And near the reservoir. Kenton took a map out to his car and spread it out across the Vauxhall's steering wheel. He couldn't help but notice how the two roads that met at the pub encircled Abberton Reservoir, which lay to the immediate south-east of the crossroads.

He made it to the Hare in under fifteen minutes, surprising the landlord. 'What can you tell me?'

'He came in late. Had a few then left without uttering a word. Never seen him before. Then when his chops pops up on the box, I said to the wife that was the mush in 'ere with the young lady on his arm.'

'Time?'

The landlord rubbed an unshaven jaw. 'Got here about nine, stayed for few, was with a bird.'

'Oh yeah?'

95

'Yeah, much younger than him. It was her that draw me eye, if you get me. We were well busy – weather draws them out – but they were up at the bar. Oh, and he couldn't find the lav – had to point him in the right direction.'

'Description of her?'

'Hair was frizzy like. Highlights. That's all I could see really.'

'If it was busy there'd have been punters either side. Couple of the locals might have overheard something?'

'Steve Moore and Dave Chadwick, both retired. Don't have their addresses, but they'll be in later. Will ask them to call. Doubt they'll know anything. Both sozzled.'

The pub was clean, spartan, with neat pine tables and chairs. Light and roomy.

Kenton turned and faced the pub windows, seeing two cars were sat at the crossroads.

'Would you notice a car pull in?'

If Hopkins had come from Spain it was unlikely he'd have his own car unless he hired one.

'Out front, yeah . . . on a quiet night. Headlight beams come through the window. But not on that night, sorry. Too busy,' replied the landlord, already turning away to release the dishwasher door. Kenton exited the pub.

There was limited space out front between the building and the road, but not well lit. A larger parking area was at the back. The snow was unbroken until the road. Round the back sat a solitary car, a Volvo 740 with four inches of virgin snow on the roof, like a layer of cake icing. There were footprints to and from the wheelie bins. There were very faint indents of tyres, indicating vehicle movement, but none with any definition. No attempt had been made to clear the snow, or to park a car recently. He returned to the front, where on closer inspection there was evidence of tyre tread on the periphery of the parking area, perhaps the kerb, where a car had either lost control or pulled in. The tracks made a soft arc, and then turned sharply back into the road, but again nothing of any use. He returned inside, where the landlord was pointing a remote angrily at a large TV screen beyond his range.

'Did he arrive with the woman? Or did they turn up separately?'

'I don't know mate, sorry.'

Kenton stood looking at the bar. There weren't that many stools. Five only. Keep the bar uncluttered, free to serve.

'Were they both seated, at the bar? If she was holding on to his arm, as you say, maybe she was standing.'

'Now you mention it . . . she was standing. Sort of draped over him. Bit sickening if you ask me.'

'If they'd arrived together they'd have sat somewhere else, right? There would have been room?'

'Yeah, yeah. Good point. The lads were at the bar. You know, I reckon he must have got here first.'

'Can I use the phone?'

He pulled out a fiver and asked for change as an enticement, and taking the Yellow Pages proceeded to work through the Colchester minicabs.

*

Ian Healey, a thin, waxy-complexioned northerner, had been stranded at the Copford Hotel. The forty-three-year-old, desperate to get home, sat waiting in the hotel foyer for Brazier to finish with the hotel clerk. Healey was on a routine trip selling marine insurance. He had held his final meetings for the week in a conference suite at the hotel. It was not until that afternoon, after a shower and a full English breakfast for lunch, that he had checked out and wheeled his suitcase towards the car park, only to discover his Sierra GL was gone.

The hotel was popular with salesmen for its proximity to the A12. Until recently its nearest neighbour was the old police garage and home to the traffic division. The hotel had a broad car park between its forecourt and the main road. The forecourt was shielded with a screen of evergreens: anyone could have stolen a car and the hotel would be none the wiser; in less than a minute a car could be miles away, heading towards London or Ipswich.

'Had cars stolen from here before?' Brazier addressed the blank-faced duty manager, who looked like he'd not slept in days.

'Not in the past two years, before that you'd have to ask the manager.'

'When's the manager due on?'

'Seven thirty.'

It was now six. Brazier thought that although it would be easy to nick a car here, it was unusual – like train station car parks and public shopping spaces, it'd likely have a steady stream of people coming and going all hours, and therefore likely witnesses. Even overnight there'd still be someone on the front desk. On the other hand, it was a transitory place; no one would know which car belonged to which guest, and there was the fact that this type of motor was notoriously easy to steal. Brazier left the desk and made his way over to Healey, sitting dejectedly with a suitcase.

Healey had stayed here at least a dozen times and never experienced theft of any kind, vehicle or personal belongings. He knew no one beyond his clients in the immediate area. Cooperative and polite, the man was nevertheless impatient to get away. The poor guy had the prospect of a train and all the hassles that involved travelling back to Manchester. 'A single snowflake lands on the tracks and the entire British Rail network grinds to a halt,' he said. 'Always done a presentation in the hotel on Fridays, thought it easier than carting the charts about if I had set up in one of the rooms here.' The man had a broad northern accent. 'Get away quicker when I'm done too. Straight onto the motorway. Otherwise I'd have noticed me vehicle'd gone first thing, I'm sure.'

'Was there anything in the car of value?'

'Nothing. It's a company motor. I need details for the insurance,' Healey said. 'My firm insure the fleet.'

'Right, what do you need?'

'Exact location – the sergeant told me the car was pulled out of a lake?'

'Reservoir. At Abberton.'

'Right, how far is that then?'

'About eight miles or so.'

'Whoever nicked it might've needed to put some petrol in.'

'Empty, was it?'

'Practically bone dry – conscientious, me, don't stop unless I need to. Always fill up for the journey home at Shell garage on the A12 slip road just over the way.'

Brazier made a note.

'Tell me, sir, did you keep anything in the Sierra's boot?'

'Suitcase and props. And they were in the room with me. There was nothing of value in there, as I said. It's easier to keep clean if it's empty.'

'Anyone other than yourself have a key to the car?'

'Fleet manager in Manchester.'

'How often do you come down?'

'Every six weeks or so, usually. Last were just before Christmas, seal the year end, like.'

Was the car stolen for the purpose of transporting Hopkins to the reservoir? There was no reason to think otherwise at this stage. Healey wasn't aware that his car had contained a dead body, and Brazier saw no reason to enlighten him yet. The car may have been singled out – but with a dry tank? Not ideal. The garage on the London Road would be the obvious place to refuel.

CHAPTER 21

A minicab from a firm in Osbourne Street had made a pickup from the George Hotel to Layer at 8:30 p.m., Kenton had discovered. The driver himself was not available for comment, being on an airport run. The concierge at the George was not pleased with a policeman asking questions around his quiet, peaceful lobby. He leafed through the bookings log with an insolent whetted finger.

'There's no one here by that name, Sergeant, for the night in question or any other.'

'All right, put it this way, any of your guests left without paying their bill?'

He bristled. 'Well, there's a B. R. Reynolds unaccounted for . . .'

'Give me that,' said Kenton, and he snatched the leather-bound ledger. 'Does the name Bruce Reynolds mean anything to you?'

The concierge shook his head. Behind Kenton was a woman in a fur coat and sparkly earrings, with an old bloke using a walking stick. 'Bruce Richard Reynolds led the Great Train

Robbery, in 1963. Remember that, luv?' he said over his shoulder. Hopkins' idea of a joke. Reynolds had been released in the late seventies, but his accomplice Charlie Wilson had been shot on his doorstep in Marbella last April; Hopkins' stomping ground.

'I'm sorry, your point is?' the concierge hissed.

'Don't you guys ask for proof of ID?'

'We are not the Hilton Intercontinental, sir.'

Reynolds' had taken a suite on the first floor, overlooking the High Street. Kenton moved slowly across the creaking carpeted Tudor floor. The room was tidy, the vacuum strokes across the beige carpet suggested there'd not been much activity. An open bottle of Metaxa sat on the dressing table alongside a carton of JPS. A leather Admiral holdall was tucked against a dressing table alongside a duty-free bag. Kenton checked the duty-free bag first; another bottle of Metaxa and more fags. Nothing had been handed over to store in the hotel safe.

'His passport must be in here somewhere,' he muttered to himself, as he emptied the holdall onto the bed. A pair of jeans, a pullover, socks stuffed with a half bottle of Johnnie Walker, presumably with the intent of fooling customs, and a paperback. Less than a third full. No passport.

In the en suite sat a wash bag and beside it a bottle of aftershave. No shaving kit. He unzipped the wash bag to find a freezer bag with a mix of sterling notes and pesetas wrapped round a UK passport. He flipped open the passport: Henry Winkler.

'Cheeky tool.'

Kenton tucked the passport into his pocket and flipped the holdall shut. He left the hotel with both the bag and the duty free.

Watt sat unhappily behind his desk. The last thing he wanted to hear was that Colchester was at the end of the line on a Spanish drug trail. He'd not had a great day. The Royal Military Police commander had complained that some pubs were refusing entry to soldiers in civilian dress – landlords identified them by their haircuts. Fear was stalking in the wake of the Downing Street attack; soldiers and their drinking establishments were becoming targets.

The February evening painted the large plate-glass office windows black, as the men inside assembled under the stark artificial light. Closing the super's door, Kenton placed a transparent baggie on his desk. Watt could clearly make out the rolled banknote retrieved from Hopkins' nose. Ignoring this for the moment, he moved the conversation on to the sighting at the pub.

'So, nobody saw him come or go – or knew how he got there, right?'

'That we know of. Apart from the minicab driver that collected him from the George; prior to that, no. Flew in from Malaga two days before using a fake passport and checked in under another name.'

'Driver have anything useful to say?'

Kenton had since spoken to the cabbie. 'He'd asked Hopkins if he needed a return trip from the pub. Hopkins said yes and that he'd call as he didn't know when he'd be done. The driver described his passenger's mood as chatty, excited, and he'd gone on about the snow – he'd not seen any in years . . .'

'Didn't give any indication of who he was meeting?' Watt asked.

'Nope. Driver thought a date. Smartly dressed, cleanly shaven. The girl he met was young, younger than his ex-wife . . . we've nothing on her. It's possible she was a honey trap for a drugs gang.'

'Why would they go to the trouble of stripping him?' Hopkins had been found in only his pants; the rest of his clothing remained a mystery. 'Strange.'

'It's not conclusive that he died by strangulation,' Brazier said. 'Exposure. Doc reckons he might have been drugged. We're awaiting test results.'

'Seems like it was drawn out,' Kenton said, 'make him suffer, maybe lying near-naked in the snow. He may even have been conscious when loaded into the boot of the car.'

'I see.' Watt's eyes were now drawn back to the bagged note, with no desire to touch it, wishing it did not exist. 'Not very subtle, is it?'

He glanced from one to the other. This might be the tip of the iceberg.

Watt sighed. Drugs. The problem that never goes away.

'Where did it come from?'

'We don't yet know – it could be the killer's or even be Hopkins' own money. He had currency in his wash bag. Nevertheless, we suspect it's possibly a calling card from a drug cartel,' Kenton said. 'They are not known for subtlety.'

Brazier nodded in agreement.

'Why do him in over here, though?'

'Make sure everyone sees it. Warning to others.'

'Very well. One of you will have to go over there, then. To Malaga. Find this Peter Hart before Scotland Yard swoop down. Cover our bases, so to speak. And make sure no one hears anything of *this*.' He gestured towards the rolled banknote in the bag.

'Yes, we'll keep that piece of intel to ourselves for now,' he continued. 'Once the drug squad are crawling over us, it will undoubtedly get messy. Right, Spain. Who's it to be?'

Neither leapt at the opportunity, both holding back for very different reasons.

'Come, gents, we haven't got all day. Well? Brazier?'

'Err . . . I can't, sorry, sir,' he said, staring at the floor.

'Can't? Why not?'

'Don't fly. Doesn't agree with me.'

'Doesn't agree with you?' Watt snorted. 'What nonsense! Never mind. Kenton, pack your bags and get a flight sorted.'

CHAPTER 22

'You are an idiot.' Mandy stared at her brother contemptuously. He sat at the kitchen table, biting his nails. A habit he'd had as long as he'd teeth. 'Weren't you even remotely suspicious?'

Once she was convinced he wasn't going to run, she immediately began to ridicule him. What their mum ever saw in him as a child was a mystery.

'No. Why should I be? Never ask questions. That's the rule. The less you know the better.'

'Can't argue with that.' She scratched a cold sore in the corner of her mouth. 'You know naff all . . . unless you really did Brucie in?'

'Why the bloody hell would I do that?' Roland knew as much or as little as anyone else – that after the Crouch cannabis fiasco, Hopkins had done a bunk to Spain with the rest of them. Roland was not in the same league. 'Our paths never crossed.'

'Well, you better have your story straight, for when the police come knocking.'

'Who says they'll come knocking?' There was no guts to Roland's answer. He'd been caught once, he'd get caught again.

On his release from Chelmsford in December, he realised that during his years behind bars, vehicle security and technology had advanced as swiftly as his nimble-handedness had faded. Now, he was like many of the cars he had once stolen – on the scrap heap.

'If I go down again, who will look after you?'

'I managed all right last time.'

'But what if you get sick again?'

'Roland, I've not been ill in years. Mum's been dead these last five.'

She had been absolutely fine, more than fine.

'Tell me again, Rollie, how did you get the job?' His sister marvelled at his self-delusion.

'Some bloke I never met before tapped me on the shoulder after I left the Friday Woods site – the day I got the boot. Came up to me on Berechurch Hall Road. Said he knew me rep, like, asked for me in the Gladiator.'

'You're sure you'd never seen him before?'

'Didn't see his face. It was near dark and miserable. He said there was two-fifty in the phone box in that envelope with the reg on it if I wanted the job.'

Mandy was satisfied with this. There was nothing to do now but sit and wait.

*

Daniel Kenton stared blankly into the hairdresser's mirror. He did not care to see himself as others surely would: a weary man, with murky red eyes, closing in on thirty-five but aged beyond his years. Instead, his thoughts tumbled into one another as the barber took up his position behind the chair and lit a cigarette. The flame's reflection in the mirror caught Kenton's eye, reminding him of the church fire at Kempe Marsh. The Hopkins case, with its Spanish link, had eclipsed his enquiries there entirely. How life tumbled from one event to the next.

The foot pump of the chair raised him from his reverie.

'Right, what'll it be?'

'The usual, please, Chris.'

The question was always the same, as was the answer, but without it the process could not commence.

Since the birth of the children, Kenton's wife, Lindsay, did not have time to attend to her partner's grooming needs, and had passed her husband's hair over to the care of her uncle, Chris. While they were courting, Kenton had patronisingly assumed Lindsay worked in a salon because it was something all girls wanted to do. It wasn't, far from it, but her uncle ran a barber's shop in Kelvedon, and trained her up so she could make a few quid (though not with him) while she decided what she really wanted to do. Lindsay's mother was in America – she'd frittered away her twenties chasing dreams of acting in LA that had ultimately come to nothing.

Daniel tipped his head forward in a bid to deter conversation. There was no telling where a chat with Uncle Chris might lead. How Spurs might fare, whether Venables would keep Mabbutt as skipper – that was fine; but there was the risk of it getting personal – asking him how the baby was, or how Lindsay was coping. He was paranoid everyone was listening in, earwigging on CID's home life despite a low radio presence in the background.

As Chris knotted the bib, the telephone began to ring. The row of waiting customers gave a start, with a general clearing of throats and rustling of newspaper pages. The winter months were the doldrums of the barbering trade. Hunkering down, many men would allow an extra inch or two, as Kenton himself had until his wife caught up with it. This was the busiest trade had been all year.

'Aren't you going to get that?' Kenton asked.

'No.' Chris spat the word out between pursed lips, cigarette still intact.

'Why not?'

'Because it'll be someone wanting their hair cut.' Tonight was the shop's late night.

'But that's what you do; take bookings on Thursdays.'

'They'll want it tonight.'

'Restaurants take bookings on the night.'

'Yes, but this bleedin' restaurant's only got one table.' He gestured symbolically as he tied off the bib with an unnecessary tug.

'So business is good. That other place not chipped away at your regulars?'

'It's a worry, but I've had customers try them and come back,' he said in a voice indicating a reaction would be required.

'Oh, you'll take them back, then, if they defect?'

'Some. Not all – one bloke I'd not seen in eighteen months comes in here, says "All right, mate" as if he'd seen me last week. *Eighteen months.* His hair'd've been two foot long if he'd stayed loyal all that time . . . "Mate." I ask you, bloody cheek.'

Their eyes met in the mirror.

'Out of order,' Kenton said.

'Told him to sling his hook. Anyway, what you doin' in here? Lindsay says you're flying to Spain tomorrow, what's that all about then? Go a bit shorter? Nice out there. Lucky sod.'

CHAPTER 23

The Elf garage on the London Road was the closest to the hotel. Gary, the acne-burdened attendant, remembered a man stopping in a Sierra early evening, because there'd been a debate on what fuel it took. 'Yeah, I remember this bloke coming in, saying. "It was the wife's" and he was unsure what it took. I knew,' he said, nodding with pursed lips, 'that Sierra model was one of the last to take four star. I told him straight.'

'Lucky you're about, eh?' Brazier said. 'We really need to find this bloke, try and think back: a coat, colour of his hair, pale, dark?'

'I don't see faces you see, only cars.'

'Gotcha.' Brazier turned around in the shop, scanning the plastic screen wash and oil containers in the hope a reflection of the thief lay hidden somewhere within their shiny surfaces. 'Age or height? Distinguishing features.'

'An average bloke.'

'What I call average and what a lad like you calls average, ain't probably the same. Know what I mean?'

Gary was no more than nineteen.

'Close to my or your age?'

'Yours.'

'Hair colour?' Brazier repeated.

'Err – he wore a hat. Woolly one, you know, army surplus, with a peak. Used to be popular five years ago, everyone wore them at school.'

'Like this?' he pulled his own from his jacket pocket.

'Identical.'

'Good. That's a start. Face?'

'Sort of roundy, nondescript.'

'Take your time.' The door tingled and customer came in and handed over a fiver. The cash till pinged out and the attendant handed over the change. 'How much did he put in? Do you remember that?'

'Oh, yeah. The minimum, a quid; he fumbled with it and his glasses fell on the floor.'

'So, he wore glasses?'

'Yeah, one of the arms were broken like, you know, I think, and they slipped off his nose when he was rooting around for change in his jeans.'

'Roland Beech, as in "Beech the Leech", the short-sighted tea leaf?' Kenton said, surprised, in a mocking tone. It was nine o'clock at night and he was sipping tea, having just finished packing hand luggage for his flight in the morning when he'd got an unexpected call from Brazier at home. 'Used to race Formula 3?'

'The very same.'

'Identified in a garage?'

Brazier hesitated. 'Not identified in the strictest sense of the word . . . but sort of . . . The mannerisms is all Rollie; fumbling about for pennies, broken glasses.'

'Well, I must say, I'd not make Roland for a murderer. Yes to vehicle theft, and yes to complicity in insurance fraud, but add a body in the boot, no way.' He was quite pleased with his assessment, given Brazier had put him to shame about the church feather.

'Me neither . . . but maybe he's in the pay of some Spanish drug lord. Anyway, thought you should know, maybe grab a mugshot before you fly. See if it raises any eyebrows. Safe flight, mate.'

Paul seldom went out, and had no interest in the world beyond the business pages. If Bruce Hopkins' death was in the *FT* it was probably not on a page he'd read, and if he had, it was not the sort of article he'd comment on. But now it was on the box, the evening news. Michael Buerk's sombre voice was accompanied by that all-too-familiar photo of Bruce with his pals on the boat on the River Crouch, the week before it all went off, followed by a shot of the boat itself, and footage of a balding grizzled policeman commenting on the haul behind. Then a long-distance shot of Abberton Reservoir resembling the Arctic tundra, his penultimate resting place. It wasn't that Chloe hadn't wanted to enlighten Paul about the situation, not even subconsciously, like with the police and Mum, but the opportunity never presented itself. Men didn't like hearing about previous relationships. They felt jealous or threatened, she didn't really know by what or why, but whatever it was, it was upsetting for them. She couldn't really be blamed.

Chloe tucked her feet up tight under her bottom on the sofa, her hand gripping her bare ankle below her jeans. She had no alternative. Work was at a remove, but there was a real chance the press might turn up on her door. It wasn't fair.

'Paul, love, there's something I need to tell you.' She muted the TV with the remote.

Paul yawned and stretched out his long arms, one brushing the back of her head. 'My ex-husband might resurface.'

'Oh, how come, where?' His face twisted uncomprehendingly.

'What did I tell you he used to do?'

The puzzlement grew. 'For a living? I have no idea. Do I need to know now?'

That was Paul, straight to the nub of the situation. Paul and she had been planning to move in together for nearly a year. Chloe was sure this was the right thing to do, or as right as she ever would be.

'He didn't do much, really, this and that. Pretty useless, to be honest. Then he got mixed up in some dodgy stuff—' She gripped her ankle tightly, fingers marking her flesh – 'in some silly smuggling caper.'

'What, cigarettes? You wouldn't believe what the estimated loss to the Revenue is.'

CHAPTER 24

Kenneth Markham closed the door as the lad hurried off down the garden path, a foot slipping outwards on the snow as he went. He tucked the money into his back pocket and returned to the front room, where Bach tinkled softly from the stereo.

He pushed the door to, so as not to be disturbed by Conor in the kitchen, making toast by the sounds of it.

'You've still not opened this.' Conor stole in, holding out an envelope. He swept his hair back, as a forelock flopped forward over his right eye. 'Sorry, spilt a drop of tea on the carpet just now. Very light nice handwriting though.'

The envelope was addressed in a neat hand, in fountain pen, and postmarked Colchester. Ken didn't know anyone in Colchester that he could recall. It had arrived a few days ago and he'd put it to one side in a rush to get to the flower market and then completely forgotten about it. He placed it unopened on the occasional table next to the lamp. Conor touched him lightly on the shoulder. 'Aren't you going to open it?'

Ken shrugged. 'It'll keep.' Secretly he was pleased at the

prospect of a surprise communication. Life was a little dull at times. Conor loitered, unsatisfied with this response. 'Oh, all right, I will. I'll get the opener.' As Conor left, Ken picked the letter up and ran it through his fingers. Wafer-thin and light as a feather. His curiosity grew. He removed his spectacles, slid one of the arms inside the envelope, and then tore it open evenly.

Inside was half a sheet of airmail paper and a cutting from a newspaper.

He replaced his glasses. Fear struck a cold prickle to the back of his neck. With trembling fingers, he reinserted the envelope's contents and placed it back on the table.

Conor breezed in. 'I couldn't find the blasted thing – under the newspaper, of course. Here. Oh, you've opened it.' He glanced at Ken, who was pale. 'Bad news?' he said.

But Kenneth Markham was oblivious. Conor moved around behind the winged chair. His pale liver-spotted fingers moved towards the light of the lamp, hovering over the envelope for an instant before withdrawing.

'It's fine, just sad news,' Markham muttered, barely audible. 'From an old friend. A bit of a shock. I'll tell you later.'

'I see, all right. Well, I'm off upstairs for now.' He stood in the centre of the room, on the faded carpet before the electric fire, the cord from his dressing gown trailing like a surplus appendage.

'Conor, do please clothe yourself on days I have students. I've told you before. It doesn't do for students to see a chap wandering around in a state of undress.'

'I am composing,' Conor said stiffly, rubbing a stubbly chin. 'And as you know, I like to do that in bed. It's warmer and more conducive to—'

'Yes, yes. Away with you then. They'll be here any moment.'

Once he heard the door click, Markham picked up the envelope and withdrew the contents. A newspaper cutting with a picture of a church. There was no date, but the paper felt recent and was not discoloured. He placed it to one side and stared at the airmail paper until his eyes lost focus.

They had smoked him out and set the island on fire.

Beyond his hand the three panels of the fire projected a fierce orange that melded with the paper as if consuming it. Eventually the doorbell roused him; it had rung several times before he noticed. Time had collapsed since he had opened the letter, and Markham had forgotten this afternoon's obligations. He sighed, folded the envelope in two and tucked it inside his sports jacket pocket. Forcing himself to his senses, he realised this would be his last ever student.

PART 2

CHAPTER 25

As Kenton's plane touched down in Malaga, he smiled. Here he was – the Costa del Sol. Following the collapse of the extradition treaty between Britain and Spain in 1978, the southern coast of Spain had found itself welcoming a substantial number of the British criminal fraternity. The *Daily Express* renamed the region the 'Costa del Crime'. These colourful, gregarious, cash-rich villains swiftly made themselves comfortable, living the high life in villas and bars and driving sports cars. All of a sudden, hitmen, conmen and bank robbers were rubbing shoulders with aristocrats and bullfighters in the nightclubs of Marbella. In 1985, the legal loophole was tidied up. There followed a series of high-profile extradition cases, fodder for the front pages of the British press. But as Kenton and other coppers knew, many remained; slipping through the net where the evidence was vague, and the process too costly. Peter Hart was such a fish, and he took no small delight in toying with his one-time pursuer and Kenton's one-time boss, Stephen Sparks, once sending him a postcard: *Wish you were here!*

And these were hardly reformed characters making a fresh start – a number of enterprising individuals had established a UK connection with the 'Spanish Dragon'; importing Moroccan hashish through Tangier across the straits of Gibraltar and up into Malaga and Torremolinos, then couriered back to Blighty by mules posing as tourists returning from holiday. The Costa del Sol, then, was never far from Scotland Yard's thoughts nor, so it seemed, from Watt's. That an Englishman by the name of Roland Beech had now surfaced in connection with the car theft made no difference: a Spanish banknote was enough – get out there and establish any link between Hart, Hopkins and the UK–Spain drug route.

Watt sanctioning Kenton's passage signalled to him that all past misdemeanours had been forgiven, or probably forgotten. In 1983, Kenton was investigated for drugs abuse, a messy and prolonged affair. Although ultimately they'd allowed him to continue in the force, his card had been marked and he had carried the stigma about him. He'd become used to all the interesting cases being passed over his head, being a deliberate blind spot with the higher-ups. To be sent abroad required trust and confidence in the individual assigned; that Brazier had a fear of flying was neither here nor there. If mistrust had lingered, had continued with the new guard, Watt himself would surely be here instead of him.

The warm dusty Andalusian air added to his good mood as he confidently gave the directions to the taxi driver outside the terminal building. They headed north along the Costa del

Sol. He stretched an arm across the back seat and savoured the change in climate from the cab window, watching the fluidity in people's movements as they gambolled along wide promenades lined with palm trees in short-sleeved shirts and colourful, loose-fitting dresses. The contrast with what he'd left behind was stark: this was paradise. Stretches of endless beaches lapped by the sultry Mediterranean. Yes, it was no wonder people flocked here in the winter; two hours from Gatwick and it felt the other side of the world.

The criminal classes might have been the first Brits out here, but now every autumn, as the clocks went back, a migration of silver-haired winter sunseekers descended on the Spanish coast to spend their pension on tapas and Rioja instead of heating bills. Pete's Place, on a dusty side street running down to the promenade in Fuengirola, was packed with such a flock; Brits stuffing themselves with olives and anchovies. They would stay until the spring, when their hitherto dormant gardens required their attention. Presiding over the early afternoon feasting was Peter Hart himself; bronzed, healthy, mulleted, with a drooping moustache beneath which large white teeth occasionally beamed.

Hart could spot a British copper a mile off and he bore down on Kenton as soon as he stepped through a bright rectangle of winter light into the mellow wooden interior of his bar.

'Afternoon. Business good?' Kenton said, taking in the healthy face of the man in his late forties.

'Musn't grumble,' replied Hart, offering him a stool at

the bar beneath a ceiling festooned with fishing nets and lanterns. A hoot of hilarity went up from a table of eight smartly dressed and already flushed elderly groovers. A waitress carrying a pan of sizzling prawns passed Hart, rolling her eyes.

'Lively bunch,' Kenton said, catching a whiff of fried garlic.

'Good folk of a certain generation; they think that if they speak loudly enough in English, the locals will surely understand.' Hart's accent was hard to place, though not Essex for sure; he spoke clearly and properly. Kenton wouldn't go as far as to say posh, but certainly educated from his manner and enunciation.

'It's the English way.'

'The English way, yes. And what's your way, friend? I guess you are not here on holiday.' Hart pulled his own bar stool closer to Kenton. The taverna lighting gave both men a deep orange complexion.

'Correct. DS Kenton, Essex CID. Bruce Hopkins, ring any bells?'

'Cathedral-size, yes. In trouble?'

'Dead,' Kenton said, prizing a pistachio nut from its shell.

'Dead?' Hart's eye skewed along the bar surface as he took this in. 'Natural causes . . .? No, of course not, why else would you be here?'

'He was found in the boot of a Ford Sierra at the bottom of a reservoir outside Colchester.'

All warmth vanished from Hart's face. His mouth set hard

and his eyes glazed. Eventually he shook his head. 'That's a shame.'

'Would you know anyone who might want to do that?'

'Well, Detective Kenton, I have been coming here since 1975, permanently since 1980, and I lost touch with carryings on in dear ol' Blighty and all of its intricacies long ago.'

'Apart from that little jaunt back you both made in eighty-four.'

Hart's mouth broke into a cracked smile. 'Now, now – there's no conclusive evidence.'

'Other than you both were photographed the month before on the boat, and the fingerprints.'

'Those dabs may well have been mine—' he made a show of placing his dark fingertips on his chest – 'but made here. I never left España, hombre – guess we'll never know who took that boat, eh?'

'I'm not here to get into that,' Kenton said. 'Hopkins had been in Spain the same length of time as you?'

'Torremolinos, up the coast ten miles, but you said he was found dead in Essex?'

'We believe his death had a Spanish connection.'

'I see.'

'When did you last see him?'

'Last month. Prior to that, we'd not spoken for a couple of years.'

'Since eighty-four, perhaps,' Kenton said.

'You know, I can't recall the date . . . but there was a

disagreement . . .' Hart tapped his golden forehead with a forefinger. 'Funny, nor can I remember what it was all about now. Memory ain't what it was.'

There were hints of grey at the roots of Hart's slick bleach-blond hair. The 'disagreement' was obviously over whose fault it was the job was botched. Still, they both got out of the UK – and Hart was right, although they'd both be nabbed if they set foot on home soil, there was not enough evidence to extradite them – or they'd paid someone off to conclude as much. None of it made much sense to Kenton.

'I don't care what happened then,' he said. 'You said you'd seen him a month back. How did you find him after so long?'

'Much changed.' He took a sip, his first, from a crystal glass of brandy.

'How so?'

Hart puffed out his cheeks and then exhaled. 'Unhealthy and fat. Obesely so. And liking a drink rather as much as he always did, which was why I assumed his death was natural causes, you see.'

'Understood.'

'I mean, Brucie always was prone to run to fat, a bit of a chubber – not like you, Detective, lean and mean – and there comes a time when you can't get away with it any longer. The high life can often be the unhealthy life, if you don't learn a bit of moderation.'

'Like you?'

Hart pulled a soft pack of cigarettes from his shirt pocket.

'Bruce had an inheritance; it was his boat that they found in the Crouch,' he said, steering the conversation away from himself. 'Money came to him in a windfall – before any of this – he didn't have to hustle for it anymore. Comfort made him lazy.'

'He repeatedly said he couldn't sail.'

'The boat belonged to his late uncle. When the old boy died, Bruce took it off the widow – she was none the wiser, in a wheelchair. All he did with it was pootle up and down the Crouch; never so much as unfurled the jib. Let one and all lark around on deck. When his auntie died, we got more adventurous, that is true.' He tapped a cigarette on the dark wooden bar. 'I was the only one what could sail it,' he said in a mock cockney accent.

'Back to January, why did he come round after all this time?'

'Got a letter from the missus. Thought she wanted to patch it up.'

'Really? Chloe?'

'You sound incredulous, Detective . . . She not mention it, eh?'

Kenton should have kept his reaction to himself. 'Does that sound likely to you?'

'She never had much time for me an' the lads. Thought we were a bad influence.'

If this guy was telling the truth, it would put Chloe in the frame. 'Did you see the letter?'

'Nope.'

'Does the name Roland Beech mean anything to you?'

'Nope.'

'A teen Billy Whizz in the early seventies, on the Formula 3 circuit – then when it didn't work out, a car thief.'

'Still no.'

Kenton wasn't expecting that. He pulled out a mugshot.

'How about this?'

'Beech? Sorry, still no.' Hart savoured the cigarette. 'He connected to Bruce in some way?'

'Maybe. We want a word with him. Worth asking. How long back did you know Bruce?'

'We were at school together.'

Kenton would have guessed him much younger than Bruce. Unlike Hopkins, fine living and decent weather had been kind to Hart.

'You said his death had a Spanish connection, what might that be?'

'That would depend on what he got up to in Torremolinos – perhaps he ran into trouble.'

'Hmm. I'd be surprised. He'd been down there long enough to get the lay of the land and he wasn't a hothead. Our North African neighbours are serious – he's enough sense to be careful.' A scraping of chairs made them aware of the pensioners' imminent departure. 'Anyway, I've got to crack on. Tidy up while this lot take a siesta. Sorry not to be of more help, but I live out here, you understand. And I'm sorry for Bruce – he wasn't a bad chap, just a bit muddled.'

'Muddled? In what sense?' Kenton pulled out a banknote. 'One not dissimilar to this was found, rolled up, poking out of Hopkins' nostril.'

Hart rubbed his chin slowly. 'Perhaps I'm wrong, maybe he took a dip,' he said dismissively and downed his drink, signalling for the bottle. 'Give my regards to Chief Sparks, won't you.'

'Oh, he's long since gone.' Kenton took a sip of his drink. 'My flight's not until tomorrow.' Hart was giving him nothing. Unless nothing was all there was, and the story about the letter from his ex-wife was legit, this was a disappointing encounter. Hart sat languidly at the bar, relaxed and untroubled.

'How far is it to Granada?'

'Granada? A good four or five hours. Coach picks up along here.' He looked at his watch, a glittering chunky timepiece. 'Too late today, I think. Stay for one more, on the house?'

'Sure.' Kenton hesitated, then said, 'You realise, Mr Hart, as best we know you were the last of his old associates to see Bruce alive.'

'To Brucie, then.' He raised the bottle.

Kenton stayed for a drink and then made his way to Torremolinos police station, where the Policía Nacional were helpful but refused to break into Hopkins' flat without author-isation, which would take several days. He then returned to Peter's Place for a meal, at 'Harty's' (as he wished to be known) insistence. Kenton was offered a room, which he declined.

Late that evening, the ex-pat grew sentimental as the Metaxa bottle emptied. Whether an act or not, Kenton couldn't say, but Hart did a great impression of a nostalgic old con upset at his old pal's demise and there was no need to while away the night with a British policeman. Kenton learnt little beyond Hart's refusal to believe a Spaniard would travel to the UK to carry out the deed. Whoever was responsible was 'on the other end'.

CHAPTER 26

In the middle of *EastEnders*, the doorbell's brash trill sounded. Mandy had just washed her hair and was sat on the sofa in her dressing gown. She put her make-up to one side, went to the door, released the chain and let in the police. She didn't have time to warn Rollie, who was upstairs plucking away at his ukulele and smoking some puff.

Brazier apologised for the intrusion as two uniformed officers charged past into the Monkwick council house. 'Sorry, miss, we have a warrant for Roland Beech.'

'What's he done?' she asked innocently, then added, 'I'm his sister.'

'For starters, stolen a car.' Brazier weighed up this woman. In her late twenties, wearing pale-blue pastel eye shadow, with a towel wrapped round her head. She had a heart-shaped face, fleshy, like her brother. Brazier noticed a scabbed cold sore in one corner of her mouth, which no amount of make-up could hide. The hallway had the faint air of damp.

'For starters? Meaning there's more?'

Brazier considered her for a moment. Sensing the

policeman's suspicion, she said, 'I care about my brother, all right, but I'm stunned at his stupidity – he's been out less than three months. Loses the first job he has ever had then gets nicked the week after.'

Several thumps sounded above them.

She sighed. 'He's not as tough as he thinks.'

'Can I take your name and number, Miss Beech?'

'Amanda. We don't have a phone. Mum didn't believe in them.'

'But you've a satellite dish?'

'Mine. Was lonely when Rollie got banged up.'

'I bet.' Brazier couldn't work her out. 'Okay to look around?'

'You got a search warrant? You can take him, but you can't trash this place – this is my house too. Bit of respect, if you don't mind.'

'Of course. Is there a phone number where I can reach you? Work, maybe?'

'I'll give you next door's. Not that she'll tell me you rang.'

He followed her through to the kitchen at the rear of the house. There was a clatter as the uniforms strong-armed her brother down the stairs. He was putting up a fight, she'd not expected that. Swearing and cursing. She picked up a pen from the kitchen drawer, then scouted about for a scrap of paper to write the number down. She heard an officer threaten Roland with resisting arrest. It was a desperate but futile struggle; he should save his strength, she thought. Her brother was done for. This was it for him and he knew it. Her eye rested on the envelope on the kitchen table for a second, before searching something else out.

'Here. Write it here.' The policeman offered his notebook.

She heard a squeal and winced, remembering Rollie's racing injuries, as she scribbled Tracy's number down. 'Do you really have to be so rough with him?'

'He could always come quietly.'

'He's upset,' she said, handing back the book.

He thanked her and left. There followed an abrupt slam of the front door, then silence as the house returned to normal. The normality she'd enjoyed before the winter came, bringing her brother with it.

Brazier checked Roland Beech into an empty cell then made himself a coffee.

He sat down and propped his feet up onto Kenton's desk, occasionally dipping into a paper bag of boiled sweets. A debrief with Watt was on the cards following Beech's arrest. Although Brazier had made the collar, he didn't fancy going it alone. Watt was too uptight for his liking: just looking at him, over in his glass-fronted office, fretting over something or other, made Brazier himself anxious. In the chief's presence, Brazier often imagined himself anywhere else, to avoid the bad vibes fizzing about. Wilde strutted past, tutting at Brazier's dirty Adidas on the clean desk. This place, though; it was the textbook definition of sterility. Brazier lit a cigarette and checked out Wilde over at the filing cabinet, her back to him.

'Fancy a drink after work?' he called.

'Take your feet off the desk when you're talking to me, you slob.'

'Well, what do you say? Bit different round here, eh?'

'I'm playing badminton tonight. You should try it, there's a court right here. More to life than the pub.'

He grinned. 'Not got a bat.' He then noticed a holdall and a plastic bag under Kenton's desk – Hopkins' luggage and duty free. Kenton had meant to log it, but with his sudden departure to Spain, he'd forgotten. Brazier reached under, lifted the bag out and peered inside.

'Nice,' he said to himself, 'nobody'll miss them.' He wrapped the bottle and fags tightly in the bag then shoved it in his desk drawer. He then opened the holdall on his lap. He rifled through the clothes, noting the Scotch in the socks. Under them was a paperback, *Lord of the Flies*. He picked it up. On the inside was a partial rubber stamp impression; a bird, maybe? And he could just make out some of a word ending *ARK*.

'Learning to read?' Wilde said. 'Or is it a picture book?'

'Come and help me with the long words, miss,' he said, flicking through the pages.

Something slipped out and landed on the toe of his trainer. A Polaroid of a boy with wet hair, naked from the waist up, taken outside. Beyond him, greenery, laurel bushes perhaps. The sun was in his face; head tilted to one side to avoid its glare. 'He's a pretty lad,' Wilde said over his shoulder. Pretty was accurate; high cheekbones and angular elegant nose, large frowning eyes just discernible under a long swathe of fringe, plastered across a pale forehead.

CHAPTER 27

The glass door swung open and in marched Kenton with a waft of cold air.

Brazier slipped the book and photo under a file. The DS had had a haircut; short back and sides. Not as severe as that of prefect Watts, and without the bald pate. They were cut from a similar cloth. Kenton had a troubled air about him too, similar to Watt but less pronounced. He was a man with a perpetual look of being in doubt about something. What was it with them here? Brazier dogged his fag and rose to follow Kenton. Wilde turned just in time to catch him admiring her behind. He pursed his lips to a small kiss. Secretly pleased, she chose not to react either way, and left him in the dark.

'He came back to see his ex?' Watt said.

'Hart told you that?' Brazier said.

Kenton nodded.

'Why?' Watt preferred a domestic; far more agreeable than a Spanish drug murder.

'Hart reckons he got a letter . . .'

136

'Did this bozo actually see it?' said Brazier. 'Do you believe him? From what we saw of her, it's bloody unlikely.'

Kenton was taken aback by Brazier's outburst. 'Hey, I'm just reporting what the man said. I didn't say it was gospel, given the man is an ex-con I take it with a large pinch of salt, but it's the reason he gave for his old pal returning to the UK. And no, he didn't see a letter.'

Watt enjoyed this little confrontation. 'Did he rule out Hopkins as a drug mule, though?'

'He didn't know what Hopkins had been up to – they hadn't been all that close in years . . .'

'So why did he tell him he was off to see his wife?' Brazier said.

'They'd lived in same country for years – he just swung by to say *adiós amigo*. Let bygones be bygones. Hell, I don't know. I was only there for a day. I don't know conclusively. He might be lying, but what purpose would that serve?'

Watt only half listened, hoping it irrelevant; they had their man already, or they had *a* man at least, though a doubt about Beech lingered.

'This was at the end of January,' Kenton continued. 'Hart didn't have the impression he was in trouble . . .'

'Did you tell him about the banknote?' Brazier asked.

'Yes . . . Hart was doubtful that Hopkins was a drug trafficker, he repeated that several times.'

'Local rozzers have anything to say?'

'The Spanish police agreed: they hauled in a few of the

local "chorizos" – petty small-time crooks that run errands for the big boys – and they all claimed he was above board. They wouldn't open up his flat, though. Hart reckoned Hopkins wasn't stupid enough to carry on a flight, not his first time back here in ten years.'

'Why the banknote, then?' Watt asked, this time addressed to the ceiling.

Kenton shrugged. 'Ask his ex, first off . . .' He made to go.

'Wait. While you were propping up the tapas bars on the Costa, Mr Brazier here has been busy.'

Roland Beech, thirty-eight years old, was an ordinary specimen, recently out of Chelmsford after a five stretch for car theft.

Well known to both detectives, Beech wore a sheepish, apologetic grimace. There was something different about his appearance, though.

'Roland, it's been a while – I don't think we've had the pleasure since you were last released. You don't look the same,' Kenton said.

'My specs,' he muttered. 'That bastard didn't give me a chance to get me glasses. Can't see bugger all.'

'Is that right?' Kenton addressed Brazier. 'He'll need them for his statement.'

Brazier shrugged. 'If he can read, that is.'

'So, Roland, technology has caught you out – again. What was it last time? A Quattro immobiliser? You need to keep up with the times,' Kenton said, retiring to a corner of the room, 'if you're to stay out of here.'

'Bit hard to do though, if you're banged up for years at a time, ain't it?' Brazier said, sitting opposite Beech.

Roland gnawed at his thumbnail.

'Be flying cars by the time you get out next time – if you get out – like *Blade Runner*,' Brazier continued.

'I didn't kill anyone,' Roland said, removing his thumb and considering it. 'I was set up, like. It's obvious.'

Brazier rose, placed both hands on the table, and loomed over Beech. 'Obvious? Why the hell do you say that? What is obvious is you stopped to fill up a car – with unleaded petrol, I believe – and then, the following day, dumped it and Bruce Hopkins' body in the reservoir.'

Beech glanced over at Kenton. Kenton was known to be straight – and soft. But Kenton's head remained bowed and he didn't say a word, more interested in his Chelsea boots stained with snow and grit.

'I'll level with you, Roland,' Brazier said. 'There'll be a line-up, of which you'll be a part. Should the attendant at the London Road garage single you out then you'll be arrested for car theft forthwith, and will be the prime suspect for the murder of Bruce Hopkins.'

'Bruce . . . wha . . . Nicetoseeyou?'

'Know him?' Brazier said. 'Of course you do. Strangled the bastard.'

Hearing those words, bringing together the image of victim

and accused was more preposterous than Kenton first thought; Hopkins was twice the size of Roland. Brazier had dropped in that mention of strangulation for a reaction.

'Wait, wait,' Beech protested. 'I'll put me hand up to nicking the motor. But I swear I'd no idea about Brucie in the boot – yes, okay, I know Nicetoseeyou. Not personally, like. We're in different branches of the trade: he's gems and me, it's motors. You know that, right?'

'But you used his nickname?'

'Yeah, but everyone called him that back in the day. It's what he'd say to his marks before he ripped them off. He could con an old dear out of her family heirloom in seconds flat, speaking in that posh way of his.'

Beech had regained his composure. He didn't talk like a man caught red-handed for murder. 'I took the car on that evening, then went home, slept, to the pub, then dumped it at dawn.'

'All right then, Roland.' Kenton sat down next to Brazier. 'So if we're to believe your version of events, how do you explain your predicament?'

'Bloke came up to me on Berechurch Hall Road. Wanted a car. *That* car.'

'What, in broad daylight? Just like that – "oi mate nick me this motor?"' Brazier said, impatiently.

'I was expecting it,' he retorted, 'Been told in the pub some geezer was looking for me, and we were alone – safe, man – hardly broad daylight, was practically dark.'

'What did he want the car for?'

'I don't know. A job of some sort.'

'Didn't you ask what he wanted it for?'

'No. None of my business.'

'Is now, sunshine?' Brazier beamed.

Beech didn't trust Brazier one inch. 'Two-fifty upfront in an envelope and another four hundred on completion, weren't it?' He spoke at Kenton. 'But then the geez changed his mind – didn't want it, just wanted the motor sunk.'

CHAPTER 28

Getaway cars were invariably stolen, used, then ditched – or if the job was clean, sold to a dodgy dealer in Southend.

'Explain?' Brazier said, moving inches behind Roland's ear, causing him to flinch. Roland's gaze remained on Kenton. Nobody was frightened of four eyes Danny Kenton. Beech had been in this situation many times before; but knowing it was a game – understanding why Kenton was paired with Brazier for the interrogation – didn't make it any easier; Brazier's dead eye could spook the worst of them.

'I said. Got a message a bloke was after me in the pub: wanted a car, a particular car, and heard I was the man for the job. Said he'd meet me after work.'

'Work? You have employment?'

'Had. Didn't work out. Labouring on the new housing estate over the road at Friday Woods. You know, next to the glass house?'

The Monkwick council estate shouldered up against MOD property. The fringe of the garrison; married quarters and the military prison tucked away in Friday Woods.

'And?'

'Well, he did come up to me on Berechurch Hall Road, as I was coming out of Lethe Grove. We walked as far as the Gladiator, he tells me where and when, then he disappeared. I couldn't see his face: in this big parka, green one like the Mods used to have, know what I mean?'

'Height?'

'About average. Anyway, he says he'll leave the down payment and the reg of a blue Sierra in a phone box, says I was to park it in Friday Woods, and he'd call me at Monkwick once I'd done the job to confirm all was good, which I did.'

'And how'd that go?' Kenton said lightly, but he locked his stare.

'I said all good, but the car was empty and I had to put some juice in, like you say, and said it was only a quid's worth so as to warn 'em he'd need to fill up himself.'

'And?'

'This spooked the geezer. Said I'd better ditch the car and ditch it pronto.'

'Really? Just like that?' Brazier said from somewhere behind him.

'Yeah, as I was near the reservoir, he said slip it in there. So I agreed to do it just after it got light the next day.'

'It's probably not as easy as it sounds, ditching a car there? You'd need good knowledge of the area – where to slide the car in the water, know of a gap in the reed beds, and that the ground would support the car – before attempting it.'

'I know Abberton like the back of my hand, fished there as a kid – pike. Double banking on the causeway – get a bus to Layer-de-la-Haye then walk the rest. Sometimes after a few ciders, we'd miss the bus back and have to walk back the whole way, following the bridleway and cutting through the woods.'

'Do you still see anyone from those days?'

'Wish I did,' he said sadly.

'What about the money?'

'Left me another two ton under the sun visor.' Beech dared to turn in Brazier's direction. 'It's still there under the bed, check if you don't believe me.'

'Don't you think that strange: bungle the job . . . and you still got paid?'

A wave of annoyance washed over Beech's face. 'I didn't bungle the job. The car had no petrol in it, how the bloody hell was that my fault? Ain't a screw-up in anyone's book, that.'

'Isn't it? You got spotted in a garage – something your employer twigged too, and so had to get rid of the car. If that's not a screw-up, I don't what is.'

'Yeah . . . but that's because *you* found the car, not because you saw *me* nick it.'

'And we found the car because someone saw you push it in.'

'Bloke with binoculars. That's cheating.'

'And we found you, didn't we?' Kenton said.

'Mush I nicked the car for don't know that.'

'Look, cretin, he told you to get shot of the car immediately, don't you find that odd?'

'Didn't at the time.' Beech was confused. They were both coming at him. 'I was glad of the cash. Didn't ask any questions. All right, I guess he was worried I might get nicked, but at the time I thought the guy was lily-livered – there's no way you lot would have gone checking out petrol stations on the hunt for a stolen motor, unless—'

'Unless maybe it had a body in it!' Brazier shouted at him.

'Calm down, this is getting us nowhere,' Kenton intervened. 'Roland, listen to me. You are going to have to help yourself here; if you didn't kill Bruce Hopkins, give us evidence that somebody else did or you'll find yourself back inside for a much longer spell than you'll get for stealing the Ford Sierra. For a start, would you recognise this man? Any accent?'

'Nope. Sounded normal to me.' Roland was perspiring now.

'Normal? What's that sound like when it's at home?' Brazier said. 'Him? Me? You?' He poked Roland sharply in the neck, sending a bolt of pain up through his cranium.

'Look, I don't know who it was! I'd tell you!'

'All right.' Kenton came forward. 'Let's begin at the beginning; height, clothes, etcetera – remember, Roland, you are the number-one suspect. Got that?'

Roland nodded. 'When do I get a phone call?'

'Soon,' Kenton said to Brazier, and tipped his head towards the door.

'Well?' Brazier asked in the corridor, out of earshot.

'I don't know . . . it'd be convenient if it was Roland, but . . .'

'Agreed. What a tool! Want to go see Miss Moran now?'

'Give me an hour. I better type this up – and the Hart stuff. Watt is adamant that we'll be asked all this business of Hopkins' life in Spain.'

'Oh, yeah. Did he have a kid, Hopkins?' Brazier strode over to his desk and picked up the paperback book. 'Was having a snoop about while waiting for you to roll up this morning.'

Kenton studied the Polaroid of a young boy in swimming trunks, in a garden, frowning in the sunlight. He looked to be clutching something, goggles perhaps. Instant cameras weren't the greatest quality and the colours made him wonder when it was taken. 'Not that I know of.'

CHAPTER 29

Roland was left to stew. Kenton went to type up the interview statement together with his report on Hart. Meanwhile, Brazier having obtained a search warrant, would re-visit Mandy Beech. But first he wanted to get a handle on the distance between the initial drop-off point for the car, and where Roland Beech lived. Brazier wasn't as familiar with the area as he'd like to be and knew this to be a disadvantage. He hadn't come across Friday Woods before, so he thought he'd get some air at the same time – even if it was three below zero outside.

DS Brazier was undaunted by the cold; he could handle pretty much anything but words. Reading or writing anything gave him a headache. For him, words were a jumble on the page that refused without utmost concentration to reveal a meaning. Filing a charge sheet was his limit. He compensated for this handicap with an enthusiasm for the outdoors and anything hands-on; whatever the weather, he'd always be outside, close to the scene.

In case the car park had since snowed up, he pulled up on the verge and pulled out a pair of knackered Doc Martens from the boot. His Adidas had a hole. As it happened, access wasn't too bad, and he soon arrived on a heath surrounded by woods. Empty. There was nothing to suggest the clearing had a function or purpose. On closer inspection there were faint tyre marks. It was here that Beech claimed the Sierra was left overnight. And Beech would have come through here again, having ditched the car in the reservoir – the bridleway he had followed was around here under the snow.

Friday Woods was military property, as was much of the land on the outskirts of town; but the ownership was discreet, and the public had access and were often none the wiser. This particular stretch surrounded the military prison, or glass house as it was known, not that there was any hint of its existence behind a screen of evergreens in the distance. The main road and the Monkwick housing estate lay on the other side. Brazier reckoned he could figure out where the path was; there was plenty of open space too, so he thought it unlikely he'd get lost. He moved snow aside with his foot until he could see the earth. He picked up a dead leaf. The shape was unmistakable. 'Oak,' he said to himself. One similar was found in the boot of the car, possibly from Hopkins' body.

Brazier sniffed. He'd walk to Beech's from here.

The woods were eerily still. Trees were dripping snowmelt, their trunks greened with algae. Far off, he could hear a male voice. He paused. Through the trees he could make out a squad of soldiers yomping deep in the thicket. It never occurred to him that the army actually used these woods for training – the firing ranges were at Fingringhoe. He made a mental note to contact the MP captain on his return. After half an hour's walk the woods ended abruptly, his route had led him to a cul-de-sac on a new housing estate. This must be where Roland had worked as a labourer, he thought. Brazier followed the road round and in a matter of minutes he was on the Monkwick council estate, feeling invigorated and alive. Approximately twelve hundred houses from the forties and fifties, wedged between the new garrison and old garrison on the southern side of Colchester. The estate was as silent as the woods from which he emerged. Two uniforms appeared from a panda car waiting in the road for his arrival.

Mandy had to take the morning absent from work, and said it was the dentist. She was paid by the hour and couldn't afford to take the time out. The panda had been sitting out the front for fifteen minutes. She watched as they got out of the car to meet the short spiky-haired policeman who had arrested Roland.

'Hi,' he said to her when she answered the door. 'Police.'

'Yes, we've met,' she said. 'You look frozen.'

'One search warrant.' He held it out.

Mandy released the door chain. 'I don't know what you think you'll find in here, he's barely been home five minutes.'

'For his sake, hopefully nothing.' Brazier crossed the threshold.

The uniform went ahead of him.

'Try not to make a mess,' Mandy called resignedly after them. 'Mind the hoover upstairs.'

'Whose gaff is this? Yours?'

'Yes, Mum's originally. Or was, she came here after the war – she was bombed out of the East End. We got it when she passed.'

The policeman was about her age and height. He didn't hold her gaze, being more intent on her house, and she felt exposed, from the faint air of damp in the hallway to the peeling skirting board.

'Your brother is in serious bother.'

'I know. You took him away.'

'Aren't you concerned?'

She shrugged.

'Do you know what he's been up to?'

'Stealing cars, you told me.'

'Correct. Only this one had a body in the boot.' He studied her for a reaction.

'He's a thief, not a murderer. You must know that,' she said, plainly.

'Believe me, miss, I hope that's so.' Brazier asked what she knew of his movements, who he'd been mixing with.

'He was skint, as you'd expect. And had a few debts from before he went inside to be settled. Even tried some labouring – working on the building site over the road there, at Friday Woods – but he ain't cut out for that. Dole money takes time to work through the system. So when he gives me a bit for housekeeping, I wondered where it came from, but didn't ask any questions.'

'Thursday night he claims to have been in the Gladiator? You too?'

'Sounds about right.'

The sound of a bed scraping across the floor interrupted her. 'When's he comin' home? Needs to sign on tomorrow.'

'Hmm . . . maybe that'll be on the forefront of his mind,' Brazier said. 'Listen, if you're hiding anything for him, it'll be in his interests to hand it over. If he goes back in again, he might not get out. Ever.'

Without a word, she turned around, entered the kitchen and put the kettle on. Brazier followed her and stared out of the window, where two blackbirds were tussling, spraying snow.

After five minutes, a constable appeared in the doorway and shook his head.

'Excuse me a moment,' Brazier said and left the room. The constable remained at the door, as though a sentry. Not that Brazier doubted uniform's thoroughness; he only wanted to get a sense of how Roland's daily life was on the outside.

There was nothing to see in Beech's bedroom, the same room he'd had since childhood. A battered ukulele lay forlorn on the unmade bed. In and out of trouble most of his adult life, Roland had no real possessions beyond those left from his youth; fishing rods and an air rifle unused for years lay resting in a mildewed corner, hiding the lifted wallpaper. A couple of scuffed Dinky toys on the windowsill, covered in dust so thick it was visible, together with a child's globe. A world this particular child was unlikely to ever see. See! Brazier went to the bedside table, where he found a pair of glasses on top of a car magazine. One arm was held in place by tape. The garage attendant had said the man he saw had broken glasses.

Brazier pocketed the specs and hurried downstairs, and ordered uniform to search the place. He himself did not hang around, thanking Mandy back politely, saying her brother was in need of his glasses and left.

CHAPTER 30

'The Bishop, sir, on line one.'

Watt was expecting visitors and didn't wish to be disturbed, and hence his telephone had on been on divert to Philips. Little point in that if all Philips did was bother him when it rang.

'Again? Jesus.' No one could have predicted the clergyman would prove such a pain in the behind.

'He is one of the country's most senior clergy, sir.'

'I don't care whether he's next in line for Pope,' Watt said. 'We are not personal security guards, he'll have to wait in line like everyone else.'

'The Pope is Catholic. St Nicholas – and indeed the Bishop – is Church of England. Administratively, at least, it's a different operation altogether.'

'I know, Leslie, I know,' Watt groaned. 'I don't give a fig. St James church in the town on fire? No. Chelmsford Cathedral? Not when last I looked. My point is, this is an isolated incident, and nobody was hurt.'

'I gather this particular church was unique in its construction, hence the vicar's mortification.'

'Yes, yes, I heard all about that.'

'Maybe it's personal, against the vicar, sir?'

'Yes, yes . . .' Watt rocked back on his overly springy new chair, palms resting on the plastic arms. He was pleased with this sprout of an idea. 'Suggest that to the good father, will you? See where that gets us. Yes, and I shall direct Brazier and Kenton to root around the vicar's personal foundations: as one should, in a thorough investigation.' Poke at me, he thought, and I'll take you to task. 'That might temper the holy grumblings. Bravo, Philips.'

Superintendent Watt wasn't accustomed to interference from anyone, but if there was one thing he'd learnt sharpish since landing this post, it was that there was no escape from front-line policing. When Brazier had reported that the Sierra had been left overnight on military land – a fact that had been overlooked – he had felt it was his duty, not that of a detective sergeant, to contact the base commander.

Watt's ascendancy through the ranks had been nothing short of meteoric. He'd not been in any one position long enough for his actions to be questioned; be it casework or community relations. A desire for power propelled him purposely through the ranks, deftly moving through depart-ments like a frog across lily pads. Robbery, drugs, murder, rape; he'd skimmed the surface of all, leaving not so much as a fingerprint on a case file. Always managing up, Watt's narrow eyes were fixed on his superiors: that was the way to succeed. Beneath him, the rank and file were too busy grafting.

This philosophy had served him well until last year. He had been the ACC's favourite and when Merrydown's retirement arrived, he was sure her job was his. But then – Blam! – out of nowhere a woman was named successor. One he'd never heard of before, from somewhere up north. Why? For equality's sake, he was told. But Merrydown *is* a woman? Apparently, that didn't count – she'd been appointed before Women's Rights and equality had been an issue. Hadn't it always been an issue? No, as a matter of fact it hadn't, he was to learn.

Watt was crushed. Merrydown swept down to soothe him, and almost stroking his arm had said: 'You want autonomy and power? I know where you can have it.'

His dark browless eyes had lit up, expecting to hear of an important strategic role freeing up within the Met, but instead he heard the word '*Colchester*'.

Colchester?

In an instant he saw career disaster: a backward town in East Anglia would be the end of him. Biting down his disappointment, he had replied civilly. 'A town, not a city?'

'Not yet. Have patience and mark my words,' she said. 'There is no city in Essex, Trevor, but there'll be one soon . . . Surprised? Chelmsford has its cathedral but is only a town. Why? Because of the rivalry with Colchester, a great – greater – town, an important one . . . Complex.'

Watt had heard her stress the word 'complex' – by which,

he was sure, she meant 'problematic'. Colchester had been a garrison town for centuries. With a 'unique' social structure, dependent economically on a massive military presence, it had to take the rough with the smooth. Drunken brawling was a mainstay, and resentment at the army was etched deep in the civilian community. And then, from time to time, terrorism would pop up on the agenda, as it had now, putting everyone on edge. On the top of this was the geography of the place; the Essex coast notorious as a smugglers' haven by virtue of its unnavigable coastline.

'Suffice to say we need a strong man out there,' the Assistant Chief Constable had said, now sternly. 'We can squeal all we like about equal rights, but like it or not, while aggression, hostility, killing and war-mongering persist in being an innately male pursuit, the army will continue to be the domain of men.'

'Domain of men,' Watt muttered to himself now as he watched Philips guide two men in the unmistakable drab olive of military uniform across the open-plan office towards him.

'I believe you were expecting these gentlemen, sir.'

He was indeed.

CHAPTER 31

Brazier and Kenton stood outside Chloe Moran's flat. She had been hesitant on the intercom. The newspapers were sniffing around.

'Why would he tell us he stashed money there, then?' Kenton asked.

'No idea. We had the mattress off, the lot. Nowt. Maybe he spent it in the pub and forgot. The sister confirmed they were in there the Thursday night. Ah, here she is.'

Chloe Moran was furious.

'If I wrote this letter, show me it. Where is it? Huh?'

Brazier, slumped against the porch wall, allowed Kenton to do all the talking.

'Who told you I wrote to him? Come on.'

They exchanged glances.

Chloe was exhausted and well aware she looked a fright. She had not slept a wink. Paul was properly upset. He didn't say anything, he didn't need to. Locked in his silence, churning it over in his mind. She'd tried to laugh it off, comparing dope to fags, but it hadn't worked. This was a world that he only understood through the movies and telly: Paul had not so much as received a parking ticket. 'Well, cat got your tongue? Jesus!' She knew she was taking it out on them.

'Peter Hart . . . I've been to Spain to iron out a few possibilities,' Kenton said.

'"Iron out a few possibilities", by which you mean listen to any old nonsense one of the country's most wanted criminals cares to spout? How could I have written to him, when I didn't even have a clue whereabouts he was living?'

'Bruce was staying at the George in the High Street under a false name. He took a taxi out to Layer the night he was killed, and never returned. The Hare. Do you know it?'

'No.'

'Being in Colchester, it's likely you'd bump into him, or at the very least hear about it.'

'Maybe – but so what?'

'Miss Moran, can you recall what you were doing the night Bruce was killed?'

'Huh.' She went quiet. 'I was at my boyfriend's place. Westland Drive, Highwoods.'

'Hypothetically speaking, how would you react if Bruce had wanted to see you?'

Chloe's shoulders tensed at the direct line of questioning.

'With dismay,' she said sourly. 'Look, I heard he was here, but didn't want to believe it. He called on my mother.'

'Your mother?'

'Don't ask me why.' Chloe wouldn't mention Sandra telling her Bruce had been spotted in town.

'Why didn't you tell us this before, Chloe?'

She met his stern bespectacled eyes. 'I told her to report it. Jesus, she's an adult. I didn't give it any thought after that – I'm trying not to think about Bruce, do you understand? I don't care what happened to him.'

It was the truth. She couldn't tell if she'd convinced them.

'Okay, your mother is presumably easy enough to find?' Kenton said eventually.

'Yes, she's round the corner. And honestly, I couldn't quite believe that he'd want to see her. They didn't get on.'

The other policeman stirred from resting against the porch wall.

'Do you know this lad?' He held out a faded Polaroid of a boy of nine or ten in swimming trunks, standing against a laurel hedge. The boy's head was slightly cowed from the glare of the sun.

'No,' she said. 'Why?'

'It was among Bruce's few possessions. We wondered if he had a son and whether it was him he came to see.'

She snorted in mock laughter. 'If he did, it wasn't with me.'

CHAPTER 32

The Avenue in Lexden was lined with grand detached Victorian houses. Grey brick, red brick, some gothic, but all of them large.

'Shines rather a different light on Miss Moran, don't you think?' Brazier said as they pulled up outside Margaret Moran's house. 'Is that a fucking turret or what?'

'A tad ostentatious,' Kenton said. Anything to do with property made him gloomy. 'Yeah, yeah – we'd not thought of her with any degree of significance . . .' And that meant they'd not looked into Chloe Moran's background. Until now.

A woman in an emerald-coloured dress contemplated them from a bay window.

'I expect my daughter sent you here,' she said a few minutes later, showing them into a reception room. 'I would have of course called in my own time, having seen the appeal on the television, once I collected my thoughts. It was quite a shock, you understand.'

Short and elegantly turned-out, Moran was composed and not troubled by her own lack of urgency.

'It would seem Hopkins' sudden arrival and almost instant death was a such shock that you've all been rendered mute,' Kenton said.

She inclined her head away, as if this remark had eluded her.

'Withholding information concerning a murder investigation is an offence, Mrs Moran,' Brazier said, 'Get me?'

'Yes, I *get you*, Detective.'

'What sort of job gets you a gaff like this?' Brazier continued, moving about the chequered tiled floor.

'My late husband was medical staff officer at the garrison.'

'And yourself? You don't strike me as the stay-at-home type.'

'I was a consultant paediatrician for a private medical company.'

'What did you think of your daughter's choice of husband?' Kenton asked.

'To start with, he was perfectly pleasant. It was only later that he transpired to be a scoundrel. Appearances can be deceiving. I'm sure you, as detectives, are familiar with that possibility.'

'Why was he here?'

'To see Chloe. That's what he told me. She had written.'

'Did you believe him?'

'I could think of no reason not to . . . why else would he come and see me?'

'But after all this time? It was acrimonious, their split. Were you happy to have him disturb her?'

'No, I . . . I was of course surprised, and upset – that Chloe had not told me, and I telephoned her immediately, thinking it unwise she meet with him.'

'And?'

'She was very cross – and denied it. I didn't know what to think, I can tell you.'

'And what *did* you think?'

'How do you mean?'

'Did you think,' Kenton held both hands out like scales, 'one of them must be lying?'

She went quiet for a moment, then said, 'I was flummoxed, but at the end of the day, it's not my life. Chloe may have been embarrassed to admit seeing him again, and intended to hide it from me. Who really ever knows what goes on in other people's relationships,' she said despondently.

'You are not alone, Mrs Moran. Bruce told an acquaintance in Spain that Chloe had contacted him and that was why he was returning to the UK,' Kenton said. 'If Chloe had written to Bruce, she would have to have known where he lived in Spain, and she says she did not.'

'Everyone knows he has an apartment in the same street as my sister in Torremolinos, my sister has seen him on her holidays there, but Chloe may have chosen not to know. I really couldn't say.'

'Did Bruce say anything else?' Brazier asked.

'Only that he wouldn't be here long.'

'He's wanted for questioning in the UK, it would be unwise

to linger,' Kenton said. 'Indeed, it was risky for him to be here at all. He used a forged passport and checked in under a false name at a Colchester hotel.'

'You reel this information out as if I'm party to it. I'm not – he was here one minute and gone the next.'

'It was in all the papers, the drug bust, for days at the time.'

'Not the sort of papers I read.'

'Back to the meeting with Chloe. Did Bruce say where?'

'No. Somewhere out of the way was all he said.'

'Do you know if Hopkins had any other family here? Did he mention anyone?'

'No, we knew precious little of his background,' she said.

'This photo was among the few items he flew in with.'

Margaret Moran barely glanced at the photo before sighing. 'I have no idea whose child that is.'

'One final question, Mrs Moran.' Brazier came close enough to smell her perfume. 'How would you describe his mood?'

'Jubilant. One of excitement.'

'Excitement?' Kenton repeated.

'Yes. The prospect of reuniting. He loved her, for all his foibles – that remains.'

'Thank you, Mrs Moran. If anything comes to mind, you'll be sure to call?' Kenton said.

CHAPTER 33

'She is one cool customer,' Brazier said as they left Margaret Moran's house. She was back at the bay window, watching them go.

'*Foibles*. Talk about understatement,' Kenton said, buttoning his coat to the top. 'There's something peculiar about all this, and I can't put my finger on it.'

'Mother–daughter thing. Complex. She didn't even ask if we thought Chloe did it. Strange how these pompous rich bastards are. Maybe Bruce had a thing with the old girl? Let's face it, he was nearer her age than the daughter's. Well-preserved, too.'

'Maybe we should get mother and daughter in a room.'

Brazier's chin sunk into his scarf as they trudged up Lexden Road towards Southway as the wind whipped across the street.

Back in CID, Kenton noted army personnel in the super's office.

'What's all that about?' he asked as he handed Brazier a polystyrene cup of coffee.

'Soldiers in Friday Woods night of the murder. He wants

to handle anything to do with the base himself. Wants us to stay put till he's finished. The Bishop has been in his ear about Kempe Marsh church, by the way. Watt says we're to go down hard on the vicar; suggest it's a personal vendetta. Shut him up, in other words.'

'What a waste of time . . .'

He propped up the photo of the boy against a framed photo of Lindsay and picked up a Post-it note to call forensics. The telephone rang as he reached for it.

'A florist for you, Sergeant,' said the switchboard operator.

'A what?'

'Flower shop in Billericay.'

'If you're sure it's for me.' Billericay was the other side of Chelmsford, south Essex, thirty-odd miles down the A12 towards London. He was looking at the photo of the boy in swimming trunks as the call was patched through. He heard a softly spoken man inform him the shop had received an item for the attention of DS Kenton in the post.

'An embroidered badge,' the man repeated.

'You're certain?' Kenton said, emphasising his location.

'Very clearly so. I'd say it's from a school blazer or cap badge.'

'Just a badge, that's all?' Kenton said.

'No, there's a message with it. On blue airmail paper, I think. Wait a second.' He cleared his throat and said, slow and loud: '"*To special people looking after the fire.*"'

Kenton repeated the words aloud to Brazier. The church fire? Could it be any clearer a message?

165

'We'll be over directly.' He scribbled the shop details down and hung up.

'"Directly" where?' Brazier removed his feet from the desk.

'Billericay,' he said, heading for the door.

'Nice. Home.'

Kenton stopped. 'You're from Clacton, no?'

'Do be brief. Worked there, not born there. Who is actually born in Clacton? Sade lives there but she was obviously not born there. Billericay Dickie, aren't I?'

He was making no sense to Kenton. 'Well, I presume you'll know the way then . . .'

Philips, who had observed their exchange, stepped across the doorway, barring their exit.

'Superintendent Watt may like a word, detectives, before you scurry away. Concerning Mr Beech.'

Kenton was hesitant; to involve Watt would be to lose control . . .

Brazier solved any internal wrangling by barging past. 'Out of the way, stiff,' he said.

'We'll be in touch!' Kenton shouted back as they hurried away.

CHAPTER 34

Billericay, South Essex.

Home of the East Ender made good. Traders, jobbers, grafters on the stock market. Leave school in May at fifteen, straight on the train into Liverpool Street towards plum jobs with brokers in the city, pulling in a wedge before their smarter O-level classmates finish in the exam hall. After a couple of years jobbing, running errands and such, the savvy ones wriggle through to the dealing floor themselves, until recently the reserve of the public schoolers.

'Your chums let them in, and here's the result: prim and proper commuter belt territory, in the Square Mile in under half an hour.'

'They were not my chums,' Kenton retorted, as Brazier messed about with music cassettes, finally wedging one in the car stereo. 'My parents worked abroad, they had no choice but to send me away, and then for only two years. What about you? The lure of the City – didn't you yearn for a Porsche, mobile phone, the yuppie lifestyle?'

'Hell, no,' Brazier replied, then, 'But fair play; they earn it. Made the town prosperous too. Might be a bit OTT, Loadsamoney, here and there, but you know . . .'

'Absolutely.' Kenton had nothing more to add. The KLF vibrated inside the door speaker as they hammered down the motorway.

Billericay was a conventional provincial town, situated on a rise, and at its heart was its high street. A half-mile stretch with a dozen public houses. At the bottom, in a dip, lay the train station; at the other end of town lay the local plod, in the middle was a church, and opposite the church, Mayflower Florists. The buildings in the centre of town were old, with preserved Tudor-beamed frontage.

The church sat on a fork in the road with a war memorial on the crux. Across from the side road was a fishmonger and adjoining that, sitting proud, a double-fronted mustard-coloured pub with car parking out front. They pulled up in the pub and crossed the road. The florists, whose signage sported a three-mast ship, was between a tandoori restaurant and an off-licence, all housed within the same half-timbered building. They stepped down into the shop, ducking beneath a 'mind your head' warning on the roof beam, to be greeted by a pungent sweet smell.

'Lilies,' Kenton commented, half crouching under the low ceiling.

'Funerals,' Brazier added, waiting for the assistant behind the counter to be free. 'Lot of flu at this time of year.'

'The boss about?' Kenton asked a puffy-faced man with

longish hair swept back behind his ears, and a day or two's growth around his chin. A bit louche, was Kenton's impression. A bit shabby and miserable – not the sort to run a flower shop.

'Me,' he said, dourly. 'DS Kenton?'

'Mr Nolan?' Kenton replied, genially, standing upright and knocking his head.

Nolan reached under the desk and produced a plain Manila envelope, addressed with elegant fountain pen script to Mr C. Nolan of the Mayflower Florist. Before opening it, Kenton inspected it closely. The postmark was Colchester. The stamp first class.

'Hmm.' He weighed it in his hand. Nothing to it. He squeezed it open. Inside was a disc of material with a slip of wafer-thin blue writing paper attached by safety pin. Kenton shrugged it to the middle of the envelope and pinched it out. It wasn't a disc, but an embroidered shield: a neatly sewn coat of arms an inch and a half tall by an inch wide. The paper bore Kenton's name and rank.

'I suggest it's a cap badge.' Nolan repeated his assessment made during the telephone call. He had large eyes, set a little too far apart. Not unlike Brazier's.

'Yes, you said. I think you're right,' Kenton said.

'A school badge; what you see on a cap or blazer,' he continued. Kenton studied it and then passed it to Brazier.

'Not mine,' Kenton said. A pale blue saltire on a white

background, a lion central, and two partridges. And the motto: '*Ducere Exemplo*'.

'Latin?'

'Lead by example,' Kenton confirmed. 'What do you reckon?'

Brazier played with the badge through his fingers, his eye on the slightly frayed edging. 'It's not from any school round here that I know of, which is the sum total of two. One I went to and the one we used to ruck with at the end of term.'

'Correct. It's not from round here. A village called Oakley, past Rettendon, south of Chelmsford towards the River Crouch,' Nolan said. The shop bell went. Nolan called behind for an assistant to attend to the customer. 'Come this way, there is something you should know.' Nolan led them through a passage and out to the back out the shop, where he feverishly scrambled for a cigarette. His hands trembled so much he could not light it. Brazier leant forward with a Bic lighter.

'Thank you,' Nolan said, composing himself. 'Three days ago, the owner of this shop received a letter in the same handwriting as yours. And no, before you ask, it's not me; obvious, huh? I'm just minding it until the solicitors decide what to do, keeping it going. The owner was Kenny Markham. Nice bloke. My friend.' The man's eyes welled up, possibly with cold, or possibly with emotion. 'I was his lodger of the last eight years. He's a retired teacher. That,' he jabbed at the envelope in Kenton's hand, 'was his school. I recognise it – he had a shield with the same colours on the wall above the piano. Bryde Park, the place is called.'

'You say the shop is with the solicitors – what happened to Mr Markham?'

'He hung himself in the garage.'

CHAPTER 35

Conor Nolan grappled with an explanation of his life. 'I used to play the French horn for the Chelmsford Phil before it disbanded. Ken was always at the cathedral, either with the school or organising some concert or another. My wife was on the arts committee and we were always bumping into one another. When Sheila died, I was a bit lonely to be honest – it's not easy making friends in your fifties, and if music is the world you know, you seldom step out of it. Anyhow, Kenny said he was leaving Bryde Park and setting up shop. I was soon to be out of work, as well as on my own, so I needed a distraction.'

'Back to the letter Kenny received. You remember it, why?'

'Because it was lying around on the table unopened for several days. I spilt tea on it and nudged him to open it. Had a Colchester postmark too.'

'Any idea what was in it?'

'Nope. And I never gave it a second thought until that one came up.'

'Do you think its contents triggered his suicide?'

Nolan drew on his cigarette, squeezing the butt with yellow fingertips.

'I hadn't thought about it until this came. Ken said the letter contained sad news – he was sullen. He said he'd tell me about it later. He never did. I searched the house looking for it but he must have tossed it out. I don't know. Kenny was a gent and a very private man. He was much the same by the evening, perhaps a bit subdued, right up until when I found him in the morning, hanging there.'

'How would you describe your relationship with Mr Markham?' Brazier asked. Kenton was visibly uncomfortable with him doing this.

'Friend or companion. Call it what you will.' Nolan was unabashed.

'Was it necessary to ask that?' Kenton asked afterwards. 'I mean, the guy was a widower, as if that wasn't enough for you.'

Brazier sat drumming his fingers on the steering wheel, not paying any attention.

'Or ask at the local cop shop,' Kenton continued, 'about Markham's orientation, if it bothers you.'

'It doesn't bother me, mate, but it does help to have an inkling about the geezer's relationship to reckon on the likelihood of him sharing whatever was in that envelope,' Brazier said testily. 'Now, we steam down to this school, or what?'

'And say what?'

'Any idea why CID were sent their school cap badge, for starters.'

Kenton wasn't sure, but his nose was put out of joint by Brazier's challenging response, which he didn't know how to deal with, leaving him no option but to readily agree.

And Brazier knew his way about. They left Billericay using a different route, passing mansions to rival Southfork – Doric columns, wrought-iron gates, even balconies, but without the surrounding land – but here in Essex they crammed shoulder to shoulder, bursting out of plots barely able to contain them on the edge of woodland.

'Where there's bankers there are builders,' Brazier said, noting Kenton staring out the passenger window. 'And making a packet too. Why have a small house when you can afford to knock it down and build one three times the size?'

'Well, quite . . .'

The landscape grew flat and bleary, a dull white as featureless as the fens. The twelve-mile drive was slow, with nothing to distract the eye. Only after turning off at Rettendon Common and heading towards Oakley was there any variation. Travelling along a lane with a brown ridge of crusted snow running down the centre, the road undulated, dipping then rising over a hillock to reveal a signpost for the school. Bryde Park sat below in a vale, where the slate-tiled roof and numerous chimney stacks were visible beyond an evergreen border. As they slowly crept their way down, Kenton had a sense their approach was being watched from the large dark windows of the Edwardian manor house.

'A "preparatory boys' school, ages seven to thirteen". Well, la-di-da.' Brazier drew hard on his cigarette, turning the tip beacon red as he read the gold lettering on the green hoarding. This was his second fag since the florists and Kenton had wound the window down. Brazier was tense.

'A prep school,' Kenton said. 'A private fee one, as opposed to a state-funded establishment, in preparation for public school.' They passed between tall wrought-iron gates and crunched up the long semi-circular drive, passing between thick laurel bushes and deep leylandii which framed a perfect protractor shape of white lawn fronted by a huge yew and cedars facing the building. They drew to a halt.

Brazier stubbed the cigarette out forcefully in the Citroën's ashtray. 'You went to one, right?'

'I told you, only for two years . . . but not as you imagine.'

'Imagine? I don't imagine anything.' Brazier parked the car near the mottled grey Doric columns of the entrance, where a man stood in a black gown. 'A school's a school.' He yanked on the handbrake. It could do with tightening. 'Although they never wore capes like Batman at mine, like that geezer.'

The schoolmaster viewing their approach turned on his heel and hurried off, and a porter instead met them on the threshold. The air was thick with moisture. Icicles hung from glossy black guttering.

'Can I help you?' the porter said, bearing down on them.

'Yeah, here to see the head,' Brazier said. 'Thinking of sending my son here.'

The man regarded them dubiously.

They mounted the steps. 'No,' Kenton said, and flashed his ID. 'We're investigating the death of a retired teacher. Now, if you'd be so kind.'

The porter turned and they followed him inside. Brazier noted the lack of children, and a strong smell of floor wax.

'Oi, mate, where are the kids?'

'In lessons, sir.'

'There's always a few milling around in a school, no? This place has the vibe of a morgue.' But there were none to be seen. 'What you do here, lock them in the classroom?'

Not that they were allowed to see beyond the hallway, as the porter briskly ushered them inside the headmaster's study immediately to the right of the large front door. The room decor was pre-war. Before them sat a lean woman, the headmistress, wearing a powder blue tracksuit; a games whistle rested on her chest. She looked modern, young and out of kilter with her surroundings. But she sat straight as a wicker cane.

She beckoned them forward over a claret Persian rug and gestured towards two visitors' chairs, made of dark wood, adjacent to a trophy cabinet of similar colour. The grand cabinet housed rugby cups, cricket trophies, statuettes of footballers, even one of an archer.

'My name is Henrietta Wintour, and I am the headmistress

of Bryde Park. Now, please, what can my school have to do with the death of a former master?' The skin around her eyes was pale, but the rest of her face was tanned, suggestive of a recent skiing holiday.

Kenton informed her of the suicide of Ken Markham.

'Tragic. But if he left eight years ago . . .?'

'Did you know Mr Markham?' Kenton asked.

'Before my time, although some of the faculty and other staff will doubtless remember him.'

'How long have you been in command here, miss?' Brazier asked.

'Ms, thank you kindly.' She squinted ungenerously. 'Four years.'

'What about your predecessor, Ms Wintour?' Kenton said, settling into the chair, making himself comfortable. 'Still with us?'

Her clear cool eyes studied him before answering, 'Charles Wintour.'

'Ah, the reins passed on from the old man,' Brazier said, toying with another cigarette, wondering what 'Ms' signified and if she was married. 'Perhaps we can have a word?'

'No. I'm afraid that's impossible.'

'Oh, I'm sorry, he's passed?' said Kenton.

'No, he's upstairs,' she said sharply. Her annoyance was firmly in Kenton's direction, despite Brazier's obvious rudeness. She was above jokers of his kind. 'In a wheelchair. My father has suffered a stroke. Now, please, what is the purpose of your visit?'

'Is this your school badge?' Brazier laid it carefully on the desk, as if it were a butterfly ready for a pin and a glass box.

'It is. Did it belong to the deceased?'

'No, it was sent for my attention to Mr Markham's Florists,' said Kenton.

'Sorry, I don't understand.'

'Neither do we,' Brazier said. 'However, it came with this message.' He handed her the envelope.

'"*To special people looking after the fire.*"' Wintour read aloud. 'To you, presumably? Are you in care of a fire?'

Kenton crossed his legs. 'We are investigating an arson attack on a church and wondered if it might be related.'

'I see. If I was the vicar, I would be troubled.'

'Yes, he's not best pleased. So could we check whether the vicar has any connection to your school? The name is Symonds.'

'Again, it's a name I haven't heard in a long time. This note – it's on airmail paper. Has it come from abroad?'

'Hardly another country – Colchester,' Brazier said. 'Now, back to Symonds . . .'

'One of the older members of staff . . .?' Kenton suggested.

'May I look at the badge again?'

Brazier reached into his pocket.

'Wait. One thing I can tell you, that badge is over ten years old. My father updated the crest in honour of the royal wedding in 1981.'

'Oh, right. How do you know that?'

'I have lived here all my life. As I said, my father is upstairs in the flat. Bryde Park is a boarding school. There are certain things one remembers. And before you ask if I knew the staff back then well, the answer is no. I was in my last year of university in 1981, but was home for Charles and Diana's wedding when my father showed me the updated livery.'

'Would you mind checking your records? I presume you have records.'

'Very well.' She rose slowly and made her way silently across the rug to a row of filing cabinets next to the door. 'Please don't smoke in here,' she said over her shoulder

'Eyes in the back of your head, like all good teachers,' Brazier quipped.

Wintour smiled faintly as she pulled out a file. 'You're in luck,' she said, returning to her desk. 'Although it is with trepidation I pass this on to you, as I fear where this may lead. Kevin Symonds. Theology student. Taught games and RE while completing his degree. Here – the Easter term of 1977 until summer of 1979.'

Excited and anxious to return to the station, they took the Southend road up to Chelmsford at a dangerous speed. The road was empty and there was little to distract them, and the Citroën motored alone, occasionally veering one way or another on impacted snow. In the distance to the west, giant lattice steel pylons marched south, their tops obscured in mist and low cloud before they disappeared, on towards

Canvey Island and the Thames Estuary. On reaching the A12, Brazier's driving caught the attention of an enthusiastic traffic cop and they were pulled over by a jam-sandwich Rover. The young officer was new to the job and was vexed to see two CID officers out of Colchester driving so badly on such a treacherous day. Making a meal out of it, he cautioned them for their own good.

Kenton didn't comment on Brazier's driving and Brazier didn't curse the traffic cop; both were preoccupied contemplating the connection between Markham, Bryde Park, Symonds and the church fire, and where it all may lead.

CHAPTER 36

Her mother had gone quiet. She must have contacted the police, as Chloe had told her she must, or else she'd do it herself. Maybe life could almost be as it was before. Because no one at work knew about Bruce, almost nobody spoke to her about him. Paul was an unfortunate exception, and had gone back to his own place and not uttered more than a few words since she had 'enlightened' him, as he had put it.

The intercom went. The first viewing at the revised price. She buzzed them in.

The prospective buyer was a young man, thin-faced, in a large coat that hung off him like a tent. Hands in pockets, his arms were lost in the baggy material. He reminded her of those doleful quiet lads that like nothing better than to sit by a river smoking roll-ups and drinking tins of lager in the summer months.

'Are you a student?' She realised the banality of the words as she said them. If he was, he'd hardly be buying a property.

'Yes,' he said, 'journalism.'

'At the university?' she said, surprised. It must be the parents forking out.

'Sure. How long have you been here?' he asked.

'Ten years,' she said. 'It's a lovely quiet block. You can't hear the neighbours. Solid old building.'

He didn't appear to be listening. Instead, his eyes were on the photograph of her and Paul on the mantelpiece.

'Are you here on your own?' He spoke with a candid easy air that she found unusual.

'Yes . . . I'm hoping to move in with my boyfriend.' She smiled. 'That's him there. Would you like to see the bedrooms?'

He followed her to her room. She stood aside to allow him in and noticed an odour about him. Stale old clothes. The coat was army surplus. Not a tramp as such, but a bit extreme even for a student; where hygiene is forgone as expensive and unnecessary. The man, she hadn't taken a note of his name, wasn't especially curious. His skin was bad, marked by poor shaving. She was having second thoughts about her initial assessment. Even the boho wealthy are clean. After a quick glance at the bathroom and kitchen, he said, 'Thanks. I've seen enough.'

'Oh, okay.' She had been smiling constantly in an effort to be welcoming, and now her face hurt.

She offered to take him downstairs, but he said he'd see himself out.

'It's nice to see you,' he said before he left, studying her with pale grey eyes.

How peculiar. She shook her head in disbelief, convinced he was a time waster. She tugged on her boots, grabbed her quilted coat and hat and made for the door. That was it – any more interested parties the estate agent could deal with; she wasn't going to spend her time trying to second-guess whether any Tom, Dick or Harry had the means – or intention – of buying the place. She was desperate to return to the office, to slip back into that persona, finalise the year-end accounts and bury herself in numbers.

'Oh Christ.' Chloe could see the cameras beyond the latticed door. 'The press.' Taking a deep breath, she went out into the cold.

'Miss Moran, do you have anything to say about Bruce?'

'Where the bloody hell were you two yesterday afternoon? Philips was paging you for hours.' Watt was annoyed, and in an effort to constrain himself he retracted his thin top lip, revealing teeth best concealed. It was late morning, and he himself had been in Chelmsford, where he was greeted with the information that two of his men had been stopped for reckless driving. He was already aware; Philips had enjoyed relaying the information the previous afternoon. The strangest thing was, Chelmsford did not ask him what they were up to. Fortunate though this was at the time, it had since played on his mind; why not? 'Well?' he said.

Kenton's pager was in his own vehicle, not that he ever needed it.

'Atmospherics, guv. You know, the weather,' Brazier said, having no idea where his device was at all. He had a white stick protruding from the corner of his mouth too big for a toothpick.

'The weather,' Watt repeated. He didn't know if this was true or not. He kept the driving caution to himself to test their honesty. Why he felt the need to do so, he did not know. 'You've been out of range.' He said this as gently as he could, controlling an anger that had built overnight. Losing it was the height of poor management.

'Busy, sir, Billericay first, then Ret—'

'Billericay? That's the other side of Chelmsford.'

'Investigating the vicar, sir; as you said. He was attached to a school at Oakley near Rettendon and might be in danger . . .'

'Don't tell me what I said, Kenton.' These words were unintentionally issued as a squeaky rasp that cut the conversation dead. Watt reached for water, gulped and closed his eyes for a fraction of a second. 'Now—' he breathed deeply – 'while you have been absent the Military Police have been in and provided useful information. It seems they witnessed a second vehicle besides the Sierra in Friday Woods car park, late on the night *before* Roland Beech shoved the Sierra into the reservoir.'

'Oh yeah?' Brazier said. Both faces reflected their surprise. 'Get an ID on the driver? Or reg, make, model?'

Watt's expression remained fixed. 'The army were on night exercises. They didn't hang about, but were sure there were two individuals present . . .' He waited for a reaction. 'It could simply be a courting couple.'

'No one goes all the way out there for a snog this time of year,' Brazier objected. 'It's the middle of nowhere.'

'Too off the beaten track,' Kenton agreed. 'Not a teenage haunt, we'd know about it. It has to be the killer dumping Hopkins in the boot.'

Watt seized on this. 'The killer? Not Beech?'

'Beech is adamant he's been stitched up,' Kenton said. 'He was in a pub on the Monkwick estate the night Hopkins was waiting at the Hare pub. The sister vouched for him, we've yet to verify it with the landlord, and there's a couple of hundred quid unaccounted for – it's likely Beech was in there until closing time, which would rule him out, and explain the money. Hopkins left the Hare at nine.'

'And what about you? Do you agree?' Watt addressed Brazier.

'Anything could have happened.' Brazier was considering the lollipop he'd just removed from his mouth. 'Reminds me of that girl in *Get Carter*; locked in the boot of her own Sunbeam. It wasn't Michael Caine that nudged that motor into the Tyne.'

Watt took a breath. 'Am I to glean from that nonsense you are in agreement with Kenton?'

'Yep.'

'Right. Release Roland Beech. Pending prosecution for the Sierra.'

'Now? There's a number of loose ends . . .' Kenton began to backtrack.

'You've had plenty of time. I've found out more than you two without so much as leaving the building.'

'Come off it,' Brazier snorted. 'We have a lead. Show him.'

Watt eyed the photo Kenton produced. 'Who's this?'

'We don't know,' Kenton said, 'but it was in Bruce's suitcase.'

'A son?'

'Could be the reason he's here,' Brazier said.

'Interesting, but has no bearing on Beech, or my decision to let him out. For now.' Watt turned the photo over, looking for a date or name, and finding none handed it back without comment, then said; 'Watch him like a hawk. Any accomplice will be out to make contact. Now then, what's all this business in Billericay and Rettendon about? That's way out of your jurisdiction.'

Watt stood examining the envelope they'd collected in Billericay. Colours from a boarding school south of Chelmsford sent with an oddly worded note triggered an association with another letter with similar calligraphy sent to a recently deceased music teacher.

'A private school, you say?' Watt muttered, dark memories of his school days entering his mind. 'Our vicar was a teacher?'

'Sort of. While completing his theology degree.' Brazier tapped the envelope lightly. 'He taught RE and games classes.'

Getting one up on the clergy appealed to Watt, but not at the expense of his detectives' work on Beech and the Hopkins' case.

'Do we know what was in the letter to this fellow Markham?'

'No, he destroyed it.'

'So there's no way of telling whether it had an impact on his state of mind?'

'No, but the lodger has his suspicions – said there was no sign whatever that the man was in distress. This letter was the only thing that was unusual in the run-up to Markham's suicide.'

'The vicar is still with us,' Watt sat back in his chair, 'and if he was in any danger, he'd more than likely know about it by now. The church was harmed, but not its minister. However, if there's a hint of a vendetta at play, we must alert him. Interesting . . . Pursue, but I don't want you scooting off over there again unless with my express permission. I need you to hand – Hopkins is top priority.'

Besides, the last thing he needed was a call from the new ACC – Castleton – asking what his men were doing poking around the Thames Estuary. An expression of bewilderment came over the two sergeants.

'Look,' Watt said, patiently, 'the church will get a new roof, but Bruce Hopkins has taken his last breath. I need you here, in Colchester.'

'What, traipsing around after Beech?' Kenton said.

'You can have two uniform. Happy?'

Brazier raised an eyebrow over his normal eye.

'That'll allow you movement.' Watt reached for the phone.

187

'Get them in position while you give Beech a final going over. And utilise Wilde. That woman has promise.'

Calm but mildly disappointed, they had a quick smoke staring out the large station window before interviewing Beech one final time. Sleet blurred the tarmac of the Southway below, black and empty at this lull in the day before the school run.

'It's like being grounded,' Brazier lamented. 'My old gaffer didn't give a toss whose toes we trod on, so long as we got the job done.'

'Watt's a control freak.' Kenton drew on his cigarette. 'But he has a point. Right, let's call the Rev. Easy does it, don't want to spook him otherwise he'll be wanting twenty-four-hour protection.' He flicked through his pocketbook and found the rectory number. Kenton's call went straight to the vicar's answerphone:

'*I am attending a seminar and won't be back until tomorrow: in the meantime, please contact the verger for any urgent assistance.*'

Kenton sighed and replaced the receiver. 'Don't they teach them not to leave details of their whereabouts when away from home? Daft bugger will be complaining he's been burgled next.'

CHAPTER 37

'Roland, there was no money under your mattress,' Brazier said.

'Yeah, right.' Pigs had had it for themselves.

'Maybe you spent it all on Thursday night,' Kenton said. 'Bought all your pals a round in the Gladiator.'

Roland said nothing. There were four people in that night; his wedge would have kept them arseholed all week.

'Don't sulk,' Brazier said. Roland glared up at him, convinced he was the one who'd turned the place over and pocketed his wedge. 'We're letting you go.'

'Eh?'

'Yes, for now. You can't have been in the Gladiator and picked Hopkins up from Layer. You're lucky the landlord spotted him. The pub was busy.'

'Righty-ho, I'll be off then.' But he felt a firm grip on his shoulder.

'Few final questions.'

'Why nick a car from the Copford Hotel?'

'Because it's easy.' A smugness flowed through him, encouraged by the prospect of getting out. 'No one expects it.'

'This is true,' Kenton said, 'but if we're going with your version of events, it wasn't your idea . . . look at this map.'

They spread an OS map before him. All squiggles and symbols. 'What am I looking at?'

'Here's the hotel.' Roland followed Kenton's finger, pointing to the fringes of the Copford Planes. 'Now, look how convenient it is from Copford to Layer, the woods and the reservoir. The proximity.'

Roland saw how easy it was from there to disappear into the countryside. 'I said from the beginning I was set up.'

'And we believe you. What we're trying to find out is: why you?' Kenton said, pacing behind him, his words directed to the wall, 'given the car's not on your doorstep. And you've been off the scene for years – at least five. Weren't you a tad surprised to be contacted now? After all this time?'

'My reputation has survived the nick, obviously.'

'Seems so – even getting caught doing what you do best didn't deter someone hiring you,' Brazier said. 'Walk us through the timing, since your release from Chelmsford, then you're out of here.'

'Out on December twenty-third. Was pissing down, icy cold, screw said, just out in time for the start of winter. I didn't do nothing until the New Year. Then spent three weeks on a building site. Sister knew the foreman. But it wasn't for me. Same day I finished there, I got a message.'

'The man who hired you left the money in a phone box at the end of your road.'

'Uh-huh. Said I'd been recommended and if I was interested, I'd find an envelope with two hundred and fifty quid
stuffed in a Yellow Pages in the phone box outside the
Gladiator.'

'And?'

'I went, found the Yellow Pages, and there it was at the
back: U for Undertakers.'

'Funny,' Brazier said. Roland blinked. He gripped the side
of the chair: already out, climbing the walls of his own mind
to get away from this.

'Where else had you been, in between time?'

'Nowhere apart from the Cherry Tree on Mersea Road.'

'What went wrong with the site job?' Kenton asked.

'Tch, I don't have the frame for it . . . Rude git told me I
was better off running courier jobs out of the Globe.'

'You're right. Puny little weakling,' Brazier said. 'Can't see
you cutting it as a hod carrier.'

Beech rose angrily – there wasn't much between the two in
height. 'Sod you,' he moaned, 'I was trying to make it straight.'

Kenton stepped in. 'How long did it last?'

'I told you, 'bout three weeks.'

'And you made no new mates in that time on site? Or
outside? Any offers of a bung for lifting materials, that sort
of thing?' Kenton asked.

He shook his head.

'Promise you, Rollie, we'd not nick you for having sticky
fingers; if you were hard up for cash, who could blame you?

But you know how word gets around on site, and a mate of a mate gets wind and Bob's your uncle.'

'I didn't take anything on site, swear on it.'

'We could nip down there, see the site manager . . . eh, Kenton?'

'Be my guest.'

Back and forth they went, discussing the development cutting into Friday Woods – 'Friday Wood Green' as it was to be known – but after an hour the detectives were no further forward in discovering who might have hired Roland to steal the car. All they learnt was that the building site was a recent development. 'It was just woodlands when I went inside.' Roland repeated this more than once. Kenton knew exactly where it was, having got stuck behind a truck leaving the site on the day of the fire.

'As a man who knows his motors, Roland, is there any reason that that car was worth taking?'

'Nope. A bog-standard Sierra. One up from the bottom rung; a GL.'

'It belonged to a sales rep from Manchester. Whoever got you to pinch the car knew the man's routine. Know anyone that works in the Copford Hotel?'

'Nope. It's the other side of town, as you said.'

Finally, Brazier was out of patience.

'All right, Rollie. Off you toddle.'

CHAPTER 38

WPS Karen Wilde heard the super out.

'It's one of my priorities here to strengthen the ties between plain clothes and uniform. You're all the same rank. Kenton can be uppity, but a good officer. And Brazier,' he paused, then smiled gently, 'comes highly recommended.'

'How exactly?' she said.

'Lend a hand, that's all. No need to be formal about it.'

Kenton, she could easily handle. Brazier, she was more curious about. Undoubtedly an oddball and an outright scruffbag, she couldn't make up her mind about him; attractive and repellent at the same time. Occasionally she would watch him at his desk twiddling with a sweet wrapper and think him interesting. Then when she caught him eyeing her up, she was uneasy. He had a funny eye that no one mentioned.

Watt sensed hesitation in her dark eyes.

'I'll have your back, don't worry.'

'I won't.'

'Good, this will be beneficial for us all. You've a bright future, Wilde.'

'Sir.'

'Only caveat, Sergeant – if you witness any improper behaviour, anything you feel uncomfortable with and contrary to the good, you're to let me know immediately, you hear? There is a liaison element, shall we say, with me.'

'Improper behaviour' – what exactly did he mean by that? The new super spoke in unfamiliar terms. He spoke often, and at length, using many words, which sounded important and serious but frequently left his audience wondering whether he'd really said anything at all.

Brazier and Kenton were at the far end of the office, mooning around by the window. Night was closing in and the dull glow of the street lights cast a misleading warm peach hue on the February grey as snow began to fall again. Kenton stood with his hands in the pockets of a duffle coat, haircut too short, revealing larger than average ears she'd not noticed before. Brazier was in a green bomber jacket and baggy black trousers like Charlie Chaplin, with white trainers poking out the bottom of them. Pegged trousers with turn-ups as well – on such short a leg as Brazier's they were not at all flattering. All this week he'd been shuffling around, depositing chunks of snow caught in his turn-ups.

'Hullo!' she called. 'Can I come and play?'

Kenton raised a limp hand in acknowledgement, while Brazier openly beckoned her over. This was going to be a hoot, all right. She joined them and together they watched

Beech scurry across the Southway from their second-floor office window. He paused at the bus stop, glanced furtively over his shoulder up at the police station, then carried on up Headgate.

'The Bull, I bet you,' Brazier said. A phone started to ring.

'You two take the Globe,' Kenton said. 'The pubs around North Station, where couriers hang out. Before he works his way there.

'I'll take the building site. Better get a move on, the day is sliding away . . .' Builders didn't work in the dark.

The Globe was an early Victorian public house midway between the train station and Colchester town centre, up via North Hill. A notorious staging post since Eastern Counties Railways opened the station in the 1840s. Arrivals, departures, a pick-up place for items on the move: the 'courier jobs' referred to by Beech meaning anything illicit, from cash to guns to people coming from or going to the Smoke – or a hiding place in the shanty confusion at Point Clear.

A bold bright corner building with pale brickwork, the Globe had seen much but gave away little. With three entrances on its two outward walls, it was designed to encourage easy movement; anyone could slip in and out.

'Trouble with a place full of drifters . . .' Brazier said as they entered through the middle double doors on the corner.

'. . . is nobody's around long enough to see anything,' Wilde finished. 'No continuity.'

'Correct. Apart from this geezer.'

A portly publican, pale with thin wispy ginger beard, stood proudly looking at them, hands at his side. He knew them, of course. Nobody else cared.

'Now, I'll bet me last shilling you'll be in here asking after The Leech?' he said.

'Word travels fast. Anything to say, Ron?' Wilde asked. This was her beat.

'He won't mind me saying, I'm sure. He came in the day he was laid off from the building site, looking for work – or mischief – and got well and truly wankered.'

'Oh yeah?'

'Site manager cut his pay packet for giving him verbals and causing a scene. Or so he says.' And then after a pause, 'Didn't mention that, did he?'

'No surprise there.' Brazier cast a glance around the place. 'What do you reckon?'

'Not a lot,' Wilde said. 'This is the sort of place you'd come to find a courier. Punters are just passing through, dropping stuff off – Beech comes here as a driver, not a thief . . .'

'Well,' elbow on the bar, Brazier inclined towards her, and Wilde caught a whiff of pear-drop infused smoker's breath, not altogether unpleasant, 'time for a quick scoop.'

'It's the middle of the afternoon.'

'Correction – it's late afternoon. Four fifteen.'

'Is it really necessary?'

'Practically a legal requirement.' The change in opening

hours two years ago was still a novelty for some, including Brazier, it seemed.

'What's this?' She tapped herself on the breast and, quickly realising where Brazier's mind was heading, added, 'A uniform.'

'Oh, yeah. Half a bitter, then?'

'No. Drinking on the job is not allowed.'

'No wonder community policing has gone to the dogs.'

'You and your CID buddies will get a wake-up call one of these days. Haven't you heard drinking and driving is history?'

'How do you feel about being assigned to us?'

'Kenton's a good copper, inoffensive enough. Bit of a dork, pulls a face if a woman says the word "wank". Girls say he clams up if you ask about his personal life. Probably not getting any.'

'Wow! You don't pull your punches. What about me?'

'The jury's still out.'

He ordered a large vodka and coke for himself and half a bitter for her. 'You're right, the world is changing, put it down to habit. You don't have to drink it.'

He tipped the drink straight back and pushed his car keys her way.

'Whoever hired Beech knew he was desperate,' he said, holding out a crumpled paper bag. 'I don't know why I know that but I do, and I bet they knew where Roland lived too; knew he'd get from the reservoir back home on foot, even in this weather.'

'Even if Roland doesn't know who hired him himself?' Wilde asked, taking a mint humbug.

'About the sum of it.' Brazier considered his empty glass, then lit a cigarette. 'Rollie knows next to nothing, his five years inside will have blurred things. A lot of time given over to rewriting his own history in that head; mistakes reassessed, blame reassigned, so he could live with himself and do his time. He may well have known *then*, but now, anyone's guess.'

She called the landlord and asked him who was in the afternoon Beech was fired. He recoiled, had absolutely no idea, and nor apparently did he spot Rollie in conversation with anyone.

'You're wasting your time,' Brazier said. 'He's said all he'll say. Helpful yet mindful of his regulars.'

The side door opened, allowing an eddy of sleet inside followed by a man in his twenties with blond highlights. He strolled in, tossing his keys in the air playfully, and offered to buy the barmaid a drink. Through the door window behind him, Brazier caught a glint of a white Sierra with a rear spoiler, gleaming under the outside light. Round the other side of the bar, Brazier watched the landlord hand over pints filled with something purple to two punk girls, hair matching the drink—

'Excuse me! Checking out the girls – they're barely out of school,' snapped Wilde.

'Do be brief,' he snapped back, then awkwardly added, 'Sorry, just people watching, you know – the job.'

'*Do be brief* – what does that even mean?'

'Just a thing people say . . . like "don't be daft", "stop wasting my time". Not sure where it comes from . . . Another one?' he motioned to the untouched half.

'God, no. Do you really care? I can't work out whether you're serious.' Head tilted down, her dark bob fell over her eyes. 'About anything.'

He studied her for a moment, not sure of the right answer. 'Sometimes.'

Wilde looked up, fringe realigning neatly on her brow.

'What about the building site – shall we go find your partner?'

'They'd have knocked off by now in this weather. Come on, what do you reckon? It is practically after hours.'

'Another time maybe. Out of uniform.'

He squinted in disbelief. 'Really?'

She was dating a fireman she'd met at judo, but it wasn't really going anywhere. One-dimensional. 'Yeah, really.' What harm could it do?

CHAPTER 39

Builders do not work in the dark nor in any form of precip-
itation. Kenton should have realised that. The Friday Wood
Green site was deserted.

Rain, sleet, and snow. Given the weather in this country it
was a wonder anything got built. He considered linking up with
Brazier before the day's end but thought it too late. For the
first time it struck him; he actually enjoyed the other policeman's company. There had been some juggling of emotions and
motives, but now he realised a fondness for the eccentric. This
cheered him up and he returned home rather than to the station.

The bad weather had kept Lindsay inside at home with the two
children, both now having caught colds. She had, however,
managed to get her paints out in the late afternoon while the
ailing infants napped. Watercolours were a pursuit that not
even the worst weather could cancel.

'What do you think?' She held up a picture of the river
she'd first sketched from the upstairs window to her bleary-
eyed eldest, who had appeared at the foot of the stairs.

'There's a lot of white,' was the snotty critique.

'Snow's not as easy to paint as you think,' Lindsay said. 'The definition is tough. Here, let's see if you can do better while I put the dinner on.'

Lindsay laid the picture on the table. Secretly, she was pleased. The art shop in Coggeshall had sold one of her paintings last week. She propelled herself up and into the kitchen to the sound of the front door. There was an uneasy conversation to be had with Daniel. She picked up the quote from the garage along with the building society letter from the narrow kitchen work surface.

'My car's had it,' she announced.

'It's the heater that's blown, not the big end.'

'To replace the heater will cost more than the car is worth.'

'We can't afford to buy you another car,' he protested.

'We can't afford to replace the heater either, then. Can't you ask your parents for help? I can't drive it in this weather as it is.' Lindsay was wise to her partner's receptiveness. Serious matters were best raised as soon he was through the door, while the top was still on the bottle.

And this was serious. Money matters were at the apex of all problems, binding all others together, squirming beneath.

'I'm not asking them for money, if that's what you mean, Lindsay.' He went to hang his coat up on the back of the door and missed the peg. It slumped to the floor.

'Why not? It'll come to you in the end, just think of it as

an advance on your inheritance. Besides, it was your father's wisdom that got us into this mess.'

'Lindsay! Don't be so bloody . . .' He stood there, forgetting about his coat. 'You can drive my car. That old banger of yours has had its day. It didn't pass an MOT even when your gran had it. Look, I know you don't like mine, but I've use of the department's, and—'

'Daniel, I've had the house valued today.'

'What?'

'Do you know what negative equity is? Huh?'

The phrase followed him into the tiny sitting room. The heat of the fire hit him from behind a guard that monopolised the floor space. The combination overpowered him.

Lindsay was holding a letter, and he could see the heavy font of the building society's insignia. A shortfall warning notice. The shame of 'Negative Equity' outweighed the anger he felt – should have felt – at the unauthorised tread of estate agents in his house. The property ladder. A joke.

'What did the estate agent say? When he saw all this clutter, I dread to think.'

'I didn't have anyone round—' she waved him off – 'phoned them in the High Street. And my painting is not clutter, thank you very much.'

'Linds, I didn't mean that—'

'Greed,' she said, bitterly. 'A straightforward repayment mortgage would have done the job. The bank lends the money, we repay it, and then we own the house. Simple. But no, we saw a financial advisor. Financial advisor! You're a policeman, what do you need a financial advisor for? Your father has a lot to answer for.'

'It's precisely because we don't have much that I went for advice.'

He thought of all the different houses he'd seen today; the grandiose mansions in Billericay, Markham's comfortable post-war semi, and those foundations at the Friday Woods development, all of them bigger than anything he could afford. Everyone was better off than them. 'We could move into town,' he said. Property was cheaper in town and he'd be nearer the police station. 'Think about it,' he stood and circled her, and slyly grabbed the bottle on top of the dresser. 'There's more to do there, nearer the best schools – within the right catchment area for a start, which will be a huge advantage . . .' It would offer her more avenues of escape from him too. And vice-versa. The Bugle! He could return to his local in New Town, the hours he'd spent there. Happy days.

Lindsey relaxed a bit, and toyed with her hair.

'Schools, yes. But bigger house, yes?'

'Of course! How could it possibly be smaller?' he said without really thinking. 'You don't get houses this tiny in town. You could get a proper easel then, not make do with the table.'

'Yes, yes, you're right . . .' She smiled her big warm smile at him, the one that used to drive him mad. 'Come here, you big sexy doofus.'

*

Mandy sipped a mug of tea at the kitchen table and stared out of the window. Lights from upstairs next door projected down into her garden. It was the prettiest this garden had ever been; the one tree, an old apple, drooping magically like out of a fairy tale, and all the junk – old washing machine, car exhaust and the like – transformed by snow into a miniature Alps.

The impression she had from the police was they didn't believe Roland did it. Not that they said what 'it' was. But she knew. Did she care? No. He was out of the way, not in the house making a mess, stinking the place out, leaving takeaway food wrappers lying around. Her eye caught the unpaid Sky bill on the table. Mandy had gone and had a BSB dish installed while he was inside. One of the first in the street. Rollie was over the moon when he got out. Good job, as it was his wedge she'd taken out of the envelope to settle the arrears.

The envelope.

That was something she'd done instinctively – destroyed it. Roland had left it under the mattress. Mandy had taken the money back and used part of it today to pay the red BSB bill at the Post Office on Mersea Road.

It was hers after all.

Rollie was getting his just deserts.

Revenge had been Timmy's idea. '*This is his fault,*' Timmy had said back then. '*Why let him get away with it?*' And then they'd hatched a plan that would benefit them both. And although she was locked up, she felt safe there, and she did meet Tim, which was the best thing that had ever happened to her.

Rollie, of course, had no idea what was going on. What *he* had done was so far in the past, he'd assumed he'd long since been forgiven. No, no, no. She'd waited for their mother to die. Mandy had told her mother what Roland had done to her only after she had been released from hospital and Roland was safely inside. But did their mother listen? No, she refused to believe her angel was capable of something that despicable. 'Wash your mouth out, filthy girl,' she'd screamed. It wasn't until Mrs Beech was on her death bed that Mandy told her straight – she was going to get her precious son the second she was out of the way.

Unfortunately for Roland, Mrs Beech couldn't alert her son to the danger.

Of course, back then in hospital it was just wishful thinking; a crazy plan made in a crazy place by two kids who were far from well. (Three if she counted Emma.) No, what she had told her mother was intended to cause the old woman pain; agony at the end for not believing her daughter and loving a wicked son. Not in a million years did Mandy dream that Tim would be let out. In the time she had known him, he'd been moved from an okay ward, where they'd met, to the acute block. But then one visit last year, he said they were letting him out, just like that. 'It's happening,' he told her. 'Together we'll get them all.'

PART 3

CHAPTER 40

Watt folded the paper and tossed to it to the floor dissatisfied. County were aware of the national newspaper headlines. It was only the *News of the World* the day before – now a far more detailed report had appeared in *The Times*, rehashing Chloe Hopkins' story and adding a full recap on the 1984 Crouch episode, including Hopkins and Hart evading prosecution. The *Express* carried a picture of Watt's predecessor, a grizzled old bastard by the name of Sparks, who happened to be in the right place at the right time – the Contented Sole in Burnham-on-Crouch – and had foiled the smugglers.

Castleton had telephoned twice for a progress report. He didn't answer the first call.

Philips dumped a pile of newspapers from the last few days unceremoniously on his desk.

'Don't just leave them there like that. Find the relevant report.'

Philips, unperturbed by his superior's tone, pulled out a chair and set to it.

The piece in the paper glorified the case; why hadn't he had

Hopkins' history in full from Kenton? Why had he resorted to scouring the press?

'The wife is all they have to go on, and she, it seems, was a little naive, took the suave Hopkins on face value,' Philips said, licking his forefinger and slowly paging through the *Guardian* distastefully. 'Had she – or the parents for that matter – bothered to see beneath the veneer, I'm sure it would have been obvious. We won't find anything leafing through this garbage.'

'Unlike you to side with CID,' Watt said suspiciously.

'Hardly. That's all there is to it.'

'Tell me, as you know so much; can detectives be done for speeding?' He genuinely didn't know. Castleton had mentioned this – to the desk sergeant.

'Anyone can be done for speeding, sir.'

He thought again it a wise precaution to put Wilde onto them. She had her head screwed on, of that he was sure.

'They were poking about in the Reverend's affairs, as you wished,' Philips continued, holding another paper open on his lap.

Watt studied his well-groomed number two, who appeared to be reading an article. 'Hmm, the Reverend's roof, intriguing though it may be, is not high priority. What the good vicar got up to in his youth really is no concern of ours – whereas Hopkins' past is.'

'An old chum topped himself, you're overlooking that.'

'These things happen. Public school masters are an odd bunch. Complicated souls . . .' Watt drifted off in thought.

'It's odd, I'll grant you, but that's not where our efforts will best be rewarded,' he said, reminded of crime stats.

'But sir, you did push them both in that direction,' Philips said.

'At the behest of County, Philips – however, the powers that be will not be anticipating a line of enquiry bouncing back to them . . .' One funny look from Brazier in the wrong quarters and Watt's chances of getting back in with County would be scuppered in an instant. His policy was simple; accept his lot in Neanderthal Colchester and either remain out of sight and out of mind – until he felt justified to demand a promotion, having put in his time, etc. – *or* pull off an act of supreme policing that would get him noticed and back on track. The latter was attractive and might be quicker, except he had no idea how such a feat might be achieved.

But in the meantime, he faced ambiguous situations like this blasted fire, and the prospect of offending his fellow superintendent. Terrified of Essex County protocol, he knew the Met and Essex didn't get on, and suspected the County's politics were many-layered too: there were unwritten rules, few of which he was familiar with. At least Hopkins' case was firmly on his patch, and so he repeated, 'The issue of the day is not the church arson. Disgraceful though damage to church property is,' he continued, 'the murder of Bruce Hopkins is our number-one concern. The wife has rather a lot to say for herself in the press – though little to us. That will have to change.'

Watt was determined to keep everything within his control. From a distance, he told himself a managerial, panoptic view of cases allowed him to evaluate evenly and dispassionately. The vicar's problems were a sop to County, no more no less. He tried to convince himself, so as to reign in the investigation.

Philips had found a piece in the *Mail* suggesting the police had someone and then released them. The reporters would have soon got wind of Beech's release.

'I wonder, sir, at the wisdom of letting Roland Beech out, without another avenue of enquiry.'

'The point, Leslie, is that he would lead us to the killer. He can't very well do that in here.'

'All the same . . .'

Watt's telephone rang. Philips answered it. Watt waved his hand to signal *not here*. Philips frowned then countered with a raised forefinger – *wait*.

'Take the good lady's details, officer, and advise her we will have a man up there as soon as possible.'

He soon replaced the white plastic handset. 'Seems the *News of the World* has jogged the memory of one of its Harwich readers.'

CHAPTER 41

Kenton was reading the toxicology report. Paraldehyde was found in Hopkins' blood. Lots of it. What the dickens was that? A central nervous system suppressant, it said. He picked up the phone to call Nelmes. She wasn't there. He left a message. She rang back almost instantly.

'Doc? What's this shit in his blood?'

Silence, then, 'Sergeant Kenton, this feather.' It wasn't Nelmes, but Sutton from the lab. For a moment Kenton was lost. 'You are correct it is pheasant. But there is some inorganic substance attached to it.'

'Oh, yeah,' he said, collecting himself. 'What?'

'Glue.'

'*Glue?*' he said louder than he'd meant to, attracting the attention of Brazier sitting opposite. 'As in, could have been used to put together a decorative display?'

'Possibly,' the other replied, 'although I'm not sure in what context . . . no, I was thinking perhaps an arrow fletching.'

'Thank you very much.' He hung up.

'What's with the glue?' Brazier asked.

'Remember the trophy cabinet at Bryde Park?'

'Vaguely, though my attention was more on Wintour, admittedly. What about it?'

'I'm sure there was an archery award in the cabinet, a silver statue of an archer about six inches high or so . . .'

'You've lost me. What's an archery trophy got to do with the price of eggs?'

'The church roof was the target – an arrow was shot up into the beams.'

'Who uses a bow and arrow these days? Where do you even get one?' Brazier said.

'Once upon a time, right here. That road running up towards Mersea, Butt Road, is named after the army archery butts. Butt is the old name for shooting field.'

'I forget you're quite the little historian,' said Wilde, exiting the super's office with a pile of newspapers.

'I have to get to Bryde Park right now.' Kenton ground his hands together.

'No chance without his lordship's express permission,' Brazier said. 'Call her instead.'

He did so. Wintour confirmed there was indeed an archery prize on display in the cabinet. Awarded to a school team, dated 1978. The school no longer practiced archery, after an incident in the mid-eighties.

Everything was pointing back to the past.

Kenton clocked an animated conversation inside the chief's

office. Wilde, being nearby, was called back. He'd had his fill of Watt's lectures.

'Come on,' he said to Brazier, 'let's go before we get side-tracked. Kempe Marsh, now.'

'Sure this is the right move?' As Kenton rapped on the door, Brazier glanced back down the garden path at the skeletal vine arch and gate through which they'd just passed. He tasted the sea in the snow flurry, and wondered if this was new or he'd missed it last time he was here. 'I mean, not telling Watt, you know, about the arrow. You know how antsy he is about Hopkins. He doesn't give a toss about this.'

'Watt was in a flap over your driving – speeding, that's what got his back up. Bet he didn't know what to do about it. He hates that, not knowing.'

'Yeah.' Brazier took a final gasp of his cigarette and flicked it into the vicar's holly tree. 'Ironic, getting stopped when I was trying to save time.'

There was movement behind the frosted glass. 'Forget it. We're here now.'

The vicar was in short sleeves and dog collar, and was surprised but pleased to see them.

'Ah, Father, we have news for you.'

'Good news.' Brazier warmed to it too.

'You'd better come in then.'

He led them into the front room. The bungalow was musty and airless, the furniture old and worn, handed down from one incumbent to the next. The pale green armchair and sofa were adorned in laced antimacassars. 'We have a lead,' Brazier said.

'Oh, yes?' Symonds asked eagerly.

'Two, in fact,' Brazier said, twitching in his trainers.

'Yes, we found what we believe to be the source of the fire; the remains of an arrow fired up into the roof.'

'See! Didn't I tell you the roof was priceless?' His eyes flitted excitedly from one to the other.

'Indeed you did. Then when we visited your old school, Bryde Park, it came to our attention that—'

'You were at Bryde Park?'

'Yes.'

'How? I mean, why?'

'The why I would think self-explanatory; we are searching for someone that wished to damage your church, or attack you.' Kenton spoke slowly, watching. Brazier moved about the room, eyes glancing over ornaments and curios.

'What makes you think—?'

Kenton interrupted Father Symonds by holding out the transparent pouch containing the charred arrow flight.

'What makes us think it may be someone connected to the school?' Brazier said, picking up a wooden angel.

'Please put that down, it's from Bethlehem. Yes.'

'Because there's nothing to suggest there's any grievance in the local community against you. And archery was a pursuit at the school.'

Symonds relaxed. 'If you wished to know my history, why not ask?'

'You were away yesterday,' Kenton said.

'We visited Kenneth Markham's shop,' Brazier said.

'Ken? I see – that's how you arrived at the school. But what business would you have with him?'

'That's *almost* what got us there. We'll come to that. What do you make of the evidence?'

Symonds peered at the arrow flight.

'A burnt offering,' he said blandly.

'The walls were unscathed and many of the pews, too. Clever, huh?'

'I told you that – the ceiling, irreplaceable. And what did Ken tell you? A disgruntled pupil was out to wreak revenge? Or a colleague? Did Charles Wintour have anything to say?'

'Charles's health's not so good. His daughter now runs the school.'

'Of course, the charming Henrietta,' he said thoughtfully. 'Look, I do appreciate how seriously you now, finally, are taking this barbaric crime, but I really can't see why anyone from my past – from what? Over ten years ago? – is going to make an appearance now.'

They did not have an answer.

'We have no idea either,' Kenton said, honestly. 'Is the date relevant, perhaps? February 15th mean anything? An anniversary, maybe?'

Symonds stopped to consider and bit his bottom lip. 'A blank, sorry.'

'Think hard,' Brazier said. 'Your life could be threatened next time.'

'My life? I wasn't in the church at the time it was set alight. If I were a target, surely they'd wait until I was under the roof before setting it ablaze – or indeed burn down the rectory at night while I sleep?'

Father Symonds might have been annoying, but in the face of danger he was calm and practical. Kenton put this down to the man's faith.

The Reverend grew bolder: 'I think you have this wrong. I'm not the focus of the attack, it's the church. Tell me again, the route of the investigation? It strikes me much has been going on behind my back.'

'We didn't wish to worry you,' Kenton said diplomatically, but contradicting what Brazier had said previously.

'Come off it, Kenton, tell the man of God the truth . . . Father, you've been making complaints to your archbishop, as a consequence of which we got a bollocking – pardon the language – so we had to circumvent any dealings with you directly until we had something concrete.'

'I see, point taken.' The Reverend lowered his head, chin resting on his breastbone. His lips emitted a raspberry-like sigh, 'I was very upset by the damage.'

'Yes, yes, we understand that now,' Kenton conceded.

'Am I . . . Am I in any danger?'

'As you say, if it was you they were after, they'd take a more direct approach . . . however, if it wasn't a grudge, we wouldn't be getting clues in the post like some sort of game.'

'Clues in the post?'

'Yeah, we didn't mention it, He—' Brazier indicated Kenton with a thumb – 'was sent a school badge through the post via Kenneth Markham's flower shop. *That's* what took us to Bryde Park.'

Symonds looked up in puzzlement. 'How extraordinary,' he exclaimed.

Kenton reached inside his jacket pocket and pulled out the envelope. 'Here.'

The Reverend shirked.

'Don't worry, it's been dusted for prints – nothing – you can take it.'

Symonds took it and pulled the contents out without looking at the envelope.

'That line on the airmail paper. Does it mean anything to you?'

Symonds shook his head vigorously. 'Absolutely not. How very peculiar. You, I presume, are the people looking after the fire? Yes, yes . . . though it simply mentions fire – not even the church – and there's no indication that there is any harm directed towards myself?'

'You are not mentioned, that's true,' Kenton said.

Relieved, the vicar said, 'Would you like a cup of tea?'

'Errr . . . I suppose?' Kenton agreed, uncertainly.

'If I'm to tell you my life story, you may as well make yourselves comfortable; it's frightfully dull. Do sit down.'

The vicar exited the room to put the kettle on.

CHAPTER 42

After an hour, they knew as much as they would ever need to know about the solitary life of Kevin Symonds. The family pressure to be ordained, the question of faith, the desire to teach, torn between the two. Even his own desire for a flower shop, such as Markham had possessed; a love of horticulture, which he'd picked up in the seminary, set as it was in the Somerset levels, where he'd learnt a deeply felt admiration of nature, if not of God the first time round.

'I have to say, I've bored myself,' Symonds said at the end.

Neither rushed to contradict him. After a moment's pause for politeness' sake, Kenton moved from the sofa. 'It's rare to meet someone with such dedication these days.'

Symonds smiled wanly. 'Kind of you to say. What happens now?'

'We wait. I realise that's not much comfort, but don't hesitate to call night or day, should anything trouble you.' Kenton retrieved one of his cards with his home number neatly added to it in biro – he kept a few aside for victims of unsolved incidents, usually women who thought they were being followed home from the bus.

The Reverend took the card, studied it carefully, memorising the number should he mislay the card, then placed it on the mantlepiece.

Kenton nodded towards Brazier.

'How well did you know Kenneth Markham?' Brazier asked.

'Not terribly well. I was only part-time, Religious Education and the odd games class. Kenneth was full-time. Music and English from memory. Used to smoke a pipe in the common room.'

'Was he a happy sort of chap?' Brazier said.

Symonds was uncertain on this. 'I'm afraid I don't know.'

'I regret to inform you that Mr Markham took his own life recently,' Kenton said.

'Oh. Oh dear, how terrible.'

'Shortly before his death, he received a note likely addressed in the same hand as the one sent to Mayflower Florist containing the cap badge. We believe the contents of the envelope sent to Markham have been destroyed, but you should be fully aware of a possible connection between this and the letter Sergeant Kenton was sent.'

'I see.'

'Again, if you think of anyone or anything that may link you and Mr Markham and your time at Bryde Park, be sure to let us know.'

'Most certainly.' Symonds' face was fearful. 'What do you think?'

'Like you, we are inclined to believe the church, not yourself, the target. So for us there is something missing . . .' Kenton said. 'But . . .'

'But what?'

'If it wasn't for the passage of time, an unsolicited letter linked to a suicide could be thought to be blackmail.'

'And so, what will you be doing now?'

'We are in contact with Chelmsford police, to see if there have been any other incidents.'

Symonds gave them a little wave from the rectory front door as they stepped out into the lane.

'Hell. He bored me, too. That's that— *Jeez!*' Brazier put his foot through a frozen-over puddle that had formed in a furrow caused by a tractor. He clutched the icy, sodden trainer as if a nail had gone through it.

'For now,' Kenton said, opening the passenger door. Had the vicar revealed an age-old enemy, then there'd be something to go on. 'We couldn't ignore that badge. But I agree, we can hardly go through the school register of fifteen years ago line by line. If the headmistress was more forthcoming . . . we'll have to wait and see. Unsatisfactory though it is.' Kenton braced in the seat.

'The headmistress. Symonds mentioned her by her Christian name, whereas she claimed not to know him.'

'She was the headmaster's daughter, in an all boys' school; it's far more likely he'd notice a slip of a girl breezing through the corridors than that she'd pay any attention to another adult male under her father's employ.'

'All right, then. We've got to crack on with Hopkins, my Jedi senses tell me we're missed at HQ.'

CHAPTER 43

'I don't want to hear any more about it. That an arrow was responsible for the Kempe Marshe blaze is no more important to us than finding a dead match. Simply log it in the main directory computer, see what that churns out, ritualistic arsonists and so forth; record it, and move on.' Watt threw his hands up despairingly. His complexion was glazed like a bun – the fan heater beneath his desk was too much. 'Never mind chasing back and forth to Brightlingsea.'

Wilde immediately stepped discreetly to one side.

Brazier nonchalantly rolled a lolly stick from one side of his mouth to the other, gazing out the window, undisturbed by the commander's agitation.

'I think I ought to get back over to Bryde Park,' Kenton said.

Watt flatly refused the request. His eye joined Wilde's on Brazier, even as Kenton spoke. Watt hasn't the first inkling how to deal with him, she thought. And, as if reading her mind, Watt's attention switched to her, causing her to self-consciously shuffle her feet.

'Right. Enough,' Watt announced, hands resting on the

desk, knuckles clenched. 'There's progress here too. A woman in Harwich claims Bruce lodged with her some years back. She recognised him from a newspaper. You, DS Brazier, are to take yourself off to Harwich without further delay. Philips will fill you in. Sergeant Wilde will accompany you.

'And Kenton, please attend to Roland Beech, below.'

Wilde watched Kenton's jaw drop. Funny how Watt rolled out Beech's name as if it was unfamiliar.

'Beech?' Kenton said, the word erupting like a belch.

'Yes, I thought it safer he were housed here.'

'Safer?'

'Yes. Right, that's it. Dismissed. Oh, Kenton, Beech has a lawyer down there with him, so be on your guard.'

Kenton's face went scarlet. Watt unclenched his knuckles and flexed his hand in the manner of Spider-Man about to shoot out a web. 'Yes, he's been assigned legal aid. Now move along.'

'Wordy sort, our guv'nor,' Wilde said, walking behind Brazier, who stopped abruptly at his desk to sit down.

'Not kidding. What a fanny! *Safer he were housed here*,' Brazier said calmly, adjusting his scarf under his chin. '*Housed?* Only a dick of the highest order says that.'

'A dick and a fanny?' Wilde remarked. 'Are you indicating the commander is a modern thinker? A model for us all? Gender neutral is the way to get ahead.'

'You what?' Brazier proceeded to remove his trainers. 'Ooff . . .' He thought he saw steam rise.

Kenton was fit to burst. 'Jesus! Bringing Beech back in only days after letting him out! Of all the stupid . . .' He fumbled with a pack of cigarettes. Empty. 'What do you think?' He tossed the pack at the bin, missing.

Brazier contemplated his soggy socks. 'Nothing. You just don't like him. It's no skin off our nose either way.'

'Only I've to interview him again, with nothing more to say – and in the presence of a blasted lawyer.'

Moving his feet up onto Kenton's desk, Brazier merely shrugged.

'Do you have to do that?' Kenton said.

'Feet are wet.' Brazier shifted his feet on the desk and pulled the end of a sock up into a peak.

'I eat my lunch off that surface.'

'Need some air. Can't roll up in Harwich with wet feet. Might get rheumatism or something.'

CHAPTER 44

'Surprised you didn't object.' Wilde pulled out to overtake a mini.

'To what?'

'Me driving; men hate a woman behind the wheel.'

'Not me. It's 1991, love. All that sexist shit is so eighties.' Brazier wound his seat recliner back to demonstrate this. In truth, he fancied they'd be up there quicker in the jam-sandwich Rover – traffic would soon get out of their way, seeing this in the rear-view mirror. Had some go in it too. Three and half-litre engine; leave the Citroën standing.

'You talk absolute twaddle – however did you end up in the police?'

'How'd you get this? Not standard issue.'

'Lads in traffic lent it me.'

'Natty. Right, what do we know?'

Philips had handed the details to her, not him. 'A woman by the name of Meldrum, who ran a B&B in Harwich, remembers him. Said Hopkins had spent a few nights with her around ten years ago then one day disappeared without trace.'

'And?'

'Woke one morning and he'd gone, years later, she recognised him on the national news, wanted by the police
in eighty-four. She called the police but they weren't very
interested. He'd left clothes in the wardrobe, she said. Then
she forgot all about him again, until she opens her paper at
the weekend and there he is, reported dead. Said he didn't
do much while he was here other than read and take long
strolls along the front. Suppose there's not a lot to do in
Harwich.'

'Apart from the ferry to the Hook of Holland. If you need
to make a run for it, round here is the quickest and easiest
way out of the country.'

'Funny, he did spend a lot of time watching the ferries. It's
what I told the police,' said Nora Meldrum, who could have
been seventy or eighty. A sausage dog with a grey whiskery
chin similar to its owner's stood beside her on the doorstep.
'Funny, he said his aunt had a yacht, but he couldn't sail it.
Just chugged up and down the river. Can't remember which
river. Then some years later, there he is bold as brass, standing
on a yacht, smiling away, with a 'wanted for questioning'
headline above him on the telly. It was that same photo as
appeared in the paper just now.'

'This was in 1980?' Wilde asked. 'When he came to stay?'

'There about – I can't remember precisely. Afterwards he
must have emigrated to Spain, presumably. The police called

for witnesses, anyone who'd been in contact with him for that last five years.'

'Had he mentioned Spain to you?'

'Not as such . . . I believed he was weighing up his options. He'd been through a bumpy spell with his wife and he'd come to Harwich to cool off, or so he said. Come on inside,' she beckoned, and continued talking, leading them through the house. 'He may even have slipped back to Colchester. Before he went away, that is.'

'Did he leave that impression?'

'At the time, I had no reason to doubt he wanted to patch things up. He never said her name. Claimed to have plans to open a jeweller's and offered to sell my mother's ruby ring. He knew his gems, taught me how to tell a ruby from a garnet. But all lies, I suspect. The police told me they suspected he was lying low after a robbery.'

'You didn't let him take the ring?' Wilde asked.

'Oh, no. I still have it. I know the papers said he was a wrong 'un, but he was always a gent with me. Once, when he was roaring drunk, he told me about his parents . . . sat right there and it all came spilling out. He wasn't telling me in particular; could've been anyone. All pent-up.'

'What about them?' Brazier asked.

'Farmers in Norfolk. Farm got into debt. Irreversible debt. The father shot himself and his wife. Why he was brought up by his aunt, who packed him off to boarding school.'

'Bloody hell!' Wilde exclaimed.

'Bruce was very apologetic.'

'Why?'

'He'd raid my drinks cabinet. Drank like a fish. I was always finding bottles under the bed. I think he was very unhappy as a little boy.'

'Did he say anything else?'

'Yes . . .'

Her eyes narrowed. Brazier, after the vicar, found this tedious, and did well to bite his tongue. 'And . . .?'

'He'd lost a child. A boy. I suspected this was the root of the problem with his marriage, but he never said as much. There was a photograph, he showed me, taken on one of those instant cameras. Always carried it.'

'This one?' Brazier whipped the photo out.

'Oh, I don't know,' she grew timid and averted her gaze, 'it's a long time ago . . .'

'Please, it'd be a help,' Wilde pleaded, her more patient tone doing the trick.

Nora Meldrum pulled up her spectacles, attached to a chain resting on her chest.

After a moment she announced it to be the same photo. 'The poor love,' she said.

'D'you mind if I give the room a quick look?'

'Not at all – it's much the same as it was then. I chucked his clothes out, though; the police weren't interested in having them. This way.' She tottered to the front of the bungalow, the sausage dog at her heel. They peered into a narrow room with a single metal-framed bed. A bookshelf ran across the length of the bed, with an impressive range of *Reader's Digest* and some old paperbacks. On the opposite wall there was a single oil painting of sand dunes. A huge dark wardrobe – the sort children would hide in – took up one end of the room. The bed wasn't much bigger than a child's. It was difficult to imagine someone of Hopkins' weight in here, even if he was slimmer back then.

'Blimey, a bit of a squeeze,' Brazier said.

'Yes, he was a big lad.' Mrs Meldrum had followed them through and was practically on his heels.

'You can say that again.'

'It was my son's room before then. He passed away when he was a boy, from meningitis. It was after I told him that when he said his own was taken from him.' Brazier turned abruptly to face the tiny woman behind him. She was not as old as he'd assumed; rather, she'd been shrunken by grief, her eyes were dulled and aged but her skin was unblemished.

'It's a terrible thing to lose a child,' he said. Her stare was fixed on the bedside table, lost in another time. Brazier stepped further into the room.

'I'm sure he was a wonderful father – loved kids, did Bruce. Made up for his own unloved childhood, I always thought.'

'What makes you say that?' Wilde, who'd been observing until now, suddenly spoke.

'He was a teacher as a young man. He regretted leaving the profession and had been permanently in between jobs ever since, it seemed. He spent a lot of time figuring out what to do next. One minute a jeweller's in Colchester, then back to Fambridge and his auntie. Perhaps if he stayed a teacher, he might not have landed in trouble.'

'Yeah, stranger things have happened,' Brazier said, doubtfully. 'Don't suppose you know where he taught?'

'I can't be expected to remember that!' she snapped. She suddenly reached across the bed to the bookshelf and picked out a volume. 'Wait, there's one of his books here. I found it, slipped down the side of the bed. Has a stamp in it. There you go.'

Inside the copy of *The Hound of the Baskervilles*, the unmistakable circular stamp of Bryde Park was legible.

CHAPTER 45

It was late by the time Brazier made it back to Colchester. The cleaner's vacuum could be heard in far-off quarters of the cold building as Wilde turned on the lights and Kenton flopped open the case file.

'Symonds is thirty-four, and Hopkins was forty-eight. The question is, did they both overlap at Bryde Park with Markham? – and if so, we have hit on something . . . something else entirely,' he said, as Kenton arrived.

'Symonds was there seventy-seven to nine,' Wilde said.

The Hound of the Baskervilles was in a decrepit state, the spine held together with Sellotape. Kenton put it to one side and began to root around the plastic trays on his desk for the book found in the George Hotel, which was in better condition. 'Let me check the print date here.' He flicked through the opening pages of *Lord of the Flies*: *This edition reprinted 1977.* The school would have stamped it on arrival. 'You can bet they were there at the same time.'

'And so . . .?'

Kenton waited.

'The fire at Kempe Marsh and the murder of Hopkins are connected. Likely Markham's suicide too, although we're not investigating it directly.'

Kenton turned the book in his hands. A demonic black pig's head lurched out of the darkness of the cover. 'This changes everything,' he muttered.

'Guess it does.' Brazier fingered a cigarette out of the pack of Fortuna lying on Kenton's desk. 'But nothing is leaping out to me . . .'

'Ignoring Symonds for now – let's focus on Hopkins. He arrives in Colchester ten years ago, remember, gave little away of his history – Chloe, his wife, knew only vague fragments.'

'True. Except she knew he was clever.'

'Why wouldn't he mention his early career to her? Teaching is a respectable profession, but she didn't seem to know. . . .'

Brazier flipped through his pocketbook. 'She did – she said he'd tried his hand at all manner of things, but stuck at none of them. Basically said he was born to be a villain, like Roland Beech.'

'But unlike Roland, who's only got one talent, if that, Hopkins could have chosen a better life, which makes him more despicable,' Wilde said. 'And I've never met the man.'

'What about his son – who is the mother?'

The distant hoovering stopped. They sat in silence, staring at the photo of the slim pale boy of about nine or ten, frame made slight by copious dark hair. The Polaroid was still propped up against the framed pic of Lindsay Kenton. A door slammed somewhere in the rapidly cooling building.

'Chloe never mentioned another woman in Bruce's life.'

'Why would she . . .?' Wilde said. 'If her own relationship failed.'

Brazier raised an eyebrow and puffed heartily on the cigarette. The situation demanded focus and boiled sweets did nothing for this, or for his temperament for that matter.

'What's our next move?' Wilde asked. 'I think let's forget here, Colchester – and focus on the school.'

'Bypassing the head,' said Brazier. 'She's less than helpful . . . Check in with the local plod first, before seeing her. See if there's been any problems at the school. Then if there has, we confront her with them.'

'Problems? Like what?' Kenton said.

'I don't know. You tell me. You know the drill in those places. Sending kids away from the age of five doesn't seem right to me. Not natural.'

Brazier didn't extrapolate, allowing Kenton's imagination to wander into a maze of uncertainty. 'Yes, yes,' he said finally, 'tomorrow. We'll go tomorrow.'

'I'm done for the day, boys,' Wilde said, looking at Brazier pointedly, then gaily announcing, 'I have a date,' before immediately leaving with a flourish.

'Am I missing something here?' Kenton said, watching her. 'Or was that aimed in your direction?'

'Beats me, mate. She has spent the best of the day with me,

to be honest. I fancy a pint, you?' Brazier said it loud enough that she might hear.

Bryde Park was a private school, a primer for public school life. What youngsters experienced in prep set the tone for their older years. What went on during the early years was seen as character building. On the rare occasions a policeman's tread was heard upon those elite floorboards, it was usually in relation to the youngest pupils; by the time of graduation to the upper levels of public school, any thoughts of escape would have been considered bad form, and the shame too much to bear. By and large, the boys eventually hit an age to know what they had, willingly or unwillingly, been signed up for – and to know that resistance was futile.

This rumination pursued Kenton into the Tap and Spile pub, along with a sticky sense of self awareness. Inside the pub, alcohol loosened his tongue.

'I can only imagine your opinion of me,' Kenton continued, 'but for the record I only went to boarding school when my father took a job abroad. I am not *posh*: my father was an engineer – not a graduate – teaching the Saudis how to look after their oil. The company paid for my education, for the period of his contract; it was not a rite of passage.'

'You have said so already. Twice,' Brazier said. 'Do speak proper, though, don't you? Like Watt, and Mrs Hoity-toity Wintour,' he continued.

'It's Ms. Sorry for not growing up round here.'

'I'm teasing you, you gigantic bender,' he said, suddenly bored with the seriousness of it all.

'That's where this will end though. Homosexuality,' Kenton said a little too loudly.

Brazier opened his mouth in mock horror at curious patrons further along the bar. 'Look, you're the one preoccupied with all this crap. All right, since you brought it up, what do you make of it? The fella Markham shared the flower shop with – *a flower shop* – was as bent as a two-bob note. You bristled when I asked about the nature of the friendship, like you can't speak these things out loud now. But there's no smoke without fire.'

Kenton swirled the bottom of his pint and glanced down at the dregs forlornly. 'What, hiding in plain sight is quite literally not being seen, you mean? Such a cliché, that no one suspected anything untoward right under their noses?' He turned to face Brazier with something like sadness in his eyes.

'Something like that, yeah,' Brazier said, with a shifting unease.

'Like birds on shingle. There, in front of you, part of the landscape,' Kenton mused, 'until the snow came down, that is.' With a sigh and sensing an ending too soon, he offered hopefully, 'Another one?'

'No, mate, you've got to drive and your missus will be wondering,' Brazier said, keen to leave now, having no idea what Kenton was on about.

'Yes, quite,' Kenton said, collecting himself. 'You go on. I need a pee.'

Kenton waited for Brazier to leave and then ordered himself another pint and a whiskey chaser. The barmaid eyed him warily but said nothing. Kenton made short work of his drinks and was soon on his way.

CHAPTER 46

Brazier pulled out onto the Lexden Road into swirling eddies of snow. They caught in the headlights and dazzled him, the contrast sharp between the snow and the black night and the Citroën's interior. He banged a cassette into the stereo.

Tomorrow it would all kick off at Bryde Park, and though knackered, Brazier knew this was his only opportunity to check in on the Copford Hotel.

He found a parking space behind the conifers shortly after seven. It may have been named Copford, but it was serviced by Marks Tey railway station, minutes across the A12 flyover. The hotel signage was illuminated, but beyond that darkness enveloped the grounds and car park, reasserting how easy it would be to steal a car. But there was more to it. He'd researched the area and learnt this was the only place offering hospitality within a mile radius. Situated as it was on the old London Road, there was no life out here, the nearest entertainment was a mile away – a nightclub in the direction of Colchester. And that was only open Thursday to Saturday. There was a village pub to the south-east, some way off the main road towards the Copford Planes, and then practically nothing but farmland until the Blackwater. To the north, across the motorway, lay Aldham and the Colne Valley. In short, in this weather the hotel had a captive audience. Only the hardy and extremely bored would venture beyond the hotel bar.

The Copford's bar area was larger than it need be, with generously spaced low tables and demure chairs. Like most early travel stops, space was not an issue, acquired when land had been cheap.

The bar itself was an oasis of light in the semi-darkness, optics twinkling enticingly. As his eyes adjusted, Brazier took in the dull sheen of lily-pad tables under the subdued glow of orange and blue lamps. So obscured were the surroundings with mood lighting, he couldn't see the enclosing walls. This lounge bar had ambitions above its station. Seating himself at a chrome stool with a large vodka and tonic, he became aware that for all its size, sound travelled easily across the space. Brazier could hear a conversation behind him over the dull instrumental music that played from hidden speakers.

'Does it ever get raucous in here?' he asked a woman with large eyes behind the bar, polishing a wine glass with a tea towel.

'Depends,' she said, eventually. 'Sometimes if there's a conference. Ordinarily it's pretty much like this.'

A cackle of laughter erupted from the darkness. He pivoted

round on the stool. A man spoke slowly and deliberately to the amusement of a companion.

Solitary individuals drifted in and out, mainly men. The lonely life of the sales rep. After a while, Brazier reappraised the bar. All right, it might be on a slip road from the motorway, but for many away from home this was the only comfort they had at the end of a long day pushing whatever it was they had to sell; paperclips, computers, or insurance like Healey, the car-theft victim.

A middle-aged man in a brown suit emerged from the darkness and headed towards the toilet signs. A second later a woman in a sleeveless dress arrived at the bar next to Brazier, the sight of her pale young arms making him shiver. She gestured to the barmaid for service.

'On *his* tab?' the inflection in the barmaid's voice told him all he needed to know.

The girl in the dress nodded. 'Make it a double.' She went about touching up her make-up in the bar mirror. If she saw Brazier looking at her, she chose to ignore him. She was working, after all. And what would a plain-clothes policeman be doing hanging about in this dismal place?

'Excuse me, luv.'

She turned, clocking him immediately as police, but fronted it out.

'Know an Ian Healey?' he said.

'Everyone knows him,' she said. 'Since last week, that is.'

'Sells insurance. Northerner,' he continued. 'Before then, was he a familiar face?'

'All the same, one becomes another. But no, I can't say I've had the pleasure.' She smiled. 'Not yet.'

'Do you know anyone who has?'

Her stare was now over his shoulder. 'Excuse me, I'll be missed. Another time, maybe. I like a policeman.'

The barmaid, who'd been observing the exchange, piped up: 'I know who you mean, comes down every few months. Loud fella, always droning on about how he runs his car on air. Uses it as an icebreaker with the ladies at the bar. You'd think he'd been across Persia on a flying carpet the way he carries on, not saving a few pennies on fuel up the M1.'

'Gotta use what you got, I guess,' Brazier said.

But this had not occurred to him previously. What if the car was selected purposely because it was empty? Ensuring Roland would have to stop for fuel and run the risk of being identified.

Brazier drove back to Southway after scribbling a sentence in the car.

- staff/guests - HEALEY - loud/boaster/regular - ROLAND set up -

He finished jotting and left the notebook on the passenger seat. Strangely, he never reread what he wrote – his aversion to words applied equally to his own – the act itself served its purpose: by recording what he saw and thought on paper, it wouldn't clutter his head – leaving him free and receptive to new information. He parked his car at the station; it was too late to get a space on his mother's tightly packed street in St Mary's.

Head bowed, and scarf wound tight, the young detective sergeant stopped off at MVC to pick up a film. He'd seen everything current, so picked an oldie. *Alien* would do. On the short walk from the video shop to home, he emptied his head of the working day. Soon, he forced open the low garden gate, dislodging a fresh wedge of snow onto the path he had cleared only this morning, reducing the risk of his mother falling, should she venture out. A small square of untouched snow lay neatly upon the manicured front lawn, its smooth surface ivory under the street lamp, matching the distinctive white lintel above the upper-floor window, a customary mark of the style found in the red-brick terraces close to the town centre. He turned the key in the latch, pleasantly weary, and shoved the door open.

He coughed as he shook off his coat and hung it on the door. Smoke reached the back of his throat. Mother was not venting the fire properly. He feared he'd come home and find her suffocated one day. As it was, she was asleep, knitting on her lap. Shaking his head, he went to the small kitchen at the back of the house and put half a dozen chipolatas under the grill and thought only of what wine would go best with his meal and the movie.

CHAPTER 47

'Hopkins had a son, sir, prior to marrying Chloe. Deceased now, we think.'

Watt nodded, but did not comment, mulling the school connection.

'So much of this man's life is a mystery,' Watt said after some time, and then added, 'People can drift through this world, wrecking lives, creating them, then *pouf!* Vanish . . .' He trailed off, catching the mystified looks from the three officers facing him, expectantly waiting for a decision.

He could not lose face, and with Wilde there too he wanted to appear supportive; she was not tainted, as the other two were. 'Righto. The school, Bryde Park. We must tread very carefully.' Unsure of whose boundaries he was about to infringe, he could feel their eyes burn into him. Was he really going to phone and ask for permission to cross an invisible line into another part of the county? Beads of perspiration were forming. There must be some other way. He had been in Chelmsford for a short period prior to his arrival here . . . in fact, think, think, wait . . . he remembered travelling to south

Essex in an Incident Control Van with a sergeant, Bradshaw was his name. Watt had been assigned to shadow this officer, accompanying him to a farm where a drug dealer had been found in a horse trough, shot dead. Watt pondered a second. 'There's this chap, of the old school, you'll like him, who mentored me for a spell. We worked a murder investigation on a farm near the River Crouch, as it happens.'

For once, something he'd done prior to his appointment here could be of use.

Wilde followed Brazier out of Watt's office and squeezed his arm lightly.

'We on for tonight, then?' she said in an almost whisper.

'Oh, yeah.' He was close enough for her to taste his sugary breath. 'Yeah, looking forward to it.'

She thought he coloured.

'What have you got in mind?'

'A bit out of town, but you'll know it.'

'Cryptic. Can't wait.'

'Speak later.' And off he went with Kenton. She'd have to do something about his dress sense if this was to go anywhere. He must own something more than a bomber jacket and Adidas trainers.

CHAPTER 48

Chelmsford police station was modern, purpose-built; a precursor to Colchester in design. Imposing, very grey and spectacularly ugly – more seventies Londonderry than nineties home counties. Sergeant Bradshaw was a genial old copper on the brink of retirement. A flicker of amusement danced across his world-weary eyes at the mention of Watt.

'Said that, did he? Bastard never set foot outside the van. December. No snow, but ice-cold, froze the tit-ends off the cows, so he can't be blamed. Yes, that farm was close to Bryde Park, that much is true. What's the interest there?'

They sat in a bustling canteen, alive with urgency, people on the move, grabbing coffees and food. A sense of dynamism that contrasted starkly with their own smaller set-up.

'How about staff misbehaving at the school? Any history of criminal activity with persons working there?' Kenton said, raising his voice.

'Nope,' Bradshaw said, twisting his teacup this way and that.

'An ex-teacher hung himself the other day,' Brazier said.

'Doesn't ring a bell.'

'Retired. Ran a florist.'

'In Billericay? Saw that . . . that wasn't on the bulletin, his being a teacher. Is that what brings you here?'

'Not as such.' Kenton told them about Hopkins and the church fire.

'Bizarre,' Bradshaw said, but his expression was unchanged.

'What about the boys, pupils? Any trouble in the community?' Brazier said.

'Nope. You've not got the picture straight: you're thinking of a liaison officer for normal kids allowed out from the local state school, nicking sweets from the corner shop, fighting on the school bus – that sort of thing.' He leant forward. 'You have visited Bryde Park, I take it?'

DS Bradshaw, like all good policemen, was curious.

'Just the once,' Kenton said.

'Then you're aware it's in the middle of bloody nowhere,' he sat back, 'though occasionally, very occasionally, the telephone will ring in the middle of the night.'

'Oh yeah, what for?' Brazier said.

He ceased playing with the teacup. 'A driver sees a boy wandering down the Southend Road. Some of the boys get homesick, try and run away.'

'That's desperate. In the middle of the night? Why then . . . and not in the day? It's not a borstal,' Brazier asked.

'It's at night when it troubles them most, missing their own bed, home. During the day, there'll be too much going on with lessons and whatnot. Alone in the dark, in a room full of strangers keeping you awake snoring and farting, gets on top 'em . . .'

'Did you ever run away?' Brazier said. Bradshaw stared across to Kenton, who did not appreciate having his personal experience raised in the room.

'I didn't board until I was thirteen, and no one ran away . . . by that age conditioning had put paid to thoughts of escape,' he said sharply. 'Sergeant, how recently?'

'Not so much these days, but there was a rash of them some years ago. One time I was on the night desk, and picked up a call. Young lad called from a phone box, asking to be taken home to his mum.'

'Oh yeah?'

'An area car picked him up and took him straight back to the school.'

'What, not to his parents?'

'We called them. His parents had gone on holiday.'

'How old?'

'I couldn't tell you. I never saw him myself. Just remember it distinctly – was a rotten night, could hear the poor little sod's teeth chattering down the line.'

Kenton said, 'When was this again?'

'Now you're asking. At least ten years back. It was late April, I remember that, after Easter. There was a period, as I say, when there was a spate of them. The old boy that ran the place thought he was still in the 1950s. Disciplinarian.'

'Charles Wintour.'

'That's him. Strode about the place in a black gown. Looked like bloody Count Dracula.'

'Define a spate?'

'Three or four in the space of a month – that same lad did it again a week later. The school would find out and call us. Or drivers passing in the middle of the night coming across kids in tracksuits and dressing gowns legging it down the road.' He passed his hand over his cup. 'But then it stopped. And not a peep since.'

'Would you have his name, the boy who was picked up twice?'

'Somewhere, no doubt. Will take a while, all the pre-computer gumpf needs digging out. Will you tell me what this is about?'

'Were you aware of any teachers leaving back then?'

He shook his head. 'Why would we know? The school'll surely have records.' He looked from one to the other. 'You think they're holding out on you?'

'There's been a change in command there, but yes, they're not exactly forthcoming.'

'Rattling skeletons in the cupboard, aren't you? Let me know how you get on.'

'Do us a favour,' Brazier said, 'and let them know we're on the way? Charming though she is, the headmistress is inclined to be tetchy.'

CHAPTER 49

'Things have moved on a tad, Ms Wintour.'

A carriage clock chimed, and seconds later the scuffing of feet on the parquet floor beyond the door indicated lessons were over.

'This is the second visit now, and I am growing concerned.' Dressed in a trouser suit, hair pulled back and neatly parted. She had three Manila files on her desk.

'Not without reason.'

She shot Brazier a disparaging glare.

As with Sergeant Bradshaw before, they presented the facts.

'It now transpires three men who were teachers here over ten years ago have recently been contacted in unusual circumstances, and two are now dead,' Kenton said in conclusion. 'Someone with a past here is after them.'

Several seconds elapsed before she raised her head. 'And so, you deduce . . . what, may I ask?'

'First things first; Mr Hopkins – you can confirm he held a post here?'

'Yes, he did a stint here as a supply teacher. History, geography, and games.'

'Did he know Symonds?'

'Yes, we're a small community and they were both keen on sports. It says on his file that Mr Hopkins lived nearby at Fambridge, but both would be residential, keeping an eye on the boys at night.'

'And did they depart at the same time?'

'Mr Hopkins left in September 1979, a month before Mr Symonds.' She stopped speaking. She turned slightly, eyes moving to the window. The pale light caught the indent of a scar on her forehead. 'There was an incident.'

'With another teacher?'

'Not as such.' She swallowed. Kenton noticed her Adam's apple move. Unusual for a woman.

'Who was involved in this incident? Hopkins? Symonds?' Kenton said.

'Mr Hopkins. Kevin Symonds was troubled by it—'

'Are you aware of Mr Hopkins' involvement with the River Crouch drugs bust?' Brazier said, halting her in her tracks. He did this to jolt witnesses and suspects alike from any pre-prepared spiel. Trying to unsettle them.

'Fambridge is a stone's throw away, how could I not?'

'What do you think about that?'

'Think? I don't think anything. It happened several years after he left the school. They say Bruce Hopkins was born with a silver spoon,' she said. 'Privilege without direction is a recipe for disaster, wouldn't you say, Sergeant?'

'Idle hands and all that,' Brazier said. 'I blame the parents.'

'If you don't mind me asking,' Kenton interjected, 'couldn't you have mentioned this connection before?'

'Hopkins was not a topic of discussion on your last visit.'

'Back to when something bad happened . . .' Brazier prompted.

She took a breath, then said, 'I said "incident". Please refrain from putting words into my mouth. There was an accusation against Mr Hopkins. A claim was made that he behaved improperly with one of the boys.'

'And did he?'

'Nothing was proved. It was his word against the boy's.'

'What do you think?'

'My father believed a boy, any boy, who was unhappy would do anything to get out of the school, even if it meant destroying a teacher's reputation. The charge, you see, was not levied by the alleged victim himself, but by a friend.'

'I asked what *you* thought, not your father.'

'The same.' Wintour was unyielding. 'As I'm sure you'll find to be the case, should you be successful in finding the boys in question.'

'Men,' Brazier corrected. 'Okay, why did Symonds quit?'

'Kevin took it badly. He and Bruce Hopkins would have conducted most of the games classes. Often together – they ran the cricket team, for instance, organised matches with other schools and so forth. Kevin was in his twenties then, and Hopkins' junior – he believed he was closer to the boys because of his age but instead of growing closer, he felt they had turned against him. It wasn't that he couldn't deal with the threat of any charges against him, you understand, but the tittle-tattle hurt. He resigned the following month.'

Wintour would have had no alternative but to reject these claims; to accept them was to admit that the school, under her father's leadership, was rotten.

'And Kenneth Markham?'

'He left the same year. My father thought it best he go,' she confessed.

'Before there were any accusations levelled at him,' Brazier said.

Wintour said nothing.

'This boy, or his friend,' Brazier said, 'any record of who they were?'

'Unlikely. It's not the sort of event the school would wish to retain for posterity,' she said, with a sliver of understated manners reserved for prospective parents.

'Chelmsford police will hopefully provide the name of the boys that attempted to run away,' Kenton said across to Brazier. 'And the year. We know the month. It's as good a place as any to start.'

'Runaways? As in boys leaving the school without permission?' Wintour said.

'Yes, if a boy is unhappy, say – what would your father have to say about that?' Brazier said, sharply.

'Well, yes, on rare occasions . . .' Wintour said, 'in any school there's always the risk, though there's usually an explanation.'

'A teacher touching you up is a hell of a good explanation for getting out of this place.'

'Surely, Ms Wintour, you must see that the police returning a lad to the school in the middle of the night is bringing the outside world in?' Kenton said. 'Waking up the other boys, stirring them to speak out, perhaps, and bring pressure on Hopkins to go, right?' *Small boys seldom rat to adults on the behaviour of other adults* . . . He'd been one himself, once. Even Wintour knew that the distress of an individual boy could be kept from leaking beyond school gates, but if a unity evolved and included the more resilient pupils, it would prove difficult to contain.

A pink tinge was visible along Wintour's neck below her face powder. 'I urge you to keep your sordid speculations to yourself. For fifty years this establishment has been held in nothing but the highest regard. If you have made enquiries at Chelmsford police station, you will know this school is unblemished – no criminal or civil cases.'

'Until now, perhaps,' Brazier said.

'Maybe we could talk to a member of staff that was here? You mentioned discussion in the common room.'

'The current staff are unacquainted with this gossip. And I'd like to keep it that way,' Wintour said, shutting the conversation down. 'Only my father was aware. All others have long since retired.'

'We need to speak to this boy – man, the runaway,' Kenton said.

'I wish I could help with the names. I was not in charge of the school then, as I have said.'

Wintour might not know the boy's name – but Bradshaw, fingers crossed, could dig out the records. Ten years was ten years, though.

'Back to the runaways. Does that still happen?'

'Yes, unsurprisingly one or two get homesick. We try our best. It's a fine balance between discipline and cosiness. No television, except on special occasions: the last Thursday of term; to watch *Top of the Pops*, a particular favourite . . .' She abruptly stopped, realising the police might be extrapolating: was there cause to investigate the school now? 'Why I am telling you this? I have no idea. Are we done?'

More of a plea than a question, Kenton thought. 'Yes, we're done.'

'What happens next?'

'Simply put, Ms Wintour, we believe someone from that period ten years ago has decided now is the time to take revenge. It could be anyone, and we'll be requiring unrestricted access to the school records.'

CHAPTER 50

'Wintour was as agreeable as she could be under the circumstances – if anything,' Brazier said, 'she was too calm.'

'Agree,' Kenton said, his breath misting as they left the
building. 'Without even questioning possible disruption to
school life. As there sure as hell will be.'

'Disruption? This place could do with a shake up. Has all
the buzz of a Victorian workhouse.' Brazier paused on the
school steps to zip up his bomber jacket and adjust his scarf.
'And what if it wasn't homesickness? What if the kid was
having his winky tugged by a grown man, who could not only
physically overpower him, but who controlled his school day
from start to finish too? Wouldn't that make him want to leg
it? Would me, I can tell you.' He lit a cigarette as two boys in
blazers and shorts hurried past them.

'Save it until we're in the car,' Kenton cautioned.

Brazier cupped his cigarette, though it was the conversation
the other was referring to, not the smoking. To the right,
beyond the driveway, against a partitioning hedge, a man
with a shovel was busily moving snow around.

'Excuse me, pal,' Brazier said, addressing a third lad with rosy cheeks passing by on the steps, 'what's that gentleman doing over there?'

The boy squinted into the crisp air. 'By the laurel bushes?' He had an impeccable side parting to his fair hair. 'That's the swimming pool over there.' He paused. 'I imagine he's clearing the snow off the tarpaulin covering.' Content with his answer, he scurried off.

'Swimming pool?' Kenton said.

The photo of the boy.

Kenton proceeded to march the 300 yards to where the deep green of laurels was evident. He crossed a low chain-link border and continued to where the snow was deeper, engulfing his every step up to the shin, until he reached the bemused shoveller.

Brazier sniffed heartily at the damp air. This was it. This was where the photo was taken. He sensed he was being watched, and turned round to see Wintour at her study window, clutching a telephone, eyes fixed on him.

'Whether Mr Hopkins had children, I couldn't say.' Wintour flexed her hands, unfurling long ringless fingers.

'Maybe his kid came here?' Brazier said. 'If he ever had one, that is.'

'That would not be permitted,' she said.

The Polaroid of the child lay before them on the desk,

cracked and fragile next to the orderly school files organised on the head's desk. In his swimming trunks, the boy's vulnerability now felt stark.

'Perhaps unknowingly admitted, then,' Kenton said sharply. 'We have reason to believe this boy may be dead – it's important that we can identify him by any means possible.'

It was fast dawning on them however, that Meldrum was mistaken – this kid was not Hopkins' son. Wintour seemed devoid of emotion, face drawn and sullen. 'Judging from the direction of the sun, this photograph could have been taken here.'

'It won't take long to identify him,' Brazier said. 'The lobby is lined with school photographs.'

'I will help you find those years with Mr Hopkins and Father Symonds.'

Circumstances had shifted, and Wintour had no option but to acquiesce. A Bryde Park teacher – Hopkins – had carried about him a photograph of a nine-year-old in nothing but swimwear for more than ten years.

'That phone call, urgent, was it?' Brazier said, eyeing her as she moved to her filing cabinets.

'Oh, no, only Cook, querying whether the boys ought to have soup again because of the weather,' she said without turning to address him.

A reasonable answer, but her manner told him she was lying.

Twenty minutes later they had identified the boy in the picture as Timothy Windows, date of birth 7 March 1969. Their search had taken them beyond the headmistress's filing cabinet, to the back of the building and the school archive, where she found a faded blue school report with a black and white photo of the boy attached with paper clip. Windows finished the 1979 summer term and did not return to Bryde Park the following September to continue working towards the Common Entrance Examination, the required qualification for public school.

'A promising young man, by the sound of it,' Wintour lifted her eyes from the file, her expression glacial, and said, 'excelled at Latin, and English. Cross country champion, two years on the trot. And won the archery tournament every term.'

'Here you go,' Brazier pulled the car door shut and dropped a greasy package in Kenton's lap.

Theirs was the only car in the lay-by, apart from an ancient Volvo attached to the grubby caravan selling bacon sandwiches. Before them the brown slush left by the tread of previous vehicles was gradually disappearing under fresh snowfall. To their left lay the bleak nothingness of the winter landscape, broken only by electricity pylons, arms stretched hauntingly, like something from a sci-fi film. Kenton unwound the window. The air was fine, sharp and still. The cold hung in stasis across the flat earth of dormant Essex fields, encased in snow, frost-hardened.

'I still don't trust her,' Brazier said.

'You don't need to – it's out of her hands now.'

'Did you notice she referred to him, Symonds, as "Father" – a capacity supposedly unknown to her until we roll up? It's as if she was elevating him, attaching respectability . . .'

'Transferring responsibility to the church.' Kenton bit into his sandwich, he was famished. Time had flown. 'She's wily, I don't doubt it, but we have the boy's name and address now; what she thinks is irrelevant.'

'His parents' address,' Brazier corrected. He had already wolfed his sandwich and was brushing crumbs off his lap into the footwell. 'Seriously though, mate, what do you think went on?'

Kenton's thoughts were loose and not cohesive. If a child had problems settling in at boarding school, these would be flushed through at the prep stage; by the time a boy had to step up to public-school life, he was hardened or at least accepting of the system. Kenton had avoided those early years and entered at the second stage, at public school, as it was then his parents had chosen to work abroad.

He'd experienced no difficulties himself; bright, athletic, he soon proved an asset to the school and so felt no hostility from those already embedded in the system. However, there were things that went on that were never discussed, but these were never matters for the police.

'I don't think you were far from the truth, in your carefully chosen words for the headmistress,' Kenton said. 'What else could it be?'

'I never met Hopkins, but from his rep, I'd never have known. And the vicar, do you make him as a nonce?'

'There is a world of difference between being homosexual and a child abuser.'

'Obviously . . . but you'll find people do like to work in environments that are attractive to them – Stringfellow likes girls, preferably dressed in underwear, so he runs a nudie bar. Scoutmasters like teaching small boys how to tie knots. One we joke about openly and one we don't talk about, why—?'

'They're completely different, but I see your point. It's hard sometimes to remain untainted by what we see and hear. I'm all for the scouts, I have to say.'

'Glad you think so. My grandpa was a scoutmaster.'

'And?'

'A diamond. Hung up his woggle long before my time, of course, but helped me get the badges when I was in the pack. Endless patience, and because I knew that he was good, I loved him even when he shouted at me for drinking his homemade wine.'

'Lucky you,' Kenton said, inwardly enjoying this strange diversion.

'Ah, I don't know why I'm saying this – I guess it's the only time I was in an all-boys' environment, you know? Made me think back.' He wiped his hands on his trousers and turned the ignition. 'And you know some things from a young age, just know them – that some people are good and some bad. Intuition. When you're a kid,' Brazier slung the car into reverse and reached his arm across the back of the passenger seat as he backed the car up. 'Anyway, enough. Right, read me the address again . . .'

'Do we check with Watt first, before charging in? You know how funny he is about protocol.'

'Relax. He knows we're here – he sent us to see his mentor,' Brazier said.

'I don't know – if there's going to be uniform tearing through the school records, those officers will be from County.'

'Let's find the boy first. You know as well as I do that once the cat's out of the bag, we'll scarcely get a look in: this could blow up big time.'

CHAPTER 51

Elizabeth and Tony Windows had occupied Willow Farm for close on two decades. The farm was in the village of Stock, a small gentrified parish between Chelmsford and Billericay, and had not been a working farm for over a century. The chalet-style abode, with broad modern chimney breast, was clearly not the original building. It was of a kind that suffered like all properties consciously envisaged as modern – tacky and out of date by the time the last roof tile was laid. Its shortcomings, however, were barely visible from the road, situated as it was in a decent plot, contained by neat white fencing barely visible against the snow. There were two large willows overhanging a sizeable duckpond, which resident mallard and moorhen families found themselves sharing with winter visitors from the Arctic Circle.

Dr Tony Windows was at his consultancy office in Harley Street, and it was Elizabeth Windows who was surprised to see two men emerge from a shabby Citroën parked behind her BMW. One, wearing glasses, had the appearance of an insurance clerk, and his companion, a trade person of some description. Elizabeth, in poor health, was unsettled easily.

'What do you want with Tim?' She trembled slightly as she answered their opening question.

'Is he here?' the informally dressed one asked.

'No . . .' After some hesitation, she said he was in Colchester.

'That's a coincidence. So are we.' They introduced themselves. 'If you look at this again . . .' He held out his ID. Brazier. She knew that name from somewhere.

'What's he up to in Colchester? Do you have an address?' the other man asked.

'No . . . I'm afraid I don't. He's not – has not been – terribly well, you see. And . . . has spent a great deal of time in hospital.'

'Oh yeah, which one?'

'Severalls.'

'Severalls,' Brazier repeated. She suspected he knew it. 'When you say a lot of time, do you mean he was an inmate?'

'A patient, yes. Until recently.'

'What was wrong with him?'

They didn't know. A sudden gasp of panic seized her. 'Why are you looking for our son?'

'We are investigating an incident related to his time at Bryde Park school.' This from the clerical-looking one – Kenton, his ID said.

'Oh, I see,' she said, relieved they didn't want him in outright connection to any misdemeanour. 'It must have happened a long time back. Tim left the school over ten years ago.'

She was then more forthcoming, and told them how Timothy, having been released from hospital in November, had not wished to stray far from Colchester. She believed his psychiatrist would be better placed to direct them in the search for his whereabouts than she. He was, after all, a man now.

'But you're his mother.' Kenton sensed the woman was ill. Not because of the ungroomed grey hair – more the pallor; something debilitating lurked within the lady's frame.

'You really are best talking to the hospital. Tim's condition was complicated . . . and I find it rather distressing even now. He used to harm himself . . . cut himself.' She rushed out the last words and started rubbing her hands together in short, sharp, frantic movements, as if washing them under a tap that could be either too hot or too cold. Brazier's own mother did this when she grew anxious, without realising she was doing it. 'Speak to the doctors, they'll know where he is.' Her voice was controlled despite the hands, and she suddenly brightened and said, 'He's better now, they'll tell you, he's an outpatient.'

'Mrs Windows, do you have any memories – good or bad – of Tim's years at Bryde Park?'

'He did very well there, a cross country champion.'

'What about archery?' Brazier mimed drawing a bow, and spun around on his heel in an unnerving fashion.

'No, I don't recall . . .'

'Are you sure?'

'Sorry. It's a long time ago.'

It would not help Tim for her to tell tales on him. Say nothing. She watched both policemen closely – they closed their notepads with satisfaction.

Shortly after they drove away, she took a tranquilliser, then telephoned Margaret.

Kenton remained silent on the drive to Severalls. Ghosts from his past inhabited the corridors of the immense hospital, opened as an insane asylum on the eve of the First World War. They passed the first Colchester turning and took the north exit for Severalls. Two of the Fox Farm witches were in here, the Cliff girls, a case that had derailed Kenton for a spell in the early eighties. He had heard of nothing but bad things going on behind these red-brick walls. Periodically, he enquired about Lucy and Emma, and then Lowry had—

'I've heard this place gives people the willies,' Brazier said as the hospital entrance loomed into view.

'Yes,' Kenton said sombrely, 'the sooner they shut it for good, the better.'

The hospital may only have been minutes away from Colchester, but the institution itself had teetered on the fringe of an archaic medical world best forgotten. At the forefront of experimental medicine in the fifties, the place was synonymous with lobotomies, padded cells, terrifying screams, and all the nightmares associated with the restraint of insanity. The size of a small town, Severalls even had its own water tower – it was a composite of low-level colony-style villas and huge Edwardian ward buildings. At its peak, the complex held 1800 patients. The length of the asylum corridors were legendary – over eleven miles in total – and many of them originally windowless, with only small holes to the outside for ventilation and to let out the stained breath of the seriously medicated. The nurses themselves dreaded these passageways at night, as they would fill with bats, cascading through the darkness.

The grounds were pleasant and surprisingly verdant in places, with trees and shrubs. Many of the buildings were in Queen Anne style, presenting to the casual observer a place of tranquil recovery; and paradoxically, as some inpatients conceded, the hospital's grounds and gardens were healing, promoting calm and safety. By the 1960s, the management had changed with the times, visually at least, decorating common spaces with murals of birds and landscapes, with art and music therapies actively encouraged among the patients.

But the effect of this splash of colour on the grey area of mental health was short-lived. Scandals of mistreatment con- tinued elsewhere, and the cost of long-term care demanded a reassessment. To the point that drastic action had now been taken: the police had been advised that Severalls was in the process of releasing its entire psychiatric patient community into the wide world. Watt had briefed his division in the summer. Early signals from the large city institutions that had forged the way suggested this was going to be an unmitigated disaster. No provisions had been made for these people, they simply had nowhere to go. But it was too late to stop: the wheels were in motion, the staff that had run these places had been given their marching orders, and the process of closure was too far gone to change.

The only concession was that Severalls, because of its size, would release its occupants gradually. Timothy Windows was in the early wave and had been released in November.

CHAPTER 52

Kenton and Brazier followed a nurse along one corridor after another and were soon unsure if they'd be able to retrace their steps without a guide. Some walls were covered in art-work – pastoral scenes, partridges, pheasants and, weirdly, a greenhouse. Eventually they were left to sit on plastic chairs awaiting an audience with a Dr Jessop.

Dr Jessop, a woman in her late fifties with dyed auburn hair, cut short, was not, it seemed, curious as to why Windows was wanted by the police. Once they were admitted to her office, she merely explained the circumstances behind his release.

'Sorry, forgive me, Doctor, we are policemen. Was he better or not?' asked Kenton. 'His mother told us he used to harm himself.'

'There were indications of a recovery, yes,' she offered slowly. 'Self-harm at such an early age is difficult, but yes, there were marked signs of improvement in some areas . . . although he could still do with putting on a few pounds.'

'You don't sound sure.'

'As sure as I can be. Severalls, as a psychiatric hospital, is closing.' She removed her glasses, folded them and placed them on Windows' file. 'You've heard of Care in the Community by now, I take it?'

They nodded.

'Unless a patient is seriously ill, and by that we mean a danger to themselves or others, they are out. Those remaining chronic cases will be moved to other institutions around the country. The hospital will continue to see those who need us as outpatients for a short spell, but those appointments will eventually move to County or the General, as yet undecided.'

'So there'll be nobody resident here?' Kenton said.

'A few – elderly, stroke patients, mainly – but yes.'

'Why would a child of ten do that, cut themselves?' Brazier said. Why hadn't the doctor raised the allegations at the school?

'Simply, more often than not, to demonstrate they can. It's a choice, a decision that the child makes for themselves.'

Brazier squinted at the doctor as if she was some distance away and not across the desk in front of him.

'You look perplexed,' Jessop said. 'It's difficult to grasp for those of us who had a comparatively normal upbringing. I imagine the pair of you made it through childhood, by and large, intact? With an element of freedom, no doubt, and were spared a confused mind in the way Tim Windows suffered.'

'Rewind a mo, if you don't mind, Doctor,' Kenton said. 'Let's go back to his admission. His mother was none too forthcoming.'

'You both know it's a breach of confidentiality for me to disclose patient information.'

'We do, but this kid needs to be found and found now, and if there's anything in there,' Brazier reached across and tapped the file lightly with his fingertips, 'that might help us figure out what's going on inside his head, you ought to let us know. We get there's ethics involved but you'd be gutted if anything untoward happened.'

'Untoward?' she repeated, then picked up her glasses.

Jessop had joined the hospital staff three years ago and prior to that was at the Maudsley in south London and, she informed them, had acted as an expert witness a number of times.

'You weren't here then, this is all history,' Kenton encouraged.

Doctor Jessop opened the file. In the summer of 1979, having reached the age of ten, Windows was brought into the hospital by his parents for observation, a period of a week: the boy's self-harming was dangerously close to suicide. 'Speaking generally, the shock of an institution such as this can have an unpredictable impact on young children, so staff aren't always surprised when some deteriorate, initially.'

The doctor had chosen to share information, albeit in an ambiguous, guarded fashion.

'What form can this take?' Kenton asked.

'Refusing to eat. Talk. Communicate whatsoever. In fact, the contrary, this can be taken as an encouraging sign; a child has spirit, rebelling at enforced hospitalisation, the loss of liberty . . .' She let it hang, while searching for her next remark.

'But? I can tell there's a "but" coming,' Brazier prompted.

'As the week passed, there was no change in his behaviour; this surprised the doctors at the time,' she continued, letting all pretence drop, 'given the end was in sight, no amount of cajoling could get him to play ball. He grew weak and was soon on an intravenous drip. The parents were alarmed – his stay began to encroach into term time. They blamed themselves, evidently. Over time, though, he did improve – eat, minimally – and slipped into a routine, spoke with other patients, even befriended some – this was observed discreetly, it says here. Still, every assessment drew a blank. The resident said, and still says, that his interactions with the other patients revealed him to be intelligent, caring and with a comprehension of his situation. He was an avid reader too. The conclusion was that he did not want to get better.'

'Or get out.'

'Correct.'

'Any idea why?'

'A trauma of some kind that frightened him. In here, he was safe.'

'He's ten. What trauma would he have experienced?' Brazier was growing restless with the knowledge tumbling around inside him. They both now saw the situation for what it was and sought ratification: that he had suffered sexual abuse. That this was not immediately forthcoming from the physician under whose care Windows had been placed was frustrating – and seeded doubt. If they could see it, why not a doctor?

Kenton, sensing Brazier's frustration, gently placed a hand on his colleague's forearm. 'How did you do it then? Make him better?'

'I never claimed we cured him entirely.'

'Do you think he should still be locked up?'

'Not under current guidelines, no.'

'Without this Care in the Community shit, though, he'd still be here?'

'Who's to say? Society evolves. The old system was ineffective. The aim is for the good of people like Tim.'

'Presumably you don't see him as a danger to anyone else?'

'No, why would I think that? He wouldn't hurt a fly. Now he has a chance to mix with normal, healthy people, build a life for himself.'

'Oh yeah, and what's he doing?' Brazier said.

'He has a place on a training scheme, at a local DIY store called TimberHouse. Learning skills to help him lead a fulfilling life.'

'Any chance you got an example of Tim's handwriting in that folder?'

'Why would we keep a sample of his handwriting in a medical file?'

'Signature?' he said, hopefully. 'No, I guess that wasn't required. No authority.'

'Tell me, Doctor, truthfully, was he ready in your opinion to go?' Kenton said.

'Yes. There's only so much an institution can do. By the time he left he was communicating, not only with patients, but doctors too. The longer he was here, the tougher it would be to adapt to outside life. You may sniff at TimberHouse, but it's a chance.'

'He's an outpatient, right? So he'll be in next . . . when?' Kenton asked.

'Tomorrow.'

'If it's okay with you, we'd like to see him afterwards.'

'You don't need my permission.' She picked up a biro and started to scribble. 'Here's the hostel address; the Wild Palms, in the Hythe, save you travelling all the way out here again.'

The doctor had had enough. It was time to leave. One last question.

'Thanks for your help, doc,' Brazier said. 'Just for our records, Tim Window's admission: when precisely was that? Is there a date?'

She spun the file around, and pointed to the date: 31 August 1979.

'End of the summer holidays,' Kenton said.

'Did you attach any significance to that? Maybe he didn't fancy going back to school?'

Brazier's antagonism was discernible to the psychiatrist, skilled in recognising behavioural shifts.

'School was discussed,' she said, 'but was not considered a

determinate in his condition, according to the file. The parents'
concern was that one day they'd return home to find their
son had made an incision too far and opened an artery. In the
first instance, as I said, he was placed here for observation,
but soon lapsed into a catatonic state, saying nothing for two
years to any adult nurse or doctor.'

Brazier leant forward across the desk, forcing the doctor
to recoil at the detective's faintly noxious breath. 'You know
how far that boarding school is from Tim Windows' home?'

'No, why should I?'

'Six miles,' he said. 'Ten, fifteen minutes' drive at the most.
Don't you find that odd? To send a child away when his home
is so nearby.'

'I'm a doctor, Sergeant, not a geographer,' she said, curtly,
'and as I said earlier, I was not present at the boy's admission.'

'Let's not debate professional boundaries, eh?' Kenton said.
'Thank you – you didn't have to tell us this.'

'There's only so much doctors can do for children, for
anyone, even now.' Dr Jessop closed the file. 'I trust, though,
I've been more helpful than the boy's parents?'

That was true, as one institution dealing with another
institution, untainted by emotion, sharing only records and
facts was straightforward.

'Yes,' Brazier said, 'that's a fact. To be frank, his mother
had no real idea where he was.'

'Since reaching maturity, the details and nature of Tim's
release were his concern alone. Further, Timothy Windows

was adopted. You didn't know that, did you? The parents were reluctant to admit it, less it be perceived they had failed. Don't judge them too harshly – the doctor's remarks here suggest they held themselves to blame for the boy's predicament in some way; he was never told he was adopted, but he intuited they were not his biological parents.'

Brazier studied the crumbling masonry and flaking paintwork of the halfway house – Care in the Community indeed.

They had driven immediately to the address Dr Jessop had passed them. The Wild Palms was, in a former life, a fisherman's lodging on Hythe Quay, on the outskirts of town. A forgotten derelict quarter that had not recovered from the recession of the early eighties.

'Where better to hide your problems,' Kenton said, 'than on the edge of the country slipping into the sea, hoping one day a tidal surge may sweep them away.'

'Very poetic,' Brazier said. 'Wild Palms; Dead Palms more like.' A gull landed on a snow-crowned capstan and cried loudly.

The hostel's lime front was punctuated by ancient lifebelts linked by a network of cracks that spread like a half-hearted spider's web across the rendering. Inside, the aura was that of a cheap hotel full of transient people. Dirty and draughty. Half the beds had been assigned to the homeless for the winter, so the police thought their boy might have stood out.

'I know the guy. Ex Severalls? He's supposed to check in and out.' The manager went to a clipboard attached by string to the wall and lifted several sheets of curled A4 paper, frowned, then moved to a card index system beneath it.

'He's not here. And I've not seen him.'

'Any idea when he's due back?'

'Nope. Wanna wait? Hot tea served nine till five.'

'Will he definitely be back?'

'Not necessarily. It's not a prison.'

'Then why do they check in and check out?'

'Them's the rules, pal. Social workers like to know.'

'Why?' Brazier asked.

'Beats me. We just do it – part of the deal. Red tape, you know.' He winked exaggeratedly. 'Anything else?'

It was nearly five and bitterly cold. They'd find their man at the hospital the next day.

'Can I have a look at that?' Kenton asked, pointing to the clipboard.

The clerk pivoted round and unattached the string. 'Here.'

'What's the card index for?' Kenton asked as he leafed through the log until he reached the date of Hopkins' death.

'Personal details, next of kin, departure date.'

'What does it say about Tim Windows?' According to the clipboard, Windows had not left the building in the period Hopkins was killed. Kenton moved back to the date of the fire; Windows had checked in and out that day.

'That he's on a waiting list for a council flat. No next of kin, and no emergency contact. That's it.'

'Is this accurate?' Kenton tapped the log.

'As far as I know. And we got that.' He raised an arm towards the hooded black lens of a camera in the corner. 'Council experiment. More a deterrent, can get oddballs chancing it in here. Runs on video tape.'

Satisfied that tomorrow would do, they left, asking the manager not to mention their visit if Windows returned later – they didn't want him spooked.

CHAPTER 53

This evening was to be his last night at the hostel; the housing benefit application had worked its way through the system and a flat in Greenstead had been allocated. Having done two hours overtime, Tim arrived back later than usual. The meal before him was tasteless, and cold – he'd only just made it in time, the kitchen finished at 6.30 and what was left in the stainless-steel tray had congealed in the half hour or more it had been sitting there. Barely touching it, he edged the food to one side of the plate, to look as though he'd eaten more than he had. Not that anyone was checking up on him here, but old habits die hard. He rose from the table, slid his plate into the rack and exited the room.

He'd not miss this place, or anyone in it. No one had spoken to Tim Windows at the hostel since the morning of his arrival, and he was not in the habit of soliciting conversation. Contact with people was limited to the transactional.

After breaking his silence at the hospital all those years ago, he quickly discovered nobody really wished to speak with him; it seemed the effort of trying to get him to talk for two years had exhausted their enthusiasm to hear what he might have to say. There were the regular review meetings with the psychiatrists, but these were conducted as though scripted, each party saying what was required. Social interchange and friends existed only in books for Tim.

Apart from Mandy, of course. She would chatter on at him endlessly from the instant she arrived. Then she wangled her way out, and his world closed in on itself. Until the time he finally gave in to Emma Cliff.

There was no need to talk to anyone at the hostel, nobody spoke; he was free and that meant nobody telling him what time to eat, to go to bed. This was the strangest facet of being out, all the fundamental decisions were now his to take. The first night here he had sat in his room, expectantly, not knowing what was wrong until he dropped off to sleep, waking hours later with pangs of hunger and the lights on.

In the morning he stirred to the familiar smell of toast. Downstairs in the dayroom with large sash windows, a cheerful social worker in a colourful jumper came to greet him and said that food was available at set times throughout the day, but nobody would come and fetch him. He should have been told this, although she did not say by whom. If he needed anything he was to ask for her at the desk; she wasn't a resident but was here every third day (the intervening days she visited similar hostels).

Back in December, he didn't know what he needed. It was just over ten years since he was last abroad in civilisation, and then much of that was at boarding school, where freedom to do anything for himself was practically nil. Only at the weekends at home with his distant mother was he left to his own devices, in a place where he had no friends, not going to the local school. Without rules, Tim's life collapsed like an upended blancmange. He had desires, though, nurtured and expanded on, growing ever more intricate as the years slipped by; desires which, due to careful planning, he had miraculously started to achieve. Thanks to Mandy, devoted Mandy. She was different outside, quieter, demure even. The first time she'd come to visit he thought her a different person. 'Adapt,' she'd said. 'You'll learn. In the meantime, just pretend.'

Pretend. That's all he'd ever done. Everything else was irrelevant, and he did only as his body urged. After starting his apprenticeship at TimberHouse – where he had, it was true, to apply himself at first, so alien was the DIY warehouse, his thin ill-formed frame not used to humping garden furniture and potted shrubs around – he soon found he had an appetite. This was a surprise, a distant pang of pain he hadn't experienced since those first grim weeks at Severalls. It was worth it, though; he'd held the job down and soon he was to have his own place. His nights at the hostel were over.

His evenings were spent in solitude, in his small damp room, reading. Only the yells of the drunks stumbling out of the Anchor at closing time broke the silence, reminding him of the howls that echoed in the hospital. (Being on the ground floor did have an advantage – he had managed to slip out through the draughty sash window, avoiding the fuss of the front desk.) He had read everything there was to read in the hospital, from *Mansfield Park* to *Not a Lot of People Know That*. His one and only excursion into town since his release had been to find a bookshop. On North Hill, he had discovered a labyrinthine second-hand bookshop and picked up a tatty copy of *The Devils of Loudon* and an ex-library *Naked Lunch*. Both of these books he'd heard about from her, the succubus, Emma, who had them smuggled in only to be swiftly confiscated. Emma was awaiting transfer. The system, broken though it was, was not about to unleash the chaos of Emma Cliff back into the world.

Tim took his pills, noticing the jar near-empty. Outside, they didn't seem to work as well, and he had taken to upping the dosage. Sometimes he woke in the middle of the night to discover the room freezing and had been unable to get back to sleep – an extra tablet taken earlier with dinner together with one before bed seemed to do the job. After a couple of pages, Burroughs' book lay on his chest and he nodded off. The overhead bedroom light remained on, casting a low-watt glow from a discoloured pendant across the prone twenty-one-year-old as mugwumps rose up, rumbled about his subconscious, disturbing his dreams.

PART 4

CHAPTER 54

'So, I understand you've been careening around Chelmsford again?'

'Yes, with your blessing this time, guv,' Brazier said. 'Old Bradshaw.'

'The school, I'm referring to the school,' Watt said, as he sipped his coffee.

'Obviously the school,' Kenton said. Watt didn't react to this impertinence. Bleary-eyed, the sergeant hadn't shaved, unusual for him. Watt's fingers formed a steeple. 'You're to desist with the Kempe Marsh fire investigation.'

The room fell silent. The rumble of traffic along the Southway was strangely audible – a sound none would confess to having previously noticed.

'Aren't you curious to know what triggered the attack?'

'Revenge?' He held up his hand. 'No, I don't want to hear any more.'

'Why?' Kenton said.

'You haven't establishment support for this route of enquiry.'

Watt's eyes met them both, nervous but hostile; courting a denial.

'The establishment? I thought we *were* the establishment?' Brazier said.

Kenton shook his head with a mock smile. 'No. We *serve* the establishment, we're the little people.'

Watt didn't contradict this, neither did he agree. 'What did the doctors at Severalls say? Hmm? Was there any mention of abuse? Did the school's name come up? No . . .'

'That headmistress knew all along. Lying bastard – swore I saw her on the phone. Stuck-up, uptight . . .' Brazier, surprisingly, reined it in.

'I don't know this woman,' Watt said, indifferently, 'but she has friends in high places.'

'And Hopkins?'

'The Hopkins' case is different – for now, pursue.'

'Why's he different?' Kenton said. 'He was at the school, she confirmed it.'

Watt released his hands from the piety they presented and rocked back in the chrome chair. He had not expressed his own view on the situation; those above were not interested, nor equally, it seemed, his own men. Curiously, he was in limbo.

'For a start, he's dead. And dead on our patch.' With this unfamiliar expression, and a seldom used inclusive determiner, Watt had their attention. 'You'll have the presence of mind to keep me informed. From the sounds of it, you'll have this man, Windows, very soon.'

'Symonds is inextricably tangled with Windows and Hopkins, it's impossible to separate them.'

'We'll worry about that when the time comes.'

Dismissed, Kenton and Brazier quietly prepared to leave the station. There was nothing to be gained battling the powers of Essex County. If they really existed, that is. 'Establishment support': it was just like Watt to blame someone else for his own decision – made for reasons unknown and devoid of any rationale . . . and if anyone was part of the system, Watt was.

'Jesus, what a mess!' Kenton laughed to himself sardonically.

'You all right, mate?' Brazier said, zipping up his bomber jacket.

'Huh. Yes. I guess,' he said. 'Until tomorrow?'

They agreed a plan of action for the following day and left the building to return to their respective homes. Kenton passed through the Citroën headlights towards his own vehicle. As he watched the Citroën disappear ahead, it occurred to him that Brazier usually left his car here overnight; where might he be going at seven in the evening?

CHAPTER 55

'Where are we going, then?'

'Copford Hotel.'

'Classy,' Wilde said without sarcasm. She was out of uniform and in jeans, sheepskin coat and Moon Boots. Her expectations were not high, but this was an unusual choice.

'Wait, isn't this where Beech stole that Sierra?'

He nodded in the darkness. 'There's a nice cosy place round the corner we can try later.'

It was Brazier's third time at the hotel and with a fresh fall of snow it appeared cleaner on the approach. From the outside, at least.

He ambled over towards reception, holding back as the woman on the desk finished dealing with a guest, while Wilde loitered in the background. The receptionist wore her blonde hair up in a neat pile and as she reached over to take receipt of a cheque, Brazier recognised her as the barmaid from his last visit. Wilde strolled around the foyer, noting the decor was tired and desperate for a refresh. The most striking thing was a zany orange carpet, which must have been thirty years old at least. She had no idea who'd willingly wish to stay here.

Brazier watched Wilde as he waited. He liked her, but she scared him a bit, and that made him silly at times, and he knew it. A waiter abruptly emerged through the double doors to the bar. The waiter too was familiar. Brazier reckoned all the staff must double up to maintain the hotel's momentum throughout the winter – maybe they ran on a skeletal staff in the lean months of January and February. It was then that it struck him why they may not have come across a lead. Healey had been here the week before Christmas too.

'Hi, Helen—' he read her name tag as he stepped up to the desk – 'do you lose any staff before Christmas as it quietens down?'

'No.'

'Oh.' He was hoping for a name that would jump out, one that was missing on the current roster of staff, someone with form.

'But we take on extra help in the run-up to Christmas, quite a few,' she said. 'Serving in the restaurant. We hire out space to companies for their Christmas dos.'

'Really? Anything happening when Mr Healey was here around then – December seventeenth to nineteenth?'

She pulled out a Manila folder marked 'Christmas 1990' and started sifting through paperwork. Helen was prim, she took pride in her appearance. A strand of hair escaped over her face. She was too good for this place. The red lipstick was a little much, but maybe she wore it for a reason – a signal, who knew?

'Do you like your job?' he asked, an eye on Wilde as he spoke.

Her fingers halted, as though frozen on the loose sheets of paper. Instantly regretting the question, he turned away. Unfortunately for Brazier, being on the job was often the only time he came into contact with civilians. He smiled at Wilde behind him, who returned a questioning look and came over.

'December eighteenth, there was a disco. CBS were here,' she said eventually. 'Staff Christmas party.'

'The record label? Amazing. Bloody hell, bet that disco was something,' Wilde said, sidling up.

'Not quite as glamorous as that – Colchester Book Supply, a distribution company in Tiptree.' She lifted her face towards Brazier's, there was a smudge of tiredness below her blue eyes, but not, he was relieved to see, any hostility. 'The disco, since you mention it, was Brian Jones – or the *Witham Waltzer*, as he likes to be known.'

'Mind if I borrow a phone?'

Brazier was shown to the back office and pulled his pocketbook.

'What you doing?' Wilde asked.

'Just checking something before going any further down this line of enquiry.' He cradled the receiver between ear and shoulder as he located the Manchester number.

The insurance salesman was home at this time in the evening and answered.

'Healey, Detective Sergeant Brazier from Colchester CID here.'

'You've got him? Got the bastard that nicked my motor!' he exclaimed excitedly.

'Not quite . . . your visit in December. Remember then?'

A moment's silence.

'Yes . . .' he then said slowly.

'One night there was a disco. Chat any crumpet up that night?'

'Am I on a speakerphone?' he asked suspiciously.

'Only me here, sir,' Brazier said.

'All right, luv, just the copper investigating the motor,' Healey hollered. His voice then dropped to a hush. 'Is it crucial, what went on that night? Guess so, or you'd not be calling . . . Listen, can I call you back in't morning from the office?'

'Just give me a yes or no and we need go no further.'

'All right.'

'You were in Essex between seventeenth to nineteenth December and you flirted with the ladies out enjoying their Christmas party?'

'Yes,' he said quietly.

'That's it for now.'

'Ta. An' guess what, fleet have signed off a new Probe,' he said, delighted, before hanging up.

Brazier replaced the receiver.

*

'Why are you back in December?' Wilde asked.

They were in a snug country pub as promised, complete with a crackling fire, as Brazier filled her in on his suspicions.

'All the hotel staff in February have checked out clean. Healey goes back and forth, right, so I went back to the last time he was down this way to see who was about then. One of the restaurant staff told me he is always banging on about his car running on air, said he's such a loudmouth the whole hotel knows when Ian Healey's in town. So, I reckon he was boring someone in his usual way, and someone dodgy at the hotel on their Christmas bash overheard him.'

'That's it – that's your theory?'

'Part of it – we know Beech didn't find Healey's car himself. Someone pointed him to it, but we've don't know who.'

'What about this kid you're looking for at the Wild Palms?'

'Windows. He just got released from Severalls. The last car he touched was a Dinky toy.'

'So where does he fit in? You both told Watt he was your suspect.'

'He is – for the fire, without a doubt. Hopkins' killing is connected, in some weird way . . . but the kid is, for the moment, out of this part of the picture.' He smiled and placed an empty pint glass down. He rubbed his hands, eager for another. They'd barely sat down.

'Complicated. I've never come across anything like this.'

'Me neither.'

'Another one?' She reached for her purse, reluctantly

acknowledging drink was the only way he'd loosen up. 'And enough about Healey's festive antics – I don't remember seeing you at the nick Christmas drinks?'

'I'd not properly started,' he said. 'Was in transition between here and Clacton.' That he was busy settling his mother into her new home near the police station was not something he wanted to share. Not yet, anyway.

'Getting all emotional over which nick to be with? Bless . . .'

'Besides, I wouldn't have known anyone,' he said into the empty pint glass. 'Other than Kenton.'

'That would have been a way in, then? Kenton should have asked you along.'

'Oh, he asked me all right, I didn't fancy it.'

'You're a bit of an enigma, aren't you, Sergeant?'

'Hardly,' he said, 'just a policeman. Like you.'

'I'm a woman, in case you hadn't noticed – my rank carries a W in front of it, to remind everyone.'

'You sound unhappy about it.'

'Urgh. It's tough, you know – of course you know – being female in this organisation. You can joke about it, but it's not easy at times.'

'Why do it, then? You must feel strongly about it.'

'It's not a reason not to,' she said, plainly. 'Anyway, yes, I did once upon a time, feel strongly – my dad was one, a copper. Not here. In Hong Kong, died when I was little, so I knew what the police were from a very young age, by his absence, if you see what I mean. By the time I was old enough to join,

I had sort of forgotten why.' She laughed. 'But I love it. Must be in the blood.'

'Mine too, died when I was a kid – not a copper, though . . .'

'Why d'you do it?'

'As a little lad I always fancied the RAF, but later discovered that flying was not for me – the uniform was closest in colour.'

'But you're in plain clothes.'

He squinted. 'I know. Bummer.'

He was shy beneath it all. Nevertheless, Wilde felt at ease in his company.

'What do you do when you're not doing this?' she asked.

'Watch films. Cinema. Like the outdoors – you know, a ramble, bit of fresh air – but no badminton or judo. Have a drink when one's going.'

'All right, all right.' She rose. 'Next time, we'll do one of mine, mix it up a bit.'

'I'll take the badders. Used to play at school.'

'Good, and by the way,' she said over her shoulder, 'do you have a different pair of trousers? You leave a trail of snow wherever you go with those. Not very becoming for a detective, is it?'

CHAPTER 56

Brazier flicked on the wipers. A bus rumbled through the late-morning mist towards the hospital approach. 'About time,' Brazier said, making to get out of the car. 'Better bloody be on that bus.'

'We can't just barge in there now, might freak him out . . . The doctor would not be impressed. Wait.'

'Nothing'd impress her,' Brazier grumbled, sitting back.

Kenton glanced across, wondering what exactly he was thinking. 'She's doing a difficult job,' he said finally, then yawned loudly. 'Excuse me.'

'Late night?'

'Something like that.'

Kenton had sat on one of Lindsay's paintings, and the whole issue of space flared up again. Never go to bed on an argument; her maxim. As long as she won, that is. He shifted in his seat. The bus was now stationary, chugging diesel fumes into the sharp air. A low beam of sunlight appeared unexpectedly as the cloud thinned and the car warmed fractionally. Kenton wound down the window a notch as the bus disgorged its passengers, out of view.

'Do you think anyone cares whether this lad turns up or not? I don't mean the doc,' Brazier said, after a while, 'although, I'm not sure she'd notice.'

'How do you mean? We care.'

'His old dear, real or not, didn't give a fig. I mean, what sort of life is he going to have had? From Bryde Park to this place . . . and why hang about here and not go home, to that huge pile in Stock? When was the last time you visited a house with a duck pond you could row across? Suck it up and fill your boots, I say.'

'It's a condition of his release to be close. To be in the area.'

'Pah, get on over there and milk that guilt.'

'Besides, he's institutionalised, severing ties aren't that easy, no matter how unpleasant.'

'Don't see Beech climbing the walls to get back into his institution.' Brazier's attention had switched to a man in a black uniform marching in their direction. 'This might not look like a prison from the outside, but inside could be straight out of *Porridge*, only on a bigger scale – don't be fooled by the colourful wall paintings. All those corridors, Christ knows where some of them led. Worse, in fact, our equivalent of *One Flew Over the*—' He wound down his own window to greet the man. 'All right, mate.'

'The doctor says you gentlemen are welcome to wait inside. Mr Windows is here.'

*

Tim sat watching Dr Jessop's mouth through his cigarette smoke as it casually twirled up to the ceiling. He raised the cigarette to his lips and nodded to indicate he'd heard her. He had informed her that he was still working in the DIY shop, sweeping the warehouse floor. He might as well have said he'd joined the NASA astronaut programme for all the interest she'd shown. But he said nothing, wanting the meeting over as quickly as possible; since she had announced the police were waiting outside to see him, he'd retreated behind his eyes to prepare himself. He'd been anticipating this moment for so long, he could barely contain his excitement. It had worked like clockwork. From inception to planning, the very day and place to find him, here at the hospital – not at the fleapit of a hostel where, with the best will in the world, they'd think him no more than a bum. At the hospital, his plight would be framed in the right way. He must be careful how he put himself across. Vulnerable, yes, but not too meek, a tiny bit scared perhaps; if he came across as a weakling they'd not confide in or believe him.

At the doctor's mention of renewing his prescription he snapped back to the present. The nights would be unendurable without that stuff. Was he having trouble sleeping? Yes. Anxiety arising from work? Definitely. She would give him something extra. Did he know where to get the prescription when she was no longer here? No, she hadn't told him. She was leaving at the end of the month, so pay attention. He did.

Kenton and Brazier paced about in the reception area. Policemen were no strangers to hospitals, but this was not what they were accustomed to: at a remove from the community, without the bustle of the general public drifting aimlessly about, folk out for a fag, some with a drip in tow, it had a different, more sombre atmosphere. The place had an air of gentle decay. The whitewashed walls were a sickly grey-yellow, like a corpse.

'Remember, try not to frighten him,' Kenton warned. Brazier was restlessly chewing gum. His appearance was different today. Still untidy, but not quite as bad as usual. Something had changed. The trousers. Muscular short legs accentuated by an old pair of light blue stay-press with the same scuffed trainers at the end of them. His eccentric appearance was matched by the non sequiturs that so often left his mouth. And what was intelligible was often only fit only for a schoolboys' lavatory. There was a direct correlation between how excited he got and the nonsense he spouted.

'I don't frighten anyone,' he said, running his fingers through spiky hair. A nurse glided by, giving him a wide berth.

'Gentlemen, I believe you're waiting for me.' Before them stood a man in an old army parka, apparently twice the age of the man they were anticipating, holding a sports bag in one hand and a plastic carrier bag in another.

'No, I don't think— unless you happen to be a Timothy Windows.'

His large eyes rolled in the near-naked skull. 'Yes, that's

me.' He spoke softly, but had a croak, like the elderly – a groaning voice unaccustomed to talking.

'Jesus Christ! Just looking at you makes me stomach rumble,' Brazier muttered.

'Ignore my friend here, we're sorry to trouble you at this personal moment, but felt you'd more comfortable if we spoke here rather than in full view of the hostel.'

'Isn't that place awful?' he said. 'At least here the radiators are on. They're always on, in fact. Keeps us mellow,' he added without a trace of irony. 'How can I help?'

'Just a few questions, if that's all right. I'm Sergeant Kenton and this is Sergeant Brazier. You arrived by bus, perhaps we can talk here then run you back to the hostel instead of the bus?'

He weighed this up.

'Sure.'

'Shall we?' Brazier's open palm directed him to the double exit doors.

The sky had grown dark with menace while they were inside, and once again it was bitterly cold. Windows stopped and breathed it in, deeply. 'Ahh. Better air outside,' he said, before moving on.

'Any idea why we might be here?' Kenton asked as they walked towards the car.

'Mummy checking up on me?' If this was meant playfully, the tone did not suggest it.

'Why would she do that?' Kenton replied cautiously.

'She can't bear to see me. But perhaps her guilt has

manifested – twisting her into a panic that now that I'm released something dreadful might happen to me.'

'Is that likely?'

'Without a doubt.' His eyes were on the ground, watching his feet crunch through crusts of snow across the empty car park.

'It wasn't your mum, I'm afraid,' Brazier said abruptly. 'Your old school, Bryde Park. Fond memories?'

Windows raised his head and broke into a thin smile, revealing brown teeth. 'Distinctive.'

'What stands out? Your mum remembers you were a cross country champion.' Brazier opened the passenger door. 'Not quick enough to outrun the Old Bill, to make it six miles or so home when you'd had enough, eh?'

They stood, the three of them alone in the bleakness, each waiting for the other to move first inside the car. Kenton watching Windows closely, wondering whether he still had the legs and might make a bolt for it.

'Schoolboy error, sir,' Windows said finally. 'I forgot to take a compass.' He climbed into the car.

'Both times? Cross country, you won only twice, unlike archery, where you were school champion every term,' Brazier said into the back of the car before shutting Windows' door. 'Funny, your mother never mentioned your fondness for a bow and arrow.'

Windows waited for them to get in the car before answering,

staring towards the hospital entrance, fearful perhaps he might yet be recalled even now.

'She knows nothing of what went on there,' he said. 'Apart from the running away, which at the time, like you, she made a joke of.'

CHAPTER 57

Brazier waited until they were out of the hospital grounds before asking anything more. He glanced at Windows in the rear-view mirror.

'Tell us about it, then. We're not here for a joke.'

'Children are not locked away in Severalls for being home-sick,' Windows said.

'Of course not, and forgive us for being glib,' Kenton intervened, twisting round in the passenger seat. 'But children do wind up in hospital for self-harm.'

'That's just to get attention, Sergeant.'

Windows' expression was unreadable, and Kenton couldn't decipher whether he was mocking them.

'You have ours – undivided, Tim,' Brazier said. 'Explain; pretend like we're simple.'

'I cut myself because I did not want to go back to school. And that's all I can or will say. If you can't work it out, you've no business being policemen.'

'And Kevin Symonds and Ken Markham were the reason?'

'Yes.'

'They . . .'

'Yes, whatever you find unsayable, they did.'

'How could you keep this to yourself for so long?' Brazier said.

'What you really mean is – why didn't I speak up before? The reason, Sergeant, is plain and simple – I could not. I can't elaborate, sorry.'

'Do you admit to setting fire to St Nicholas's church in Kempe Marsh?' Kenton asked.

'Archery was, for centuries, the quintessential English sport, don't you know, and they taught me to be such a good shot. "For behold, the Lord will come in fire, and his chariots like the whirlwind, to render his anger in fury, and his rebuke with flames of fire." As they say in the Gospels.'

'Ah, so were they biblical references, in the letters you sent?' Kenton asked, thinking of the two notes.

'No. What I sent you and Master Markham was from *Lord of the Flies*. He taught English – why would I send him the New Testament? I sent the Reverend something from Luke this morning.'

'So, your plan is to take him down?' Brazier said. 'Symonds.'

'*Take him down*?' Windows started laughing in the back seat, hard, like his slight frame might fracture. 'Why do you think he's with the Church? He's untouchable there. But his precious building isn't, and he knows it. I have destroyed the only thing he prizes in the world, and it is irreplaceable.' The words came tumbling out.

'Only the roof. All right, it was a very old wooden one,' said Brazier.

'He was gutted,' Kenton said.

'I bet,' Windows said sharply. 'And tell me, did he behave exactly how I predicted? Drawing attention to himself?'

'He was a bit of fusspot, yeah,' Brazier said. 'How did you trace him, after all this time?'

'Yes, a fusspot,' Windows muttered derisively. 'Tracing them both was easy. A letter here and there. Not what you call the old-boy network, but polite enquiries in the right direction were answered. And setting up a flower shop in Billericay High Street is not what you might call deep cover. Mr Markham, without the protection of the Church, feared the worst, and took the coward's way out.'

'Was there another?' Kenton asked.

'You mean charming Master Hopkins?'

'Yes, Hopkins.'

'He's dead.'

At this, his stare met Brazier's in the mirror. 'How do you know that?' he said.

'The newspapers. They have them in the hostel. Pity.'

'Did you want to kill him?'

'No, I'm more for shaming and ruining lives than ending them. Kill him like that, then pouf! He's gone.' He released a clenched hand between their seats. 'Over too soon. Like Markham – that's very unsporting of him, don't you think?'

Brazier nodded, sternly, his eyes back on the icy road down

to the Hythe. 'Strange, that Hopkins picked now to come over, after all this time, don't you think? A few months after you were released.'

Windows considered this and adjusted his shoulders against the seat. 'You say that as if I were the reason for his departure. He preferred a life of more lucrative crime – I remember now he was wanted in connection with drug smuggling.'

'You heard about that too?' Brazier said.

'They do have televisions as well newspapers in hospitals, you know.'

'He married, after leaving the school.'

'Really?' he said, distastefully. 'He's not the first and won't be the last.'

'But you knew Symonds and Markham also left Bryde Park. How?'

'The school, through my parents.'

'They did visit, then?'

His gaze moved to the car window. 'At first, but then I told them not to bother.'

Kenton, who was still watching him, said, 'Did you have help from the outside?'

'In what context, Sergeant?' Windows spun round. 'The postmarks on the letters to Markham and Symonds will confirm I was free to post them myself.'

'What's with the airmail paper?'

'You don't need to be crazy to stay at Wild Palms. American

backpackers left it at the hostel. I don't have the funds for Basildon Bond right now.'

'Whoever killed Hopkins had an accomplice.' Brazier stopped the car. 'Here we are.'

'Do you think I did him in with assistance, then?' Windows said. 'I didn't know he was here, in the country. If I knew, I wouldn't send you clues in the post, would I? Besides, he was a wanted man and with what you know you'd have found him first.'

Nobody got out of the car. What Windows said made sense; it just wasn't what they were expecting to hear. Even though the Wild Palms records showed Tim Windows hadn't left the building in the twenty-four-hour period Hopkins was murdered, they still had him connected. He had to be.

'Why d'you say that?' Brazier said.

'Because it's your job to. Justice. Drug smuggling is taken seriously, not some crazy kid making wild allegations.'

'Yes . . . but what do we really know?' Kenton twisted round in his seat.

'He was obsessed,' Windows said simply. 'You found my picture, didn't you?'

'You know about that?' Kenton asked.

'I remember the day it was taken – last week of the summer term. Hopkins said, "Need something to remind me of you over the hols, darling boy".'

'Why do you think he had it after all this time?' Kenton said.

'Hmm, let me ponder that – because he's a crazy, dirty

pervert? And maybe it should have been Master Hopkins locked up for the last ten years instead of me?' Windows looked Kenton in the eye, challenging him to deny it. 'But shit happens, eh?'

Kenton, uncomfortable, withdrew from between the front seats and sat facing the windscreen. His heart went out to the boy – if all this was true, and he believed it so, how could he remain objective?

Nobody said a word for a moment.

'So, Wild Palms, here it is,' Brazier said, breaking the silence. 'Be sure to stay in touch.'

'No,' Tim remained seated. 'I've left.'

'Not the hostel, then?'

'I'm moving. Today.'

'Luggage?'

Windows made a token gesture of lifting the carrier bag next to him on the seat to say, 'this is all I have.' Then, staring vacantly beyond the passenger window at the drab outside world and its browning snow, he started to talk, animatedly and loquaciously once he got going, clearly and without hint of an accent. A flat had been found to rent on Greenstead Estate for which he'd pay a peppercorn rent. He aired his views on the Youth Training Scheme he had been assigned. It was a start, or a chance of a start at least, he conceded.

'And soon I will have day release and go to college,' he said as they made their way back over the Colne Bridge.

'Oh yeah, and do what?' Brazier asked.

'Finance.' There were rudimentary classes in the hospital but he'd have been better prepared for the outside world had he been in prison, he said without a trace of bitterness. 'At least you can do O-levels there. My education stopped at nine years old. Apart from the books I scavenged, I doubt I have progressed much at all. Aha, here we are.'

His new lodgings were in a 1950s council house set back from the road, similar to Roland Beech's. He got out and thanked them. 'Be in touch,' he said, 'no doubt.'

They watched Tim Windows fumble with the unfamiliar lock and eventually let himself in.

'There's nothing crazy about him. I don't know what I was expecting,' Brazier said to himself. 'What a waste.' He banged the wheel with the base of his palm.

'If he didn't kill Hopkins, who did?' Kenton scratched the back of his head and sighed. 'We should take him in . . . for arson, he's more or less confessed.'

Brazier shook his head 'Uh-huh. Let's not lock the poor sod up again just yet. The Reverend has some questions to answer, don't you think?'

'But Watt said—' Kenton began.

'Screw Watt.'

CHAPTER 58

The Reverend was pink-faced and exhaling great plumes of breath as he laboured with a shovel, shifting snow from the garden path.

'Father, we come with good news.'

Symonds paused, wiping a hand on his navy duffle coat. His face glowed with exertion, not anticipation. By now, he knew the investigation was not going to end favourably for him.

'You had better come in.'

'No, here in the open is fine.' There was not a sound to be heard as snow started to fall in great chunks, effortlessly filling the surrounding murk.

'As you wish, though I'd be more comfortable inside – my poor back.' Symonds appeared to have acquired a stoop since they last met.

'We have found the culprit,' Brazier said flatly.

'The culprit, eh?'

'Yes, the man who shot an arrow into your roof.'

'An arrow,' he repeated, although he'd already been told the cause of the fire and seen the evidence.

'Do you remember teaching archery to a young lad at Bryde Park by the name of Timothy Windows?'

'Windows, Windows . . .' He gave a show of searching his memory. 'No, can't say that I do.'

Symonds didn't bat an eyelid. The situation had altered; a shift in dynamics. Moreover, as he scanned the treetops watching the snow collect, the Reverend's manner was now that of an altogether older man than the one that demanded their attention only the week before.

'He credits you with instructing him in the sport.' Brazier riled him.

'Does he now? Well, it's possible, it's possible.'

The three stood in silence as Symonds' navy-clad shoulders slowly turned white.

'You'll be arresting him, I dare say.'

'Are you pleased we caught the man – and he is a man, just – who damaged your church?'

'Of course—' his mouth upturned into a strained smile – 'if you are sure he did it. Be damned if I know why.'

'Oh, you know why.' Brazier wiped snow from his eyes.

'No, I haven't a clue, but please do tell me?'

They should leave now. Kenton thought enough had been said; leave it there.

But Brazier wouldn't let it go.

'Did you know what happened to Tim Windows, the summer before you left – were asked to leave – Bryde Park? Where he ended up?'

Kenton shot warning daggers at Brazier.

Too late.

'I was not asked to leave! Ask someone who was there before making wholly inaccurate assumptions – Charles Wintour will tell you—'

'Did you know what happened to Tim Windows?' Kenton repeated, seeing no option now.

'What sort of question is that? How should I possibly know what happened to that boy? Any boy! But what I do know is that if you cast any more aspersions towards me, I'll . . .'

Symonds didn't clarify his threat.

'And what about your old mucker, Bruce Hopkins? The news can't have escaped you he was pulled out of Abberton Reservoir . . .' Kenton said.

Symonds collected himself. 'Yes, I heard. You must remember Bruce was my elder, I was enthralled by him – yes – but I was only twenty-three, a student myself, young and gullible. I was told he was dismissed because he lied about his qualifications and was deemed unfit to teach.'

'Yep, I bet that was the official spin old Wintour put on it,' Kenton said.

'He'd had a troubled upbringing,' Symonds continued. 'It's no surprise he turned to crime.'

'And Tim Windows didn't kill him – he only set fire to your roof,' Brazier said.

'That's right. Whoever went after Bruce is still at large,'

Kenton said. 'But no, we won't mention it again, Father. Get any post today?'

'Wha—?' The vicar, out of puff, stood like a flogged donkey.

'Be on your guard,' Brazier said, and they left.

At the car, Brazier brushed snow angrily from the windscreen.

'Okay,' Kenton said, 'we have to back the boy, support him any way we can. It's not going to be easy, though.'

Watt sat and heard them out. His faults were many, but not listening was not among them. Brazier noticed the commander had failed to blink and interpreted this patient intensity as a bad sign.

Watt turned from one to the other, adjusting his small red-veined eyes. The oncoming disagreement was tangible. Even so, he waited a full ten seconds after the report had ended, giving the impression he was considering a response, which he wasn't – he'd made up his mind several minutes earlier.

'Forget it,' he said, quietly.

'I'm sorry?' Kenton said.

'I said forget it.'

'You're joking,' said Brazier.

'Put that cigarette away. No, I'm not. You are wasting your time.' Simultaneously, they both started to raise objections. 'Hold on. Rather than get emotional, think about what you're suggesting.' Their bewildered look said this was not possible, and that he would need to elucidate. 'Listen. That boy has spent nearly half his life in a mental institution. Does that not signal anything to you?'

'Like what?' Brazier said.

'That just maybe if he'd been abused by a teacher it might have come out by now? Even—'

'Hey – wait—'

'Allow me to finish.' Watt said curtly. 'Even if you're onto something, who's going to back you up? The doctor, an expert witness, right? Conceding that this, the cause of the boy's illness, has eluded them all this time – that's a pretty big admission. How'd that look on her credentials? Then the school. You've got no proof there, whatsoever. And why?'

'Because fondling the boys wouldn't add much to the school prospectus,' Brazier said.

'Correct.'

'But that's so obvious, any judge would have to see—' Kenton began.

'*Any judge*,' Watt almost spat, 'would more than likely have been through the system and know the score.'

'So you acknowledge that it exists,' Kenton stated.

'What's the matter with you two?'

'But guv, this is not mere fondling – it's rape.'

'Against Hopkins and Symonds?'

'Windows hasn't said precisely what Symonds did, but it's not hard to imagine . . .'

'And Hopkins is dead, needing no imagination at all,' Watt said simply. 'You've got sweet FA. This Windows, poor unfortunate that he is, has in his mania overlooked his own predicament; recently released from a mental hospital, years of harbouring a grudge – who knows what really happened? – it's not shaping up for his to be the most credible testimony. Bring a proper case. Remember, first and foremost, you're hunting a killer, not looking to catch perverts. But crack *how* Hopkins was murdered and the rest of this sordid mess will fall into place even if Windows didn't kill him. Hopkins had the kid's photo, right? And second, remember, the letter to Markham is linked through the book, the *Lord of the Flies* line . . . have either of you read it, by the way? Standard text at the sort of school this lad went to.'

Brazier frowned at the ceiling. Kenton meekly half raised two fingers.

'Preadolescent boys survive an airplane crash on a tropical island, make a fire to attract help. A signal. Such as a church roof ablaze, seen across water. Symbolises at first hope, then later turns to destruction. This boy isn't stupid and has been doing more than twiddling his thumbs. Read it, teach you a thing or two about the need for order.'

CHAPTER 59

'For once, he's right,' Kenton conceded. To his shame he'd read the book but had failed to see the connection. It was over twenty years ago. Brazier had not attended any English lessons from the age of twelve, where books like this may have cropped up on the syllabus. His teacher had refused to have him in the class for disruptive behaviour.

Dismissed, they loitered in the CID office at their desks.

'And it would give a reason for Hopkins to carry this book about, if he too had got a message in Spain, recognisable . . .' Kenton said, tossing the paperback on the desk.

'But Windows said he hadn't reached him – besides, why would Hopkins come back here, even supposing he did get a cryptic message like Markham's? Markham topped himself – fearing the worst, exposure. All Hopkins needed to do was ignore it – if anything, it's a reason to stay put. For ever,' Brazier said, waving a ruler around absently. He needed to do something with his fingers and had left his sweets and fags on Watt's desk.

'We've overlooked that: Markham. Maybe he tipped off Hopkins that Windows had been in touch. All the time we were thinking it was Chloe. Find Wilde, get her over to Billericay, check the florist's correspondence and phone bill, see if there's a Spanish number.'

'And? I get Chloe Moran luring Hopkins back as a possibility, but not Markham warning him the victim of their abuse is about to be set free.'

'It's an angle. And would establish if Hopkins and Markham remained in contact.'

'You know,' Brazier said eventually, flexing the ruler, 'does it really matter at the end of the day who killed Bruce? I mean, if he's a nonce, screw him – he's dead, good riddance, and saving the taxpayer the expense of him serving at Her Majesty's pleasure, right?'

'You don't mean that. We have to trace Hopkins' last steps.'

'No. Not last steps. Attack it from the beginning.' The ruler, being brittle, gave with a crack, causing heads to turn. Brazier tossed the pieces in the bin. 'Bit like the boss, that ruler. Tense. Ready to snap, like that. Come on, back to Healey's car. I have something.'

CBS was located in Tiptree, eight miles west of town on the Maldon Road. For such a large operation it was impressively hidden from view. The distribution company was located in the centre of the village, behind the High Street, where no building was much higher than a modern semi. Yet articulated delivery lorries managed to snake through a small residential estate and slip away up a side road and out the back of the village, thundering off through the countryside along the crumbing Braxted Hall wall to disappear on to the A12. CBS's visitor entrance and admin departments were housed in a two-tier prefabricated building, much like a 1960s comprehensive school, reached from the High Street itself by a discreet lane between a café and the village hall.

A sign pointed staff vehicles into a snow-carpeted area between the High Street shops and the CBS offices, while visitors were directed up towards the long narrow office block that ran the length of the lane, lined with white-capped rose bushes, erect like festive Chupa Chups. Brazier sported two colourful transfers from those particular sweets on the back of each hand. Kenton had brought him back a bag of them from Spain. The visitor parking bays were in front of the building, alongside half a dozen allocated to 'DIRECTORS ONLY' nearest the entrance, only two of which were occupied.

'Nothing like progressive management,' Kenton sniffed as they marched to the door.

'Got to remind them who's boss,' Brazier said, eyeing the two management XJSs.

Inside, they were greeted from inside a windowed reception office by a woman with bright peroxide hair, wearing peach lipstick and large red-rimmed glasses on a chain. They were expected, but still had to wait. The gentleman they were to meet, they were advised, was a Mr McCreadie, Customer Services Director.

'Maurice, please.' A puffy, ring-laden hand was offered with a flourish before a besuited stout man in his fifties was fully through the swing doors beyond the reception area. They were led swiftly to the first floor and through a door marked EXECUTIVE, where in a short corridor a bank of labelled doors presented the occupants' names. Maurice McCreadie stopped at his own. Brazier continued on, passing him to a door at the end of the corridor, where a small porthole of a window looked out onto a sea of regimented desks, populated by office workers bustling about business and holding telephones. He reckoned there were forty-odd people in there, the odd vacant desk presumably down to the weather. Mostly middle-aged women and a couple of young lads in shirts too big for them, wearing long colourful ties.

'Sergeant, if I may?' McCreadie's polite mellifluous voice called.

'Sure, sure. What goes on out there?'

'Telesales, my dear chap; orders, to you.'

Kenton was already inside McCreadie's office, inspecting various framed certificates on the mahogany panelling, a mixture of trade accolades and several attesting to McCreadie's capabilities in his field.

'Now then, how may we be of service?'

'Your staff Christmas bash was at the Copford Hotel on the eighteenth December, correct?'

'You'll forgive me if I consult the ol' diary. Last year is but now but a distant sales budget.' The man had dry sagging skin around the eyes, the toll of late-night client entertainment.

McCreadie pulled out a leather-bound desk diary from the lower desk drawer. 'Now then . . . hmm, no, our party was at the Lakes golf club on the fifteenth . . .'

'The hotel was insistent it was CBS. Monday eighteenth. Are you sure?'

'A Monday? Wait.' He held up bejewelled finger and picked up the phone. 'Some of the other departments; like finance,' he hissed conspiratorially, but nevertheless betraying he was not as grand as he portrayed. His was a fiefdom, not the entire kingdom. 'Ah, Alan, when was the bean counters' bash in December? The police are interested . . . No, not in you, old son.' He winked and then gave the thumbs-up. 'Well, actually, if it was the eighteenth, they might like a word. Incoming.' He hung up. 'Number bods always go for a Monday; cheapest night of the week. And the nearer it is to Christmas, the better – less hungry mouths to feed, having taken extra hols.' He rose. 'Come on, I'll guide you. Last year they held a Christmas party in January, but it proved a damp squib, even for them.'

The accounts department were in demountable huts back towards the entrance, beyond the staff car park. The chief accountant sat alone, hunched in a corner office with a cigarette hanging over a deep ashtray and full enough to be the devil's singed blancmange. Alan Doughty did not once engage in eye contact. To his credit, as he listened to the nature of their enquiry, he merely maintained a lugubrious stare into the snowy car park, bottom lip a slight pout, damp with spittle.

'I'm sorry, you asking me who went?' he said.

'Yes, that a problem?' Brazier said. 'Can you recall?'

He picked up a sachet of sugar, tore it open and emptied it in his mouth. 'No. Not forty-odd people I can't. Hold on.' He picked up the phone.

As they waited for his secretary to root out a list, Kenton stretched, arching his back, turning his head this way and that. And it was then that he saw her through the glass. The shape of her hair and shoulders, as her figure moved about the coffee machine beyond the accountant's office, chatting with a man with bouffant hair and an earring. In the moment, he froze. He brought his elbows down, clumsily alerting Brazier's attention towards her.

Meanwhile, a short plain-faced individual arrived, placing two sheets of A4 before the chief accountant as ash caught on his navy tie. As Doughty ran a yellowed finger down one of the sheets, mumbling to himself about whether he remembered such and such, Kenton interrupted him to ask if he could confirm who the woman was.

'Chloe. Chloe Moran,' he said.

'What does she do?' Brazier said, quickly.

'Cost accountant, next door.'

'Was she there? At the party?'

Only then did he look them square on, taking on board they were the police and not here without good reason.

'She's on the list,' he said eventually.

CHAPTER 60

Tim swept at the warehouse floor listlessly. His new abode was freezing cold and damp and so shortly after the policemen had dropped him off, he came to work. Why had they let him go just like that? He expected to be detained immediately – not necessarily charged but held and awarded legal aid.

The system protected vicars like it did schoolteachers. More so – Symonds had the entire might of the Church behind him. Tim was desperate to be arrested; from there, a solicitor would be assigned him and he could begin to destroy Symonds, publicly humiliate and shame him. Then, if Symonds had a shred of decency, perhaps he'd hang himself too . . .

Tim didn't know the intricacies of the legal system but knew he needed the establishment's support to legitimise his case, to challenge the authorities that had wrecked him: a solicitor would *have* to help him. Although now, doubt slowly arose in his mind. What if nothing went according to his plan? The familiar tension of anxiety was clawing at his neck. 'Abject stress', the doctors called it – though it didn't matter what it was called, the fact he couldn't think straight was all that mattered.

A voice echoed out from the dark recesses of the warehouse, disturbing his volatile thoughts, and reminded him his fingers ached with cold. Tim had no gloves on and the wood of the broom handle was hard and aggressive against soft tissue not used to contact more challenging than holding a spoon and fork. The warehouse was like a giant freezer. One of the lads had brought in a thermometer to confirm it was colder in here than outside; he was proven correct. Tim had every layer of clothing he possessed under the two dust coats he was wearing. Nobody had thought to see he if was equipped for the wider world when he left the hospital. What need had he for a winter coat inside Severalls, where the heating was on 24/7 and outside activity restricted to fine-weather days? And he had no money until he was paid by TimberHouse. The parka, which wasn't lined, he found under the bed at the hostel. Two months he'd waited for this job, and now he was due to receive a wage packet: his first experience of possessing cash since he was a little boy in the form of pocket money. For two months, he'd sat staring at the walls in the hostel, with less to do than in hospital, which at least had been warm.

When Tim's teeth began to chatter, it was a signal: enough was enough. He placed the broom up against a stack of redundant artificial Christmas trees, and went in search of his supervisor to ask directions to the police station.

Chloe Moran could do little to hide her surprise. At first, she was confused, as often happens when a face is familiar but can't be placed, being in the wrong surroundings, but then a wave of panic hit her. The police were here, at her place of work. Doughty shut the door to a room in the main building, leaving the three of them at a table. There were no windows and nothing in the room apart from a box of Kleenex on the table. The room's purpose was usually for the delivery of grim news.

'I'm sorry, I didn't expect to see you here, so forgive my reaction.' She held her hand to her chest to emphasise her surprise and the apology. 'Is there news on Bruce?'

'You could say that, yes,' Kenton said.

'Your festive bash in Copford, good one, was it?'

Her mouth hung open. 'Oh . . . the car. Crikey, I can't remember that, was quite boozy as these things are . . .'

'The reason we ask you, see, is the car your ex wound up in was that of a salesman who happened to be staying at the hotel that same night in December.'

'Yes, I seem to remember that.'

'But didn't think to mention that you'd been at the hotel yourself?'

'That was over two months before . . . why would I? . . . Wait, are you suggesting I stole that car, and . . . murdered my ex-husband?'

'Are we saying that?' Brazier turned to consult his partner.

'No, but we are saying that a chatty sales rep from the north of England, on his last trip of the year, might have shared details of when he might next be down.'

'It was the staff Christmas party, why would I be talking to a sales rep?'

'I know you have a partner, Chloe, but everyone lets their hair down at Christmas.'

'How bloody rude! What business is it of yours what I do?'

'Did you have a smooch with a stranger?' Kenton said evenly. 'Did you meet a man by the name of Ian Healey that evening?'

She shook her head violently. 'Oh, I don't bloody know – or care! Now, do you mind if I return to work or are you arresting me?'

'No, you're good to go. But try to cast your mind back, will you? Bear in mind we'll be interviewing everyone from your company that was there.'

Chloe turned on her heels and all but slammed the door.

Brazier tutted. 'Reckon she had a fling?'

The door no sooner closed than it opened.

'Your list, gentlemen.'

'Cheers.' Brazier reached for it. He screwed up his face in disbelief. 'Bloody hell!'

'What?'

'Mandy Beech.'

The police station was not as Tim imagined it would be. A new, almost sci-fi building, fringed in blue, that to him was more imposing than the old psychiatric hospital. The pristine tiled floor and clean polished glass were a stark contrast to the familiar and worn paintwork of the Edwardian labyrinth.

'I'd like to hand myself in, please.'

The desk officer did not look up from what he was doing, typing on a keyboard in front of a television screen. Though it could be a computer – Tim had heard of them but never seen one.

'Excuse me—' he raised his voice – 'I am here to admit the to the arson attack on St Nicholas's in Brightlingsea.'

That got the officer's attention. And everyone else's in the station. Within minutes, he found himself in custody. Soon after, he felt the cold he'd endured since he left the hospital finally take hold of his body and consume it. Shivering uncontrollably, he slipped off the chair and lost consciousness.

Downstairs in the cells, Roland Beech, having been charged for vehicle theft, was awaiting release. His solicitor had them bang to rights; it was on record that he could not physically be in two places at once, he was to be released immediately. But now the solicitor had gone the police were dragging their heels in letting him out. Ruminating on his lot, word of a commotion upstairs reached down below and he swore aggressively at the walls at the further delay. Fed up with being treated like scum, he was determined to make someone pay. He had nothing to lose. He wondered where his bloody sister was. She should be here pressing for his release, yet there was no sign of her . . .

CHAPTER 61

Outside the CBS offices, waiting for the windscreen to de-fog, Brazier and Kenton sat deliberating their next move.

Two women connected to the Hopkins case were in the Copford Hotel at a party in December the same night Ian Healey was spouting off about his empty fuel tank. They'd had only minutes to consider Chloe Moran as a serious suspect before she was replaced by the more obvious Mandy Beech. Only Mandy was no longer working at CBS – hers had been a temporary assignment and she had left in January.

'Mandy fixing for her brother to steal the car seems a distinct possibility, but with the knowledge he'd run out of fuel instantly, and in all likelihood he'd get recognised filling up. Why?' Kenton said. 'What's he done to incite her hatred?'

'Makes the house untidy,' Brazier said impatiently, wiping the screen with the back of his glove. 'She didn't want him back.'

'He's been in and out of prison his entire adult life . . . it's not the first time he's been out for a spell. He came out first of December – it's only ten weeks, was he that much of a pain?

No doubt he'll be back inside soon, but there must be more to it than that. Is there a link between her and Hopkins? But she was in the Gladiator the night Hopkins was killed, same as her brother. Or so we think . . .'

'What about *her* getting off with Healey? Can't picture Chloe groping his Man at C&A behind – even just a quickie under the mistletoe.'

'I wouldn't rule it out yet – she was pretty angry when we brought up Healey's name, which signals a guilty conscience to me. Nobody is the person we took them for in this. What do we know about them both – next to nothing? And it's time we did. Damn it. Should have thought of this before.'

Brazier cast a sideways glance at Kenton as he reversed the car out. He was quite a character when he got the bit between his teeth. It was true, they knew nothing of Chloe before her meeting Bruce, apart from her being an army doctor's daughter from Lexden. Maybe the mother required closer scrutiny too. Mandy Beech they knew even less of, only that she had wound up at CBS through a recruitment agency in the town.

'Maybe Mandy works for somebody, scouts easy pickings, before her unwanted bro got out and she didn't want him in the way, mucking things up,' Brazier said. 'Get uniform to check her past employers.'

McCreadie had said there hadn't been vehicle thefts from CBS's staff car park, so they'd start before Mandy had that job. Kenton grabbed the radio handset to leave a message for

Wilde, directing her to help on the background checks, only to receive a curt response from the desk sergeant. 'Seems there's been a bit of a to-do involving a Timothy Windows – fella handed himself in, then promptly collapsed.'

Fifteen minutes later, they were in Southway and being served a lecture from Watt.

'Do you two know anything at all about Care in the Community?'

Yes, they did, having heard it from him in a briefing with the entire force not long ago, but that in itself meant nothing. Until confronted by a real-life incident, officers rarely digested hypothetical difficulties. And who could blame them? Crime on the street today, in the here and now; they'd no room for what might happen, only what was under their noses. Watt, with his background, was more comfortable with the hypothetical, and was in his element regurgitating risks to society. However, a dramatic incident in London had unhelpfully coincided with the arrival of Windows at Southway. It turned the hypothetical into the real: the station chief began to relay what they were not privy to – a bulletin from the Met received last night on the impact of hospital closures in north London.

'In the capital, when the city's institutions were among the first to roll this out,' he continued, 'the transport police soon discovered ex patients travelling up and down the tube all day long because they had nowhere to go. And though an alarming thought in hindsight, it was considered a good result at the time; no one really notices, apart from spooking the occasional commuter. Where's the harm? No, we could live with that. But last night a schizophrenic stabbed a man on the Victoria Line. The whole thing is suddenly considered a massive fuck-up, nothing short of a scandal waiting to blow up in the government's face.' Watt seldom swore.

'What's your point, sir?' Brazier said, disingenuously, seizing an opportunity to rile the chief. 'Sounds to me like this was on the cards. It's not our fault.'

'No, it's not your fault, but that's hardly the point! Do you know how many patients Severalls still holds? Over 700. How do you think that will affect everyday people? They'll be scared out of their wits when this breaks. And this Windows setting fire to a church in Brightlingsea is hardly an auspicious start. Jesus, it's like a bloody . . . I don't know what . . .'

'A beacon, sir?' Kenton said.

'Yes,' Watt scowled. For Watt to be concerned about the impact on the community was a welcome new aspect to his philosophy on policing. Except, Kenton thought, his blanket assessment on the mentally impaired lacked compassion. But one thing at a time.

'What do you want to do?'

'Make it go away.'

'Sorry?'

'It? Meaning what? Not the boy?' Kenton said.

'Yes, I mean Windows. Get rid of him. Call the doctors.'

Nobody spoke. The sound of Brazier twiddling a sweet wrapper in his lap was audible.

'What else is there?' Watts lowered his voice. 'We can't have him roaming the town, shooting incendiary arrows into ecclesiastical rooftops.'

'He's not a serial arsonist, he is only after Symonds. He's been locked up literally half his life, analysing what put him there, stewing, plotting . . . There's no way he's going to go quietly. He's nothing to lose,' Kenton said, 'but we can't send him back. It's not fair.'

'Life's not fair.' Watt leant forward. 'We have to. He's handed himself in? Jesus, what's he expect? With nothing to lose, he may torch the vicar himself.'

'Let's talk to him. Once he realises the options, he may value his freedom.'

'No. You're not a psychiatrist. Lock him up and call the hospital; there are still places, if not here then somewhere else. Like Broadmoor, where they can evaluate whether he should be let out. It's not our call.'

'I must say—' Kenton began, angrily.

'You're a detective, and the job has been done, and done well. The decision hereon is not yours to take. Make sure he is not a danger to himself or others,' Watt said. 'Now, the case of Bruce Hopkins, any news?'

'Nothing,' Brazier said quickly, wanting to be out of the building. Mention of Chloe or Mandy Beech to their chief was pointless until they had concrete evidence.

CHAPTER 62

Chloe found Alan alone in his department, punching numbers intently into an adding machine. A huge coil of paper spilling over the desk. She waited for her boss to finish before interrupting. The ticker of the machine stopped and Alan compared his tally to a computer printout that must have been six inches thick. The accountant grimaced.

'Al?'

He raised his head to her as if disturbed from a dream.

'Sorry about that, with the police. My ex was found dead, I didn't want to tell anyone.'

Reaching for a pack of Superkings, he pushed himself back from the desk. 'Don't worry about it—' he waved her off limply – 'the fella in Abberton. We knew, one of the girls is married to a hack on the *Gazette*.' He raised a cigarette lighter. 'You can be forgiven for keeping that quiet.'

'Oh. I feel so stupid.'

'Don't. It was a long time ago. We all make mistakes.' He smiled. It was the first time he'd looked on her kindly for ages, it seemed.

'I don't know what to say . . . I was very young. You won't tell head office?'

'What do you take me for? I don't tittle-tattle.'

'Sorry.' It was true, for all her misgivings of the old grouch, she never heard him say a bad word against anyone.

'What happened, anyway? With the police? You don't have to tell.'

'Nothing.' Chloe hadn't yet considered the implications of her interview with CID, only the embarrassment of being questioned by the police at the office. 'Actually, nothing at all. I think they were just surprised to see me here . . . they're looking for someone connected with that hotel, as . . .' She trailed off as she saw his expression change; he knew something. 'Wait, what was that piece of paper I saw you carrying as I passed you in the corridor?'

'A list of people that attended the party. Sue always keeps it in her party folder along with the bill, for the food and what have you.'

'And?' She moved closer, shutting his door behind her.

'They saw a name they recognised. A temp. Gone now.'

'Who?'

'I can't say.'

'Oh, come on . . . wait. A woman. When I went to the loo, there was someone talking to that sales rep whose car was stolen. He was next us when we arrived, remember? Who was she . . .?' Then she spied a list of names on the corner of the desk. 'The computer room had temps until January.' Then she made a lunge and snatched the paper. She needn't have been so aggressive, though – Alan remained seated, gently tapping his cigarette into an ashtray, and returned his attention to the year-end trial balance.

Chloe thought back to that night in December, the man with the moustache, winking. She had returned from the bathroom . . . Who was that woman – did she know Bruce?

Outside Southway station, the two detectives stood, alternating between breathing in cold air and cigarette smoke. When there's been a confrontation with the boss, distance is always useful, even if it's only the car park.

'Windows doesn't strike me as the type receptive to care. How many years had he been banged up and not mentioned Symonds or Bryde Park once? That doctor didn't have a clue that the kid's parents were just down the road,' Brazier said.

'Watt's right about one thing – the mother must have had input, she led us to him. We don't know their story. The parents have got off lightly in all this mess.'

Brazier considered the glowing end of his cigarette, mottled orange in the fading light. 'You know, I always fancy a menthol fag in the cold. Sort of feels cleansing.' A pointless remark, because he was at loss to find any good in the world at this moment.

'You've sacked trying to give up, then?'

'Hell, yes. Nobody gives a toss about New Year's resolutions past Valentine's Day. Home and dry,' he said half-heartedly.

'On that basis, then, it's been a success. Congratulations.'

'Thank you. Right, let's do it.' He forced himself to be positive. 'Tell Windows the Church won't press charges, which is true. Drop it or back in the looney bin.'

'Watt's anxious – terrified it'll all kick off here.' Kenton's mind had not moved on from the commander's orders. 'He can no more trust another officer than he can handle a screw-up. County will be breathing down his neck – he's no experience for this sort of thing.'

'So what?' Brazier flicked his cigarette at Watt's Calibra windscreen. 'Who cares about him? While Windows is with us, he's not in the nuthouse. Let's see what we can do before calling the men in white coats. If he can't get Symonds, maybe we can.'

'Agreed. Fob Watt off for an hour,' Kenton said, though he was not as optimistic as his colleague sounded. 'Hello, what's going on with her?'

Wilde was walking stiffly towards them.

'What the hell are you doing out here, when there's a sick man sat in there, waiting for you? Nearly cracked his head open, he did.'

Her reproach was towards Kenton, but Brazier interpreted a smile penetrating the cold in his direction, as she beckoned them to follow. This tiny human signal, at odds with the situation, had perked him up more than he could say. He quickened his step to be in out of the cold.

CHAPTER 63

'What happened? Are you okay?' Kenton asked. Windows' complexion was sickly, jaundiced and very pale. Prominent verdigris veins at the temple added to his look of fragility. He'd been placed in a waiting room. The strip lightning was not flattering, as cold as the snow outside.

'My medication is reacting badly to the weather.' He smiled, holding a mug of tea. 'Apologies for the drama. After years of doing nothing, I'm perhaps a tiny bit impatient.'

'These things take time.' Kenton pulled up a chair and sat hands on knees, head lowered.

'Time passing is something I'm accustomed to. But why must it wait? A crime has been committed. I did it, and have a motive.'

'The Church . . .' will not pursue the matter, was what Brazier wanted to say. He sighed and scraped the chair back, sitting next to Kenton, fidgety to hide his discomfort at not finding a solution to help the lad. Instead, he said: 'Is a huge organisation, and this takes time to process. And let's not forget, the building is their property, so we can't force it.'

'Oh,' Windows said. 'I suppose I could go to the newspapers?'

'If you do that, there's the possibility you may end up in an institution again.'

'Do you think that bothers me? Why would I present myself here if so? You have to arrest me for criminal damage.' He stamped his feet beneath the table.

'If we arrest you, the doctors will be called – you must realise that. Can't you try to put it behind you? Symonds knows, is frightened.'

'It's not enough.'

'Think about it, do you really want to relive that horrible time? Is starting again beyond the realms of possibility? Why put yourself through it?'

'To stop it happening to others,' Windows said angrily. 'Don't you see? This will keep happening, again and again.'

'You don't know that's true . . . Chelmsford police said nobody had been picked up from Bryde Park in years.'

'That woman probably fenced the perimeter off to stop people getting out. There were no gates back then, you could just come and go.'

'I'm not sure about that,' Kenton said, pushing the tall wrought-iron gates from his mind.

'Even so, why should I let it go, him living a virtuous life, pillar of the community? While I sweep floors until the end of my days. I might have been anything.' His eyes blazed up at them.

'And you still could be – channel that energy elsewhere, not in here, you're a bright lad . . .'

He sat unflinching. The mood was dangerous.

'Give us more,' Brazier said. 'Give us something to nail Symonds.'

'What? Like what?'

Brazier looked to the floor. He'd never been in a case like this and couldn't figure out what he needed. All he could feel was instinct of the old school and a desire to kick the crap out of the vicar. Kenton sat helplessly next to him. They needed time. 'Hey, been meaning to ask, where's your bow?' Brazier asked, switching the conversation to a more amiable tone.

'My bow?' He was thrown for a moment. 'Oh. Yes. That's in safe-keeping.'

'Where'd you get it? If you don't mind me asking.'

'I made it. Lemonwood on the belly, and bamboo on the outside.'

'An exotic sort?'

'No, not at all, a cheap longbow.'

'Any reason for—'

'It won the English all their wars in the Middle Ages. Agincourt is reason enough. Don't look surprised. I did learn something at Bryde Park.'

'Made it? Where?'

'At the hostel. There was some benefit working at a DIY store. I'd have preferred yew, or ash, bamboo is a touch springy for the lemonwood, but beggars can't be choosers. The tips were stainless-steel rivets.'

'The flights though are pheasant feathers?'

For a moment he was stunned.

'Charred remains,' Kenton said.

'Ah, very good. Yes, I picked them up in the hospital grounds.'

'Okay, wait here. We need to talk to our guv'nor.'

'May I use the toilet?'

'Sure.' Kenton opened the door and nabbed a passing uniform to show Windows the lav.

'Think, think, think,' Kenton said desperately once Windows had been escorted out. 'We can't hold off for long, what if he passes out again? I didn't think of medicine – what's he taking . . .? Maybe it's best we just call the hospital . . .?'

Brazier too was at a loss. They left the waiting room and paced the corridor anxiously for a couple of minutes.

'Pretty clever, though, crafting his own weaponry while at work,' Brazier said.

'Exactly.'

'We need to press him on where he's stashed the bow. It wasn't at the crime scene and he didn't have it with him when we dropped him at his new digs. It's more evidence, if nothing else.'

'Agreed. Let's . . .' Kenton trailed off as the uniform who'd taken Windows to the toilet passed them, alone. 'Hey! Where's the young fella in the parka?'

'Dunno, Sarge, left him in the khazi for a minute and he wasn't there when I came back. He not come back here?'

CHAPTER 64

Windows had disappeared. He'd left the station without a word.

Kenton was cagey with what he told Brightlingsea police – and avoided admitting they'd let a potentially dangerous man simply walk out of the station – only saying the man responsible for the fire was at large. The Brightlingsea police, on hearing such vagueness, were sceptical about placing a guard outside the vicarage. This man had been at large since the day of the fire, after all.

'Why don't you warn him yourself, Sergeant? We're not a protection service. I doubt he'd listen to us anyway, knowing him. But if he thinks he's in danger, he'll be sure to let us know.'

'I'm telling you, damn it – if the vicar ends with an arrow through the neck, you'll have to answer for it,' Kenton raised his voice, 'so get two men down there now and keep them there until we find Timothy Windows, and suggest to the vicar it'll be in his best interest to remain at home.'

Windows would only try to kill Symonds if all else failed.

The question was what that 'all else' could be – what were his alternatives?

Kenton hung up. 'Protection,' he muttered. 'Someone is protecting Tim. He must have a friend out here.'

'Someone with a motor? He needs to get around. How else would he get to Kempe Marsh? Wait—' Brazier banged the desk with his fist – 'geezer in the pub saw two people walking on the sea front – a couple – man and woman?'

'Well remembered.' Kenton dialled the hands-free. He realised by now how mercurial his colleague was, and right now, Brazier wouldn't lift a finger to save the vicar. When it boiled down to it, Brazier would quite happily see the vicar skewered against St Nicholas's door.

The phone at Severalls rang and rang before he was told Dr Jessop was unavailable and the remainder of the dwindling hospital staff appeared to have no clue of Windows' existence or if Jessop was even returning. With a growing sense of panic, Kenton then called a social services number he found on a memo giving details of those responsible for assigning council housing to patients. Vulnerable patients were in wardened flats and those deemed more capable in shared housing. Community workers would still check on a regular basis, helping ex-patients adapt to life outside: how to cook, where the launderette was, day-to-day tasks that had hitherto been done for them. Even though they'd dropped Windows off, the community worker wasn't authorised to give out details and confirm that it was the correct address.

'Can you at least tell us whether he has support – or is he living alone?'

'How do I know you're the police?' he snapped in a squeaky voice accentuated by the speakerphone. 'I need authorisation.'

'You phone me back then, Colchester nick, ask for Detective Sergeant Kenton. And do it immediately. We're very concerned for this individual's well-being.'

'Our guidelines are precise,' the voice continued, 'no information over the phone. These people are vulnerable, and for many of them, it's their first experience of normal life in a very long time. They don't want old acquaintances dropping in on them out of the blue—'

'We're not old acquaintances, we're the police—'

'And we are ever mindful that some old acquaintances may bear grudges. We, as carers, leave it for the patients to make up their minds whom they wish to see, and if they need assistance, we are only—'

'Right, you – don't move an inch. I'm coming down there,' Brazier said.

An hour later, they were no further ahead, other than terrifying a very inexperienced clerk, fresh out of college, who'd frantically confirmed Windows' address, and worryingly that he lived alone.

The TimberHouse store where Windows worked was on St Andrew's Avenue. Tim's manager there was a lean man in his fifties and was guarded, seemingly not wanting to jeopardise the young man's future. He said little beyond commenting on the young man's attitude to his job. Windows worked hard, without complaint, and was eager to learn what he could, especially in the carpentry department, where he had mastered both saw and wood plane. 'No kidding,' Brazier said. Wasting no further time, they headed south on the A12 to see Windows' mother – only to sit for an hour outside the empty Willow Farm as they waited for someone to return home.

Eventually, Elizabeth Windows rolled into the dark drive, emerging from a BMW with several shiny plastic bags from a Chelmsford department store, which she appeared to struggle with.

'Please excuse me, I need to catch my breath,' the woman said as she sat them in the front room, without removing her coat, bags either side under the wings of an armchair, visibly exhausted. They explained that Tim had turned himself in but then absconded before being either charged or released, and that his whereabouts was now unknown.

'I don't know what you expect from me,' she said eventually.

'Have you no concern for Tim?'

'On a human level, yes. But as your investigation will have no doubt revealed, we are not Timothy's natural parents. Although we received him as a baby, he never took to us.'

CHAPTER 65

'Can you elucidate?' Kenton asked. Elizabeth Windows had divested herself of coat and hat, and now sat with a glass of water. Lank grey hair lay plastered across her forehead. Behind her was a large open-hearth fireplace, big enough to stand in.

'Do you have children, detective?' she countered, bravely.

'Two.'

'You?'

Brazier shook his head.

'I was unable to have children, to have one was all I ever dreamt of. Tim was a nervous child, and the local schools are – I don't want to a be a snob – rough and unpleasant. We thought in a small, caring private school surrounded by children his own age, he would find learning easier and he might thrive. When he did not . . .'

'I think that's enough, Elizabeth, time for a rest. Gentlemen, Tim's been in the hands of the best healthcare in the in world, the NHS.' A nattily dressed, narrow-shouldered man in a waistcoat had appeared from nowhere; the husband, who had been in the house all along, was now suddenly protective of his wife.

'My husband, Dr Windows.'

'Ah, a medical man in our midst. And you work for the provider of the best healthcare in the world, presumably?' Brazier asked.

'No. I am an ophthalmologist. Eye specialist. The NHS has always been the best when it comes to diseases of the mind.'

'We'll have to take your word for that, Doctor,' Kenton said.

'Am I to understand you have lost him?' the doctor asked stiffly.

'What makes you say that?'

'Why would you be here otherwise?'

'We don't think he'd come to you,' Kenton said flatly. That Tim had not, even for mercenary reasons, sought out his adoptive parents sent a chill through Kenton: Windows' mission was all-consuming. But then that had been obvious from the moment they met him. 'In fact, I'm sure he's not strayed far at all.'

'Quite. Timothy is where he was meant to be,' the doctor commented.

'Oh?' Brazier said loudly.

The wife's pale face pinched. The doctor had slipped up.

'You wouldn't happen to know Timothy's birth parents?' Brazier placed his hands behind his head and stretched out his legs, digging the heels of his trainers into the plush carpet. 'Being a doctor, you must – could – have had access to this information.'

Husband and wife exchanged glances.

'You best tell them, Anthony,' Mrs Windows said, her voice growing weak, though her eye lingered on a hole in the sole of Brazier's trainer.

'You must know that until recently, pregnancy out of wedlock was completely frowned upon.' Anthony Windows lifted a cut-glass decanter from the sideboard and poured himself and his wife a drink. 'The sixties may have been promiscuous, and the seventies full of hippy sentiment, but in decent homes, a schoolgirl getting pregnant was forced by her parents to give the baby away.'

'Yeah, yeah, spare us the lecture . . .' Brazier said.

Dr Windows remained standing, resting his glass above his elaborately waistcoated paunch, and did not hide his contempt for the unsightly policeman slumped on his £5,000 sofa. 'A colleague in the profession called me. Their fourteen-year-old daughter, a young tearaway, found herself in the family way. Knowing of our desire for a child, we offered to help. Her husband held a senior post on the army garrison, a medical officer, at Colchester, the wife also in medicine, private practice, and they were fearful of repercussions . . .'

'Name.'

'Major Richard Moran.'

The enormity of what they were hearing was shocking. Kenton turned to gauge Brazier's reaction – his expression was frozen, eyes staring into space.

'Dead now,' Windows continued, unaware, 'at least five years ago.'

Brazier snapped out of it and said, 'The daughter. Would she know what happened to the boy?'

'Good lord, no. Nor Tim. Only the girl's mother will know. Unless, of course, she chose to share, which ethically—'

'Ethics.' Brazier snorted. 'Screw ethics.'

'And that teacher, remember?' Elizabeth Windows spoke barely above a whisper. 'When Tim wouldn't go back to school, flatly refused, rebelling without a reason, this teacher – I can't remember his name, very nice – called on the telephone, in September. His form tutor or house master . . .'

'Continue,' Kenton said.

Ignoring the drink poured by her husband, she took a sip of water. 'He suggested a meeting. I asked him round to the house to try and talk Tim round, but he felt that too invasive and suggest we meet for coffee. In Billericay, I think it was. So long ago now. In an effort to be kind, he said that with such wonderful, successful parents such as us, he was sure that Tim would pull through.' She sighed. 'He could tell from our expression that something wasn't right so I told them our son was adopted at birth.

'Mr Hopkins was his name, said would we mind if we kept him abreast of the situation regarding Tim's health. At that time, we still held out hope for him returning to school . . . however, events then overtook us, and the doctors were brought in, when Tim started to . . . hurt himself.' Elizabeth

Windows faltered. Only now did any sign of emotion come to the surface. 'I telephoned the school and spoke to the headmaster, explained that Tim was not going back to Bryde Park and that we were seeking medical help. Soon after, Mr Hopkins called to say how sorry he was and asked if he could help in any way. I was particularly vulnerable at that time and Anthony was in London at the flat a lot—'

'Liz, that's not—' Windows motioned for her to stop.

'No, Anthony, I will tell it. I was lonely and miserable. He offered to take me out to dinner, which I agreed. And I told him how we had failed. That was when I told him we had helped a friend out in Colchester.'

PART 5

CHAPTER 66

The following morning, Roland Beech let himself into the cold and empty house. He had not gone home directly after his release, instead he'd surprised Fat Roger sleeping off a lunchtime session and together the two had worked through the latter's supply of puff and strong cider late into the night.

He shook off his heavy wet leather jacket and chucked it over the banister despondently. Now home, he had nothing to do, and the relief of release swiftly faded. He'd hoped to get back before Mandy had left for work so he could cadge some money, but he'd missed her, even though it had just gone eight. He was skint and his spirits were low. The police had treated him as a sap – he'd been set up. Who, though? Who had a grudge against him? He'd not given it any thought until now. Jesus, he'd been locked up for five years, who could he possibly have offended? Someone on the building site? No, they thought he wasn't worth the trouble: Beech was 'useless', as the site foreman had said. Wretched from the night's excesses, there was nothing for it but to go to bed. He dug into his jean pockets and emptied the contents on the kitchen table. If he could just eke out the price of a pint, that would take him out of the house, come lunchtime . . . but only the seventy-seven pence he already knew to be there was revealed, dull and disappointing before him. He stared at it. Fifty pence of this was from the meter pot, and so the house would remain unheated until Mandy got in. Without cash, he couldn't move, tap people up, find out the name of the bloke that set him up. He shoved the kitchen drawer shut, where he'd looked for the umpteenth time for some cash only to see the same manky Ever Ready batteries and radiator keys.

Mandy was working. She must have money, he reasoned. She'd not begrudge him a couple of quid. Her room at the back of the house was neat and tidy, the counterpane on the bed folded back smooth without a crease. He never ventured in here. At the foot of the bed was a dressing table and mirror. Lipsticks, hairspray and make-up stuff. Among it he saw some loose change, sitting on a bill. He went over and scooped up the silver and coppers, counting into the palm of his hand – there might just be enough. The bill beneath was red, for the satellite TV. He picked it up and studied it: paid with cash the day before the police called. Mandy had a bank account and cheque book.

Why had she allowed it to go unpaid for so long? An innate breeze of mistrust swirled about him, prompting him to poke around his sister's room. Was it her that nabbed his money and not the police? At first, he moved about carefully and cautiously, fingering the contents of the wardrobe lightly, but soon his

354

search became clumsy with a mixture of anxiety and anger, until he didn't care whether he left a trace or not. Finding nothing to either calm his clamour or provoke it further, he whipped up the counterpane, sank to his knees and peered under the bed.

At first he thought it was some old fishing rods, but no. 'What the . . .?'

He reached underneath.

Since Hopkins' return, Margaret Moran had been anticipating something like this would happen. That he'd bring all the misery back, bursting forth into the here and now. Yet somehow, when she heard the police sirens growing closer, she still did not expect them to arrive on her own doorstep.

On her drive were two police cars with flashing lights.

'Heavens, what will the neighbours think?' she mumbled. It was eight thirty and pupils en route to the grammar school had stopped to stare.

The two plain clothes officers emerging from the car were those that were here before. This time they were accompanied by uniformed officers. She checked her hair in the hallway mirror before answering the door.

'Mrs Margaret Moran, we have come to arrest you on suspicion of the murder of Bruce Hopkins. You . . .'

She didn't hear the rest. Her eyes misted, a lack of focus rather than any emotion. When her vision returned, the policemen were motionless on the doorstep. 'Why?' she said simply, this word apparently signalling to the men they could enter the house without being asked. One, in uniform, held back to shut her front door and remained there, arms crossed, close enough for her to smell his cheap aftershave.

'Now, off the record, I can't say that I blame you.' The voice of the one with bed hair echoed from the hallway. She turned and followed them into her house. 'But we need you to sit down and help us understand what the fuck is going on. Because from where we are standing this is too weird to make any sense.'

'On what grounds are you arresting me?'

'Soon, Mrs Moran, soon. The case goes back years and years, let's not rush, eh?' Brazier flopped down in an armchair, as if home after a hard day's work. 'Did you read about the church that was set ablaze?'

'No, I can't say that I—'

'Out near Brightlingsea, place called Kempe Marsh. A man confessed – you may know the name. Timothy Windows. Your grandson, we believe.' Brazier spoke quickly to get the words out in the open.

Margaret looked blankly at them both. 'What are you talking about?'

'Now, it doesn't matter how we know him to be a relation of yours, the question is, how much you know.' Kenton remained standing, but opened his coat and loosened his tie, feeling hot. 'About what happened to Chloe's kid after you gave him away in the September of 1969.'

Margaret had come to terms with her decision, a decision made over twenty years ago.

'In those days,' she began, 'if your daughter got pregnant at fourteen you gave the baby away, it was as simple as that.' She addressed the policeman with the loosened tie. 'It seems cruel, but that's how things were done. In polite society. Did I know of the child's fate? Yes . . . Elizabeth told me. Tragic, tragic. I didn't know he was—' she was going to say 'better' but stopped herself – 'out. What do you mean, he set fire to a church? As in arson? And what does this have to do with Bruce?'

'Everything.'

Margaret sat and listened. She heard a harrowing story of a boy's experience at a boarding school. Part of it she knew, from Hopkins. Two other men she'd never heard of, also teachers, were involved in an unspecified way. One was now the vicar of the church set alight. When she spoke again, her tone was detached – she couldn't get any words out without somehow removing herself from what she must say. 'When Bruce came, the other day, I saw him for what he was – a twisted, evil man disguised as a debonair bachelor. I asked to see this letter that he claimed brought him back. No, he didn't have it. Did it ever exist? I doubt it. Nevertheless, I quizzed him, on what, quite frankly, was an unwanted and unexpected return to this country. But Bruce was jubilant, empowered by Chloe's *letter*, its magnanimity. Revelling in her forgiveness.'

'And what did he say of Tim?'

'Barely anything at first.' She cleared her throat. 'He spoke opaquely – said . . . he said our secret had . . .'

Margaret Moran paused.

'Had what?' Brazier prompted.

'Given him "joy". I think that was the word. Then I ordered him to leave the house. He wouldn't go – insisted I hear him out. So . . . so I did. Listen to him explain how he came into our lives . . . that he was once a schoolteacher at a private school, the one you mention, and that this one pupil in particular had difficulties, and Bruce developed an interest in the child's well-being, just as you tell it. The child's plight led him to my daughter.'

'Joy?' Brazier spat.

'Go on,' Kenton said.

She nodded.

'Following the summer holiday of 1979, the child did not return to school for the start of the new term. Bruce contacted the parents. They explained the situation, that the boy was in hospital. The mother eventually revealed that the boy was adopted. And thus Bruce found his way here, as have you.'

'Except by a different route.'

'Yes. I was partner in a practice here in Lexden. It was not difficult for Bruce to trace Chloe, who at that time, being in her twenties, was rather disappointingly still doing mostly bar work and still living at home. And him, much older – at least ten years – I never asked – lurking in the street beneath the trees, he said, engineering a meeting. Most unsavoury behaviour. They were married in May 1980 after courting for only six months, after his ceaseless urging her on – and for what? He was gone by the end of the year. You could laugh if it wasn't so sad.'

Brazier and Kenton exchanged glances.

'So, Hopkins confesses this to you the afternoon he arrives. Go on.'

'Yes. I telephoned Chloe immediately after to find out if it was true that she had written to him. She did not answer the telephone and didn't call me back until the following day. She denied writing. I wondered if she would lie to me, but she is fit as a fiddle, not ill as Bruce had claimed the letter said . . . I wondered what Bruce's game was, but by then he must have already been dead.' She paused, awaiting questions.

'Why would he tell you all this?' Kenton asked.

'Must I spell it out?'

'I think it's the very least you can do.' Brazier added.

'He took pleasure in telling me – about what he called his "relationship" with Timothy – I think he was threatening me. I was to remain silent or come to his aid should he wish it, otherwise he'd tell Chloe everything.'

'How much of this does Chloe know?'

'None of it, she has no idea. That's the point. The adoption has not been mentioned since that day.'

'And did Bruce touch on why Tim Windows had been in an institution these last ten years?'

'He said the boy was disturbed, that from an early age he

began to self-harm and sadly the hospital was the best place for him. This, regardless of what you think, was hard to hear, and it's why I was dubious of Chloe finding out.'

'But now, what do you think?' Brazier asked.

Margaret Moran's face was granite. 'Nothing. I think nothing.'

'Right,' Kenton said. 'Time we moved this to the station. Mrs Moran?'

'Wait,' Brazier interrupted, 'did Hopkins know Tim was discharged from hospital?'

'No, he didn't mention it. I didn't know either, until you said Timothy had confessed to setting fire to a church.'

CHAPTER 67

'In the beginning you encouraged Hopkins to court your daughter, according to Chloe. Would it be fair to say you were equally taken in by him?' Kenton asked. As Brazier had blithely remarked, the police were not going to rush things with Margaret Moran, the situation was complex, and they must be thorough, certain that everything added up. And they still had no lead on Tim's whereabouts. Uniform were watching his address, and hunting anywhere they thought he might be likely to show; Kempe Marshe, Billericay, Stock, even Bryde Park was put on alert. Nothing. He'd simply disappeared.

'Correct. We all make mistakes, Sergeant.' This woman now struck them as old, and out of place in the interview room; her terracotta hair obviously dyed and sprayed into place; her neat turquoise dress somehow old-fashioned. Yet she was not intimidated and had not requested legal representation. Or asked to telephone her daughter. All she desired was a cup of tea. 'Similarly, he may have charmed Elizabeth Windows, I dare say.'

'What was it about him?'

'Clever, intelligent. Witty. Not like the yobs round here. Clearly well brought up, spoke well, good manners.'

'Good education opens many doors,' Brazier said, lighting a cigarette. 'Did he say he'd taught, back then, before he'd met your daughter?'

She stared hard at him across the table, as if trying to elicit something, then said, 'Among other things, yes. But it soon transpired he didn't have a job, work, do anything – he proclaimed to be a gem expert.'

'He stole your eternity ring. And that's not all.'

'My, you have been digging.'

'Not really. We were out to establish the relationship Hopkins had with your family. Understandably, you feel resentment – taking you and your daughter for fools, it's not surprising you were keen on revenge.'

'You really think I killed him?'

'There's a motive,' Kenton said, frankly. 'Your daughter has a future now, you'd not welcome anyone messing it up. And let's face it, you didn't come forward and shout, "Hey, this bastard is back and has been to my house."'

Brazier leant forward and blew smoke in her face as she lifted the teacup. 'And you know, *you do know*, Mrs Moran, what he did to that kid, your grandson, and still you did nothing.'

The woman blinked. 'I was protecting my daughter. Had I called the police, there was a risk it would all come out. Tim is now a man. I'm as outraged as you at what Bruce Hopkins has done – you talk to me as if I planned it! Good lord, the outcome might have been the same had the child stayed in our family and was then sent to that school. I did what was the done thing at the time and can't rewrite the past.'

'No, just cover it all up, like you've done all along. Yes, I think you killed him.' Brazier was annoyed – annoyed with her attitude. And in turn, that attitude gave him misgivings about her guilt, despite what he had said.

'Okay, but just suppose it wasn't me – that I didn't possess the supernatural strength to kill a man twice my size. What if it was my grandson?'

'He was in sheltered accommodation at the time. They keep a record of the comings and goings. Besides, he can't drive. He'd not know the Hare.'

'Yes, I suppose.' She sighed. 'Let's hope not.'

Her tone of foreboding pricked Brazier further. They had taken Windows at face value: that he had confessed to the fire, yes, but they had only made a summary investigation into whether he had killed Hopkins. They'd not even checked the video tape at the hostel. Now Windows had vanished.

Margaret perceived unease in the room and continued: 'But if my grandson *were* responsible, and it's not beyond the realms of possibility, given he's set a church ablaze, he would need to have a friend on the outside helping him get about.'

'Yes, that has occurred to us. We're investigating all avenues,' Brazier said. 'Likewise on Hopkins' movements – a cashier from a department store came forward, said he bought a coat in the High Street, and someone else thought they recognised him briefly in a wine bar not far from here. Pretty careless behaviour but then we have reason to believe his health wasn't great. It's possible he was making his last farewells.'

'Hmm. He looked dreadful,' Margaret Moran said. 'In that case, I wonder who else he's spoken to? I pray Timothy has not discovered Chloe had given him away as a baby. I dread to think what might happen.'

'Had he done so,' said Kenton, 'you'd be in the firing line too.'

She turned her gaze on him and said stoically, 'I don't doubt it for one minute.'

CHAPTER 68

When Mandy was released from Severalls, the first thing she did was check out everything Tim had told her. Piece by piece, she had built his story. Here was a person that had never known affection, like herself, and was owed.

However, Mandy did not want him to go to prison or return to hospital and would do whatever it took to keep him out of both. Mandy had picked Hopkins up at the pub in Layer and driven him to the wood, having spiked his drink. She was not present at the end, having gone to bury Hopkins' clothes in the snow, and missed it. When she came back to the car, Tim said that it had been easier than he thought with all this snow. She handed over Hopkins' wallet, where Tim found a Spanish note. He had smiled at her in the dark and said, 'Ah. This will be a nice touch.'

Now she was here, outside Colchester's Castle Park in the centre of town, waiting for him. She'd told Tim it'd be okay, that the grounds would be full of people sledding on the slopes and chucking snowballs about beneath the castle walls. There he was, standing outside the castle gates, where she could swiftly collect him. And though having Tim incarcerated again was the last thing she wanted in the world, she could not prevent herself doing anything he wanted, anything at all.

'Where did you spend last night?' she asked.

'Somewhere warm, and familiar,' he said, 'and the last place they'd look.'

'You didn't!' she squealed, 'the hospital!'

'The old wards have never been so peaceful, I only had to turn the radiators on.'

'Clever,' she said, 'Where to? Kill the vicar?'

'Not today, Mandy,' he said calmly. 'They will expect me to go to Kempe Marsh, perhaps not straight away . . .'

Whatever Tim did next would alter the rest of his life. 'It's a joke,' he said. So many days, endless days had passed amounting to nothing – only to this point, where in an instant it could all disappear after one rash act of madness.

'Snug though the hospital is, there is nothing to eat on that particular wing. I need to get off the street, as they say on television. I can't go to the flat.'

'I'll take you home.'

'What about your brother?'

'I'll deal with him.'

'Is he still clueless?'

'As the day he was born.' They crossed St Botolph's round-about and headed up the Mersea Road. 'I'll say you're my boyfriend.'

Tim prickled at the suggestion. Any reference to sex, even

indirect, with anyone – man or woman – was abhorrent. He couldn't allow himself to be touched. Even so, he said, 'Yes, say that.'

He caught Mandy turn to admire him, but he didn't respond. His head buzzed and his sight was fogged – he was not 100 per cent and was having trouble keeping his thoughts in order. With Symonds eluding him, he went back to Hopkins' last moments alive. What the fat disgusting pig had mumbled drugged to the eyeballs, near naked and freezing in the snow behind Mandy's Opel, he had not allowed into his conscious, until now. It had seemed so far-fetched.

He was adopted, that he knew – Emma had discovered that in Severalls. That explained the lack of attachment with 'Liz and Tony'. But Hopkins, pleading for his life, said he himself had married the woman that gave him up for adoption. Hopkins did it to try and save him, he said. It had to be a lie. Begging for his life, he'd say anything. Who was his real father, then? But Hopkins wore a wedding ring; he couldn't have slipped that on in anticipation of what was to befall him. And unwanted though he surely was, Tim was born to someone after all.

Tim had kept this from the police as he had kept it from himself. He'd seen the woman though, visited her in her flat just to see if she existed. And there she was. Pretty, with eyes that—

'Tim?' Mandy's voice was distant. He wondered how long he'd been elsewhere. The car was stationary in a housing estate, where the snow sat unmoved. 'I will kill the vicar for you.'

And then he saw her. 'I knew you would.' He sparkled as he said that. 'But there's someone we need to find first.'

'The woman? The one Hopkins mentioned.' She couldn't bring herself to say the word 'mother'.

CHAPTER 69

Gophering for CID was not the same as actually working with them, as Watt had planned, but Wilde wasn't going to make waves. Not while she was interested in Brazier, at least. First, they'd asked her to investigate a Billericay florist's phone bill for overseas calls, which she'd not yet been able to do, and now, this afternoon, she'd been tasked with finding out Amanda Beech's work placements from the last twelve months and checking on unresolved thefts in the immediate vicinity. If she found nothing, and this stolen car at the Copford hotel was a one-off, what did that mean? Mandy Beech was out to get her brother?

The temp agency in the town was forthcoming on Mandy Beech's work record. Recruit Right was in the High Street, and the women wore stuffy uniforms; white vertical ruff-stroke-frilly blouses under navy blazers. They looked like a cross between an airline stewardess and Adam Ant.

'You're the second one to ask after her,' an agent with very long nails said, reaching below her desk for a file.

'Oh yeah?' Wilde said.

'Lady came by from Colchester Book Supply, saying she had jewellery belonging to Miss Beech. It had been left in the loo at a Christmas party . . .'

'What did you say to her?' Wilde said. Highly unlikely: who else was after Mandy Beech?

'I gave her the home address. Not work, of course, that's confidential.'

Baffling logic, thought Wilde. 'Mandy Beech left CBS over a month ago – don't you think they might have found it and tried to return it a tiny bit sooner?'

The agent, untroubled, said, 'It was returned from a hotel, doesn't matter when, the fact it was handed in is all that counts.'

Wilde hurriedly made a note of the past employers, except instead of following up afterwards, she made for the Monkwick estate. It couldn't be a coincidence that someone else was hunting for Mandy Beech.

CHAPTER 70

Chloe had known a boy once from Monkwick, before she was going out with Phil. She'd caught the bus to the estate to see him before his older brother drove them to a Pink Floyd gig at the university. Now, she parked her MG outside the estate's row of shops – which struck her as having the same facades as they had back then in 1969. She tried to get her bearings. Deciding she had passed the road she wanted, she got out and walked.

The house was identical to every other red-brick one on the estate, except the Beechs' boasted a satellite dish. She marched up the path and rapped on the door. It opened sharply, and she was greeted by an angry man in a woolly hat.

'What do you want?' he snapped.

'Is Amanda in?'

'Amanda,' he repeated, not so loud now, and then peered over and past her as if checking she was indeed alone.

'Is she, then? In?'

'Not right now, no . . . But I expect her any minute. Come wait inside?'

*

Beech saw someone better off than him. Nice coat. Made up well, not like his slapper of a sister.

She was hesitant.

'Come on, you'll bloody freeze out there. Make you a tea.'

'No, no, I don't want to put you to any trouble . . .'

'No trouble. Kettle's on the hob already.'

'All right then.' She walked ahead of him into the kitchen at the back of the house. The shift in temperature from the outside was negligible.

'Know me sister well, do you?'

Rubbing her gloved hands for cold or nerves, she said, 'No, we've never met.'

'Take a chair.' He pulled one out from the table.

'Thanks. Wow. These look very real. Do you compete?'

'Ha, yes . . . I mean no.' He looked at the arrows he'd found under Mandy's bed. 'They're not mine.'

Chloe noted his mouth harden as he said it.

The kettle started to whistle.

She was certain she had made a mistake by entering this house. She felt trapped, and yet she still took the proffered chair. The stainless-steel tips of the half dozen arrows lay only inches away, glinting under the dull overhead light.

'So what do you want with Mandy?'

'She might know – have known – my husband.'

'Oh, yeah. Who's that?'

She looked up at him as he held the steaming kettle.

'Bruce. Bruce Hopkins.'

He remained motionless, kettle held out, like a statue.

'Sorry, I didn't catch your name,' she said awkwardly.

'I didn't say.'

Uneasy now, she said, 'Look, I think I better go after all.'

'My name's Roland.'

'Eh . . .'

'You know, like the rat that used to be on morning telly.'

'Oh, ha, yes.'

'Bruce Hopkins. Well I never!' He returned to making the tea, his back to her as he reached into a cupboard. 'I knew who he was, but didn't know he had a wife.'

'We split up a long, long time ago. He was found dead in the bottom of—'

'Abberton Reservoir, it was on telly and everything.'

'How did you know him?'

'He was a face around town, knew *of* him more – our paths didn't cross. Too posh for the likes of me. Never spoke. Mandy knew him, you say?'

'Oh, I don't know for sure. Mandy worked at the same place as me, in Tiptree, and was there when the car was stolen, the car that Bruce was found in.'

'The car was from Copford,' Roland said, 'from the hotel.'

Her pale forehead creased. 'Was that in the papers too?'

He'd made a gaff, and said quickly, 'Abberton's not far from here, the word on the estate is it was pinched from over there.'

'Oh, I see. Well, anyway, our Christmas party was there, and— I'm not sure I should be saying . . .'

'If my sister is involved,' he stared at her, 'you must tell me.'

'Can I use the loo?'

'Top of the stairs, but it won't flush – the water has frozen.'

It was dark now in the hallway. He'd not fed the electricity meter.

Chloe rose. He couldn't stop her leaving. All the same, her shoulders tensed as she moved down towards the door. Halfway, the door opened and she met the surprised face of a woman in her early twenties.

CHAPTER 71

Margaret Moran remained in the cells without complaint.

While Kenton had been interviewing her, Dr Jessop had returned his call. This time she had helpfully left a number that would reach her directly.

Kenton dialled the number.

'Doctor, good of you to call back. Things have escalated a tad . . .' He explained simply that Tim had confessed to an arson and, to be blunt, might need to be sectioned. The doctor heard them with good grace, and said, 'I see, well, you better bring him in.'

'There's a snag there. We've lost him.'

'Oh.' She paused. 'Well, when you find him let us know and we'll see what we can do.' The doctor was as matter of fact on the phone as she had been when they'd met.

'Yes, thanks. But before you go, you mentioned patients that Tim had been close to . . . any that were released prior to his own release?'

'Perhaps.'

'Can you look in the file – it mentions he mixed with patients later on. It maybe names them.'

He heard movement down the line.

'It does mention two other patients, back in 1987.'

'Great.'

'Except their names aren't given – only their patient numbers.'

'Oh, so we're stuffed.'

'Not entirely. One is still here.'

Mandy recognised the woman immediately, first having staked out Hopkins' old flat, and later by chance at CBS. Moran was a high flyer, nose up the bosses' arses and was oblivious to the likes of her. Mandy stopped short on the hall rug and felt Tim's closeness, his chest touching her back. Beyond the woman, who was between them, loomed her brother. Rollie had a sort of mischievous leer about him, which was unsettling. Something had changed. His posture was odd – his hands for some reason were behind his back. Mandy couldn't see him straight because Moran was in the way.

'Mandy,' he said, 'who's your friend there?'

'My fella.'

Chloe, thrown by the confrontation, wanted out fast and stepped forward, seizing her chance. That the purpose of her call was to find this woman, Amanda Beech, meant nothing; she knew it was a mistake. What did she care if they had done Bruce in? 'Excuse me,' she said. Mandy moved aside but she was blocked by her companion. Chloe did not look at him, only repeated her request that he let her get by as she moved closer to his shoulder. She picked up a mouldy canvas odour which she had smelt before. Head ever so slightly to the side, she saw an army surplus coat. This man had been in her house.

'Who's this in a hurry to be off?' Mandy said. The woman was about her height.

'Says she's a friend of yours, would you believe,' Roland said.

'A mate of mine?'

'CBS. I work at CBS – you were at the Christmas party. A car was stolen,' Chloe said. 'My ex-husband ended up dead in it. I wanted to find out why you—'

'You bitch!' Roland screamed.

Chloe flinched and spun round to see an arrow less than ten feet away, pointing in her direction. She tried to flee but was jostled by the other two in the hallway and couldn't get clear. An almighty thwack reverberated against the door and someone screamed. It might have been her.

CHAPTER 72

Wilde knew this estate – one of the earlier smaller ones built in the borough soon after the war with its own shops and school. She parked behind an Opel Manta clear of snow, noting the car had recently arrived. The path up to the house showed fresh treads. Several pairs, both coming and going. Wilde continued, crunching the soft snow with her heavy police shoe. The door was ajar, several inches. Just home and left the door open? Not a sound from within. No lights either. Alarm bells rang in her mind. She moved to peer through the window but net curtains hid the inside of the house. Moving back round to the door, she gave it a gentle push. It didn't give much – something was blocking it.

She called inside. 'Hello! Amanda? This is the police – we have a couple of questions for you.'

Nothing.

Leaning her shoulder against the door, she shoved hard. As it gave, something brushed her thigh – she recoiled with a silent gasp on seeing a hand hanging limply by the door's edge. Regaining herself, she poked her head round the door. A body was pinned to it by an arrow.

Wilde's heart was thumping, then a noise from the back of the house nearly caused it to jump out of her throat. The kitchen at the end of the hall. There was blood on the floor. Lots.

Patient 111's room was some distance away, in a far corner of a remote part of the complex. They were escorted down ice-cold corridors by an orderly in a thick jumper. Not just cold, but smelly – there was a definite clinical whiff down this end of the hospital. No murals here, the walls were institutional yellow. Brazier noticed air vents punctuated the corridors' outside walls.

'What's the weird pong, mate?' Brazier asked the orderly.

'Paraldehyde,' he said over his shoulder. 'Helps some of our troubled patients sleep.'

'Holy hell . . .' said Kenton quietly. He leant into Brazer and whispered, 'The stuff Hopkins was pumped full of. Damn it.'

'Here we are.' The orderly stopped and shot a glance through a small square window in the door before entering.

'Checking she's in there?' Brazier said.

'Know she's there, all right. Just where.' He unbolted the door.

The room had a dual aspect and was exceptionally bright, the sun announcing its presence for the first time in weeks by streaming through two large, barred windows. A young woman sat cross-legged on a steel-framed bed in a shadowy corner, head bowed, with a book in her lap. The odour was particularly strong here.

'Visitors, Emma,' the orderly said, then stepped back. The doctor had said for safety he was to remain in the room.

'Excuse me, miss, we'd like to have a word,' Brazier said, noting Kenton hung back too.

'Policemen.'

'Sorry about that. Yes, we are.'

'Timothy wreaking revenge on those that landed him here, I expect. And you want my help to catch him. That's a big ask.' She lifted her head slowly then turned sharply, her white forehead catching in the light. 'Is that you, Detective Kenton?'

Kenton had known the identity of the patient from the moment Jessop retrieved 111's file.

'Hello, Emma. Tim handed himself in. We are trying to help him; trying to keep him safe.'

'Someone on the outside could endanger his chances by leading him astray, and we don't want that.'

'What's your name?' She leant forward. 'I do like your hair.'

'Thanks. Brazier. Detective Brazier.'

'Don't be so formal.'

'Julian.'

'Julian,' she said softly to herself. 'A wonderful name. The first woman to write a book, in a cell smaller than this. Well, Julian, I don't think Tim needs any encouragement to do bad things, do you? Acquainted as you will be with those beastly men that turned him into a demon. I suffered too, Julian, a grown man put me here as a child. Talk to Kenton about that.'

Nuts, thought Brazier, unable to hide his surprise.

'We're wasting our time. She's not going to tell us anything,' Kenton said.

Emma Cliff swung her feet off the bed, her bare legs lost in the light apart from green nail varnish. 'Oh, but Daniel is the good guy, Julian. It's the other one who is *bad*.'

'Have you anything useful to say or not?' Kenton said.

'Roland Beech put his little sister in here,' Emma Cliff said directly to Kenton. 'He used to . . .' She paused, rolling her eyes in thought. 'What's the word? *Fiddle* with her. And as we know, fiddling is not a crime, not now, not yet, and Mummy wouldn't believe her little angel would do that. But if Mandy stopped eating, Mandy could get away. She'd seen it at school. When Mummy came to say Roland was arrested, just like that, Mandy got her appetite back and out she came, cherishing her Tiny Tim's dream. Waiting for Mummy to die and Tim to be free.'

Brazier, who found this whole exchange too much, said, 'Are you for real?'

'Don't get it, do you, Julian?' Cliff tutted. 'Didn't bargain on screwed-up kids, did you? Big tough policeman like you signed up to chase bank robbers, not deal with the hurt of the little people. It goes unsaid, unreported, and unless *you* change it, we will all continue to wash up in here – no, now there's not even a proper "here". Evil pervades society, silver-tongued serpents out in broad daylight, without a care in world, like Hopkins, Markham and Symonds to riff–raff like Beech.'

'Thanks for the sermon,' Kenton said, although he knew it to be true. 'We're on it.'

'Are you? Who do you think is in danger right now?'

'Not Symonds. He wouldn't kill him, we know that at least.'

'The church man,' Emma sneered exaggeratedly, 'there in his pulpit, basks like an adder warming himself in the spring sun, under the Christian God's holy gaze. One of the many.'

'No Sunday school for you then,' Brazier said.

Kenton could now see her influence on Windows, steering his thinking. He wondered whether Windows was bluffing and planned to kill Symonds all along. 'And what about you, Emma, how are you?'

'Oh, I can leave whenever I like. I fly through the window at night and join the bats in the labyrinth . . . Have to, otherwise I really would go mad.'

Kenton searched her eyes for recognition. 'It says on your file you get out at the end of the month.'

'Do you think that's a good idea?' she tilted her head to one side.

He couldn't find an answer. Finally, he said, 'Be sure to look me up.'

'What was all that about?' Brazier said as they left the ward block. It was sleeting now and they both wondered if they had imagined the sun in the room at the far side of the hospital.

'In good time,' Kenton said. 'You go to Beech's, take backup – Tim must be hiding out there . . . and Roland might be in trouble from the sound of it.'

'What about you?'

'The Reverend.' He thought Emma was goading him. 'I think we'll have to take him in for his own protection after all.'

'Won't that create a hell of a stink?'

'Let's hope so.'

'And Chloe?'

'If we get everyone else, she'll be safe and need never know.'

CHAPTER 73

Wilde called into her radio for urgent assistance, her voice even but raised, alerting whoever was in the house she was there also. Only when she finished did she proceed towards the low whimpering coming from the kitchen, where she found Roland Beech at the table.

She hesitated. There was blood everywhere on the floor, mostly under the kitchen table.

'What the—?' Wilde exclaimed.

'Can't even do myself in,' he said with a macabre grin.

His wrist and forearm were both slashed. Wilde sought desperately for a kitchen towel to use as a tourniquet. He was right – he'd failed to make the vertical incision necessary. 'Hold your arm up.' She found a scrappy tea towel in a work surface corner.

'My sister chose that motor, knowing it was bone dry, you know. She fitted me up like—'

'Shut up. Where's the phone?' Wilde said. 'We need an ambulance to save your pathetic hide.'

'Don't have one. Stitched me up, she did . . . knowing

all along that nicking that motor would tie me to Hopkins. As soon as I saw that freak in the doorway, I knew he was her special friend. Mum told me – Oww!' He winced as she tightened the towel – 'that she'd made one in the looney bin.'

Wilde could hear sirens in the distance. They could bundle him in the squad car and speed him off to A&E without calling an ambulance. 'What freak in the doorway?'

'The one from the nuthouse. Where she . . .' He stopped talking.

'Why did your sister stitch you up?'

'You will never know.' He grabbed for the knife lying on the table, but he was too slow – she landed a kick to his right shoulder, sending him and the chair flying. Beech's fall was broken by the kitchen bin, its contents spilling over the floor.

'Jesus,' he moaned from a sea of rubbish. 'Why . . .?'

Wilde's mind worked quickly. 'Timothy Windows. Was he alone?'

Beech slumped over. 'She'll be dead too.'

Wilde burst onto the street in a panic, the knife still in her hand. Outside it was an ordinary street on a quiet winter's day. Which way did they go? She scanned the snow-laden path for answers, trying to differentiate the footprints leaving the house from those entering. A fresh fall was already obscuring most of the tracks. Absorbed in examining the pavement, Wilde failed to notice the siren, and it wasn't until she heard a familiar voice call from the squad car that she realised help was here.

''ello, 'ello,' Brazier called from the car window. 'You okay?'

'In one piece.' She was, but the concern on Brazier's face made her crumple a tiny bit inside with relief. 'Glad to see you, but don't get carried away – it's not over yet.'

Once she'd barged her way out of the house and into the street, Chloe realised she was being followed by Mandy's bloke. Breathless, she pleaded with him to stay away, accusing him of stalking her, but he was white as a sheet. In fact, he looked as terrified as she was. He pathetically went to his knees, as though about to expire. He looked ill, anorexic or something, in any event certainly not to be frightened of. She took pity. They heard an almighty scream from Beech's house and she scrambled into her car, dragging the feeble boyfriend with her.

'We should really get the police,' Chloe said.

For a while she drove and then pulled into the lay-by at Donyland Woods, in the dip on the Mersea road just south of town, where they sat, the car idling. Why had she come here? It was as though they were fugitives themselves. After impaling his sister to the door, Beech had exploded in grief and anger, yelling at them to leave, get out. Her hands were still trembling on the wheel.

'We've not been introduced yet,' said her companion, trying to lighten the mood.

She spun round, 'Yes, who the fuck are you?'

'Tim.' He offered her a pale thin hand. She took it limply.

'Are you a friend of Roland's? You are quite shaken,' he said calmly.

'No, I'm not his friend. I'm not anyone's friend,' Chloe said sharply. 'I'm shaken because I just witnessed a woman shot through the heart at close range with an arrow. That's enough to shake anyone – don't you think? You were her boyfriend, right? You seem . . .' *Not bothered*, she wanted to say, but didn't finish the sentence. 'What were you doing in my flat the other day? You dress like you've not got two pennies to rub together.'

'I'm an investigative reporter. I was in the middle of a piece on Bruce Hopkins, but then he went and got killed in the middle of it. Seemed inappropriate after that to quiz you, too. I just wanted a look at the flat . . .' He hung his head. 'It hasn't hit me yet – Mandy.' His voice was even and untroubled. She shoved the MG into reverse.

'What are you doing?'

'Going to the police.'

'I . . . I'm not ready.'

'I'll drop you in town, then.' She wanted him out of the car.

Moving the MG into first, the wheels lost traction, spinning uselessly on compacted snow. 'Shit.' The lay-by was on an angle, on a slight decline from the road where it met the woods. The car slid backwards. The old sports car was impractical at the best of times, and hopeless in bad weather. She yanked on the handbrake and got out of the car. Immediately, she was blinking at the whiteness. They can't have driven more than half a mile outside town, but it felt like the middle of nowhere, with snow coming down silently in thick flakes. She started trudging up the road, her feet slipping as she went. There was no traffic on the road.

'Wait.'

She felt a hand clutch her arm.

'Wait for me, we're not done yet.'

Chloe turned and looked at the gaunt man. 'What do you mean, we're not done yet?'

There was something familiar in his eyes, behind the anger.

'Like I said.'

'Let go of me.' He was still holding her arm. 'I said, let go.' His grip was strong for a skinny lad. She struggled to move forward through the snow. 'You're hurting me.'

He released her, then drew back his arm, theatrically, childishly – similar to drawing back a bow, she thought for an instant, ignoring the punch coming. It caught her on the corner of her jaw and sent her sprawling into a ditch. The next thing she knew, he was on top of her, his knees pinning her into the layers of snow. She could only see flashes of this strange, terrifying individual – the shape of his jaw, the narrow nostrils, clouds of breath. 'We're invisible. Nobody can see us,' he said, as if to the dazzling white sky.

Catching her breath, Chloe started to scream. Immediately, she felt her mouth fill with snow.

'Hush,' he said, a finger before his bloodless lips, 'or I will choke you. It works a treat.'

Again, he pressed snow into her face, this time the wet ice finding its way into her nasal cavity too, and she thought she was going to die.

CHAPTER 74

The roads were gritted and he'd made good time, having decided against informing Brightlingsea nick of his decision. Kenton drove at a snail's pace along the remaining half mile to Kempe Marsh. Emma Cliff was playing on his mind, her appearance was an omen. He battled to keep her face out of his head, telling himself once the vicar was sorted, he'd go back and see her.

He reckoned Watt may combust on discovering the vicar in his cells, but it would be worth it. Even if they let him go immediately, the rumours were enough to unsettle Symonds in the short term. He'd already let the word out in the Tap & Spile that they'd soon have an ecclesiastical guest at Southway.

Kenton recognised the uniform posted outside the vicarage as the one that found the feather fragment in the church. He called the man to his car window: 'A word in your shell-like, Officer.'

The constable was more than pleased to be relieved of his post.

Kenton banged aggressively on the vicarage door. He pushed

his face up against the frosted glass. 'Come on, I know you're in there.' He attacked the door again. 'St Nicholas is the patron saint of children, how ironic, eh? But then . . .' Behind him, he heard a blackbird call out in alarm. He turned and saw snow disturbed, loosening from the bushes. A figure was making off towards the marshes. Excellent, Kenton thought, and hollered for the constable at the top of his voice.

Symonds wouldn't get far. With the PC as a witness, so much the better. Kenton exited the garden and, at a slow jog, breathing hard, set off after the plodding clergyman.

Beneath him, Tim did not see a frightened woman, nor did he see a mother – he saw himself. Until that moment he was sure he was going to kill her. Ram her full of snow and suffocate her and make his escape. A just punishment for the callous woman who abandoned him. With no murder weapon and no clues left behind, he could do it – no one would ever know he'd been here. But now, as he studied the pink wet face, he could see a reflection; not of the young man he was, but of the contorted face of the terrified nine-year-old he'd been. The creased eyebrows furrowed up in fear, the angle of eyes: it was like a mirror.

He clambered off her. 'Get up.'

She remained on her back in the snow.

'I'm not going to hurt you.'

'Who are you?' she cried.

'No one. I'm no one.' He levered himself out of the ditch

and made his way towards the road, looking for a lift. He was distinctly light-headed. When he'd written to this woman's ex-husband, pretending to be her, he could not have imagined this outcome. Hopkins begging that night in the woods, that it was for him that he'd married Chloe, just to be close to him.

His biological mother had been responsible for everything . . . and strangely nothing.

CHAPTER 75

Watt considered Chloe Moran, as she sat wrapped in a blanket holding a coffee in the first aid room, intermittently telling her version of events. He looked to Kenton for guidance, but the CID sergeant remained mute. Wilde, who had excelled herself, sat close by, her neat-fringed bob a contrast to the others' wet straggled hair. Moran wasn't stupid, but had sailed through life attracting bad luck wherever she went – a doctor's daughter who, in the finest tradition of those from comfortable upbringings, had gone off the rails early on in her teens. There was nothing wrong in rebelling, except it was harder on girls, falling pregnant; not like boys, sowing a few wild oats. But then to have recovered and fallen prey to Hopkins, a suave older man – could you blame her for not seeing his ulterior motives? Regardless, he thought, to be confronted by both Hopkins and this child like that, out of nowhere, was hard to take for anyone.

'I was fourteen years old,' she said. 'A child myself.'

'And who is the father, Tim's father, if you don't mind me asking?' said Watt.

'Phil Patterson. I met him at the Colne Lodge on Crouch Street, he played in a band. Bass, I think. They supported Pink Floyd at the university.'

'Impressive,' Watt said. He himself had played in a band at university.

'And where is Phil now?'

'Australia. A carpenter, in New South Wales, or was last I heard. A ten-pound Pom, as they called them. He went after, you know . . .'

'I see.' He glanced again at Kenton for support.

Chloe clenched her knuckles and buried them in her eyes. 'I can't believe it.'

'Obsession takes many forms, Ms Moran,' Watt said. 'Hopkins was fixated with Timothy Windows; everything else was irrelevant. You were the closest he could get, and in some way that sufficed. Until . . .' Watt didn't know what. Hopkins hadn't grown bored or moved on from Tim – one of the few items he had on his person was a school library book with a photo of the lad. Watt saw fit not to mention this.

'He felt safe enough to move on?' Chloe said bitterly, 'I doubt he was "fixated". I think he just wanted to ensure the boy wouldn't be let out to point the finger. Bruce knew the adoptive parents had given up, from what you say, and in Colchester, he could keep an eye on things for himself, with my mother aware all along, no doubt. Then the aunt dies, he inherits a pile and a boat, and is off. No chance by then of Tim getting out. Both of us forgotten, and a new life for him in Spain. Until now. He's ... he's a bastard. That is all I know. And—'

'A chameleon,' Kenton said, stepping in. 'Adapting to whatever the circumstances dictate, drifting from one unlikely position to another without settling, be it teaching, smuggling weed, or stealing jewellery. He was without attachment or purpose, at the whim of his own vanity, and why he didn't question the veracity of Tim's letter purporting to be from you, we'll never know.'

'And all you can do,' Watt nodded approvingly, 'is remember where you are now, what you have achieved since. He didn't have long, you know, to live.'

'Yes, yes. But what about my son, what happens to him now? Is he my son or not?' Her face was distraught. 'This damaged individual has burst on the scene now. What am I supposed to do? Who will help me?'

A WPS hove into view through the glass door. Watt beckoned the officer to enter. A driver for Chloe Moran. Watt was done with this bedraggled creature before him. Nice enough, but like everyone else, interested only in herself at the end of the day. 'Thank you, Ms Moran,' he said. 'We'll be in touch. It's time for you to see your mother. Wilde, be good enough to escort Ms Moran to ... where do you wish to go, Ms Moran – home?'

'No.' With an air of resilience she ran her fingers back through her hair, 'the boating pond, at the bottom of Castle Park. I'm meeting my mother.'

*

'Where's Brazier?' Watt said brusquely as soon as the door clicked shut.

Kenton stiffened. 'With the lad. He's not to answer for this, I am.'

'You're a chippy fucker, Kenton, you know that.' Watt tapped a forefinger on the desk lightly as though in tune with music, before opening the case file. 'Think you could do this job?'

Impervious, Kenton sat, ready to take whatever Watt dished out. 'No sir, nor would I want to.'

'Not to be drawn, eh? Very wise.' He pushed his chair away from the desk, preferring distance from the other. 'Well, it ain't no fun putting up with arses like you who think they know better, and deserve this or that, and sulk. So listen here – you damn well *should* know better in the field, because that's where you are, and me? I'm here behind the desk, getting your back. Understood?'

'Sir.'

'I doubt it. We'll see.' He rocked back in the chair. 'Now, on to this clergyman.'

'He tried to run off across the marshes, treacherous out there. He got stuck. We're lucky to still have him.'

'What's he doing downstairs, then, why's he not in hospital?'

'He's fine, a bit of a chill, that's all,' Kenton said. 'Right now, he's taking stock of the situation.'

'Meaning?'

'His future.'

'I see. Do the press know he's here?'

'They might have noticed him, yes, sir.'

Kenton waited. This would be the clincher. If the vicar made the papers, then the whole thing would blow up. Watt did not know the minutiae of detectives and tip-offs to hacks, but was savvy enough to know that the vicar could have been taken into custody – or protection – without so much as a whisper to the outside world. If the press knew, someone had told them.

But the chief let it pass. 'And Windows?'

'He's with Brazier, ironing out one or two things.'

'Yes, you said. To what end, I wonder . . . The medical authorities are informed?'

'They are . . .' Kenton moved his jaw from side to side as though adjusting it, before speaking again. 'Windows will be assessed, and then before charges are brought, we'll await the Church's response to the vicar's . . . err, position.'

'The vicar's unscheduled public appearance,' Watt said. 'But the outcome of the assessment will not be influenced by how Symonds plays out. That Windows did his mother no serious harm will stand in his favour against the murder of Hopkins, but that's about it.'

'Yes, he's banking on taking the vicar down with him.'

'Uh-huh. It's inevitable, I think.'

Kenton was disconcerted that Watt had no issue with him fitting the vicar up. 'Mind if I smoke?' he said, knowing the chief was anti-cigarettes.

Watt flipped up his hand. 'If you need it,' he said magnan-imously. 'Finally then, on to Beech?'

'In breach of his parole,' Kenton said. 'In hospital under guard.'

'I'm sorry about the sister,' Watt said. 'That is tragic.'

'It's not always a happy ending.' Kenton puffed on his cigarette. 'Roland would rather be dead. There is that.'

'Could we have done anything?' Watt asked. 'Don't answer, it's rhetorical. I don't think so . . . the police are not equipped to deal with mental health or abuse yet.'

'That would appear to be the case,' said Kenton. 'It's com-plex.' He thought back to Emma Cliff's speech.

'I'm glad we agree on something,' Watt said. 'There will be a review and enquiry. The Beech girl had similar problems to Windows, and this was allowed to go unchecked.' He closed the file. 'That will be all.'

Kenton dogged his cigarette in the previously unused ash-tray and rose.

'Oh, Kenton. I'm not sure on the case-sharing – split respon-sibility doesn't really work, eh? Sure you'll agree. Not my idea, but willing to give these things a go. You'll be hearing in due course.'

'Sir,' Kenton said. He left the station in a buoyant mood. Fancying he'd reached an accord with Watt, and had an inspector's wage coming his way. There'd be no overtime though – that was left behind with the sergeant's stripes. Would he actually be better off? Yes, surely. He had a passing thought to buy Lindsay some flowers and patch things up, but settled on a bottle of bubbly, that being more of a shared celebration.

'I'll be fine, honest, thank you.'

'I can wait.' Wilde didn't think Chloe Moran was fine at all. They had driven across town and had pulled over near the bottom of North Hill, where a side street led to an entrance into Lower Castle Park. 'You've been through an ordeal.'

'So have you.'

'I chose mine. My job, I mean.'

Chloe sniffled. 'Choices. Yes. We all have them.' Her raw red lips broke into a small smile. 'Goodbye.' Wilde bid her good luck and watched her cross the road and head towards the park before climbing into the waiting squad car. Her head slunk onto her chest and she sighed heavily. God, she was drained.

Chloe was early, and had wandered along the river that flowed gently down through the bottom of Castle Park, carrying with it small babbling ducks. Her mother had asked for them to meet here, a place they would visit regularly when Chloe was a little girl. Margaret Moran was not sentimental, but her daughter thought perhaps she wished to invoke more innocent times – that, or the older women thought an open space would avoid a slanging match. Her mother was tough but did not enjoy confrontation. There was a crack of pink light on the horizon. Was the weather on the change, finally? Was it getting warmer, or was it her imagination? Her imagination – was that at fault? The reason she was where she was? At worst she was naive, tumbling through life taking what it gave out on face value and asking no questions. It sounded naff in her head and it was undoubtedly a cliché, like everything else. But she had lived. Lived an eventful life, and hopefully was only halfway through it.

Having confronted her past in the flesh, she grappled for an emotional response. Chloe wasn't alone, hadn't been alone: hundreds, maybe thousands of girls like her had been forced to give up their babies like that. How many of them, though, had faced what she had just been through twenty years after the event? Had nearly been killed by their child? Nobody, she'd bet.

All that was clear were the facts; Tim, whose existence began inside her, had not lived at all. Whoever was responsible for the first ten years of his life had given him as good a start as any. (A private education, like her own. Until she fell into disgrace.) Who was to blame for good intentions? The only one responsible for anything was Hopkins – a pervert, and one she'd been suckered into marrying. He'd wrecked her life too. After Phil left, Chloe didn't settle with anyone, bounced here, there and everywhere until she met level-headed, sensible, charming Bruce. Did anyone know his story? The police tried telling her that, to Bruce, she'd been the next best thing to her son. How wrong was that?

Chloe heard two women moving giddily through the snow, arm in arm and laughing as they made to cross the bridge. They swerved to avoid a pedestrian coming from the other direction. It was her mother, Chloe could tell. The fur hat. Chloe was sure her mother would try and make her feel guilty for being such a terrible daughter. But if anyone was to experience guilt it should, if there was any justice, be Margaret Moran.

CHAPTER 76

Hopkins' notoriety as a hash smuggler was well known, even in Severalls. The television had brought Tim's old schoolmaster and torturer back into his world. Mandy and Emma witnessed the expression, horror and trauma, spread across his face. They persisted until he relented and told them everything. But how did that slot into the River Crouch drugs haul? Hopkins was always on at the boys to come swimming off his boat at North Fambridge, or to see the horses at his old aunt's place nearby. At the weekends, he had his chums there too. Naive though the Bryde Park boys were, it was obvious to them that these fellows were up to no good. When Bruce left Bryde Park with his tail between his legs, he saddled up with those chums. Tim remembered the boat on the early evening news, and then the shock of seeing the beautiful ex-wife, Chloe. That he, Tim, was the son of this woman, defied belief. Bruce had no interest in girls, and neither did his friends. There were never ladies on the boat. He shuddered as he recalled those swimming days. The men, Symonds and Markham among them, ogling him from the deck.

'What made you such a good bowman?' Brazier asked, bringing Tim back to the present.

'You don't need to be marksman to hit a church roof bigger than the proverbial barn door.'

'Come on, you were a crack shot at school.' They walked slowly under the St John's Abbey Gate, the medieval stone's solidity resonating an aura of calm. The surrounding grounds were snow-covered, creating a sense of timelessness.

'I draw and aim with my left hand and eye, that's unusual. It's normally one of each. Mr Hopkins used to tease me that I didn't use the right side of my brain at all.'

Brazier noted the subservient 'Mr' prefix.

'You're thinking about him now, aren't you?' Windows said. 'Arms around me.'

That huge sweaty mass he witnessed on the slab encompassing the small child, tactile and crouching as the boy took aim. 'It's hard not to.'

'He wasn't the wreck of the man you found. Then, he was suave and witty, a charmer, not some ogre in the physical sense, and that's why he got away with it. In plain sight, at the butts, and we all took it, that mint humbug breath tickling your ear; a miracle we'd hit anything. And then those in the team sports, those times in the sweat-stink of changing rooms, were more intimate . . . Who knew a cricket box would need so much adjustment to sit just right?'

'I'm sorry.'

'Why? Did you hire him? Was it you that witnessed his

behaviour and chose to do nothing? No, I don't think so. Then don't apologise.'

Two soldiers in uniform walked past them, their chatter trailing mist in the air as they went. There was no point going over what had happened, or what might happen in the future. A sad state of affairs it surely was, but Windows had chosen his path.

'I was pretty good, though,' Windows said. 'With a bow. Bullseye every time, practically.'

'Mate of mine was a good aim,' Brazier said. 'Hit me in the eye with a catapult.'

Windows stopped and faced Brazier. They were about the same height. Windows looked deceptively taller, being slender.

'Oh, yes,' he said, frowning. 'It's like your pupil has leaked into your iris. Nasty. Were you in a fight? What was it, a stone?'

'Conker. A disagreement over a champion conker. Should have let him keep it, eh?'

'Does your eye work? Can you see?'

'Miraculously, yes. Except when I get tired.'

'Lucky he didn't blind you.'

They stopped. Brazier turned and glanced back at the fore-boding abbey defence. Windows had asked if they might not collect him from the station, and had suggested this fifteenth-century fortification nearby instead. Brazier had facilitated it, but there were half a dozen uniforms in shouting distance just in case. The walkway was like a gaping mouth, the pinnacled turrets like horns above two mullioned eyes; a face of a defiance through the ages.

'They say the monks built it to protect themselves after the Peasants' Revolt,' Windows said.

'Is that what they say?'

'It's still here, the church; goes on and on.' Windows sighed and breathed deeply on the chill air. He gazed into the distance, towards town. 'Ahh. Our time is up. The men in white coats.'

Brazier turned to see an ambulance waiting at the top of St John's Green, flanked by two uniforms.

Windows held out his hand, 'Thank you, Sergeant. It was kind of you to let me have a last gasp of fresh air.'

'Don't give up, mate.' Brazier took the hand and placed his other on Windows' shoulder. Shaking hands gently, he said, 'Stay calm, you hear?'

'I am sure there will be little opportunity for anything else.'

Windows shoved his hands into the parka and strode off to meet his gaoler. Brazier felt in his own pockets for his fags as he watched them leave. Disappointed, he found only an old bag of sweets. Mint humbugs. He tossed them into a bush and began to walk back to the station, where his intention was to rummage through lost property for some sports kit. He was to meet Wilde in the gym at six. The cold nibbled at his toes, reminding him that he had the right footwear at least.

ACKNOWLEDGEMENTS

Sarah Neal, Jon Riley, Sarah Castleton, Felicity Blunt, Victoria Hughes-William, Fraser Crichton, Jasmine Palmer, Olivia Hutchings, David Shelley, Charlie King, Helen Wood, Clive Parsons, Jane Richardson, M. M. Archibald, K. Boonus and Lottie D.